Full Sail

by
Annie DeMoranville

Deco Skyline Publishing

www.AnnieDeMoranville.com

Deco Skyline Publishing
Boston, MA

Publisher's Note: This is a work of fiction. Names, characters, places, and incidents are a product of the author's imagination. Locales and public names are sometimes used for atmospheric purposes. Any resemblance to actual people, living or dead, or to businesses, companies, events, institutions, or locales is completely coincidental.

Book is formatted in Calibri for accessibility

Cover by Larissa Gibson

Full Sail/ Annie DeMoranville 1st ed.
ISBN 978-1-7325070-6-7

TJ Wilde Mystery Trilogy:

Book one: Run Aground

A Sexy, Witty, Murderous Adventure

My life was not going as I had imagined. But I had a plan:

FIRST, in between being chased by Scary Dudes and frequently dodging bullets, I was determined to solve the murder of mysterious lawman, Mike Fraser. He died in my arms after involving me in a criminal investigation, so this was personal.

NEXT, I was going to get my Soon-To-Be-Ex to sign our divorce papers (a divorce he had insisted on, by the way). Then I would be free to take full advantage of the well-muscled U.S. Marshal that was now guarding my body, day and night.

Finally, I was going to find my dream job as far away from Peoria, IL, and as close to an ocean as I could possibly get. It was a simple plan. All I had to do was live long enough to implement it. And I was definitely not going to fall in love with the sexy U.S. Marshal sitting at my kitchen table. Even if every cell in my body was saying he was too good to let go.

For TJ Wilde, it was difficult to tell who was more dangerous, the men trying to kill her or the man she was falling in love with...

RUN AGROUND is a wild ride through a small town. Corrupt cops, illegal gambling, lascivious morticians, contract killers and one sexy U.S. Marshal keep TJ Wilde on her toes while she tries to solve a murder. She's also on the hunt for the jerks who keep ransacking her apartment. All while she tries to ignore the hunky man with the potential to mend her broken heart...or shatter it irrevocably.

Book Two: Underway

A DANGEROUS, SEXY, INTERNATIONAL ART ADVENTURE

A new job, a new home, and a new outlook on life. But, of course, it could not be that easy.

A cute loft with a great view would be enough to bring me back to Boston. But add in a great job with my best friend, an adorable lost kitten, and a neighborhood filled with art and artists, then there was no question I was right where I belonged.

Unfortunately, missing Cuban art, a vandalized gallery, and a gallerist who has simply vanished are making the return to my favorite city troublesome. Not to mention, someone keeps sneaking into my apartment. This was not the marvelous return I had envisioned. Add to that, my sexy lawman, who is both persistent and much too far away. He definitely is not taking no for an answer.

For TJ Wilde, moving back to Boston felt like coming home, but home was never this dangerous...

Book Three: Full Sail *You're reading it ☺*

To My Dad

That Top Secret Clearance really sparked
a young girl's imagination

It seemed like a good idea at the time -
RICK O'CONNELL, THE MUMMY

ONE

Murder is my favorite crime - LAURA

Fuck! I thought it wasn't supposed to rain in Southern California. I was soaked to the skin standing in a torrential downpour underneath the fishing pier at Venice Beach. A few miles down the road from the ritziest of Malibu mansions and the kitschy fun of Santa Monica Pier's Pacific Park. Grateful Colby convinced me to buy what had to be a military-grade phone. It was holding up to the deluge better than I. Of course, I would never tell him he was right. Keep him guessing. That was my relationship philosophy.

I had been following the ping of my best friend Mimi's phone, but it had suddenly stopped, leaving me anxious and stranded, dodging the incoming tide. I tamped down the growing dread. She was in serious trouble, but I wasn't sure what kind of trouble. Was she a fugitive on the run, or had some harm come to her? Either prospect was frightening.

I tracked her phone to this all-but-abandoned location when it abruptly went dark. Either a dead battery or someone saw me and suspected her cell was giving away her position and shut it off. I shook my phone in some irrational attempt to make the little red dot come back.

Dammit, Mimi, where the hell are you? And why hadn't Colby responded to any of my texts? What kind of fiancé was he, anyway? Oh, yeah, one with a stressful and, at the moment, very demanding job as a U.S. Marshal. Still, I felt deserted and desolate, and it was pissing me off.

A gust of wind howled under the dock, blowing sheets of rain at me, just as an enormous wave crashed inches from my drenched running shoes. I dashed toward the sand berm, scrambled over it to the walkway, and onto the pier. Striding the length of it, I looked from one end of the shoreline to the other, searching in vain for any sign of Mimi.

Squelching my growing panic, I replayed the previous night. What was the mysterious meeting that was so important she would be late to our dinner? Why didn't she wait until I could go with her? Why was she always so impulsive? And yes, I was self-aware enough to understand the irony in that question.

Two weeks ago, my phone rang, and Mimi, breathless as usual, asked me if I wanted to get paid to fly to Los Angeles. I didn't even wait for the reason. I said yes.

I should have waited for the reason.

TWO

I have to warn you, I've heard relationships based on intense experiences never work - SPEED

I am a medium girl. I'm medium height and medium weight. My hair is medium brown and medium length. I live a medium life. I take walks in the forest. I'll never hike the Appalachian Trail. I cycle on groomed paths. I'll never ride down the Rocky Mountains or race on a BMX track. I run a decent mile, but I'll never run a marathon. I quit kendo before going much further than the average tween. Though skilled, I'll never master.

Sure, I have had a few adventurous moments, but no more cloak and dagger for me. No more being shot at, held at gunpoint, stalked, and terrorized. Now, I live a quiet life. I was conflicted on the merits of that.

These days, I have a nice, unassuming position at a museum near Arlington, Virginia. A middling, nine-to-five job, researching and authenticating art acquisitions for a modest, quite ordinary collection. My life at this juncture was unremarkable.

Maybe I was having a midlife crisis. That might explain my dissatisfaction with...everything. And why, after one phone call and with little thought, I jumped into what would become a very dangerous situation. I was definitely having a midlife crisis.

Even my marriage had been mundane. I married my best friend right out of college. It wasn't a passionate relationship, but it was comfortable. Until it wasn't.

This could be why the engagement ring I now wear weighs heavily on my hand. And why I vacillated when Colby probed for an answer to his proposal. I didn't fully understand the reason I couldn't take that leap of faith into marriage with him. I didn't doubt Colby. All the doubts began and ended with me and my ability to commit. I was content with being engaged, or at least that's what I told myself.

There was nothing ordinary about our coupling, though. We met in a hail of bullets, and our relationship intensified as we fled corrupt cops and wannabe gangsters. The sex was spicy, even as we moved from a hot and heavy long-distance courtship to living together in the suburbs. Our conversations were always stimulating. Every day with him was an adventure, and I loved him more each day. That scared the crap out of me.

I tried to tell myself I was wary because of my previous catastrophic nuptials. Colby and I had a blast together, but we were so very different. Despite our obvious chemistry, our disparate experiences gave me pause.

Before our lives collided, I was a nerdy art major. Raised by a widowed (or so I thought) single mom who sold real estate by day and moonlighted as a wedding singer on weekends. Colby was a badass lawman with a Presbyterian minister father and a civil rights attorney mother. I had experience with matrimony, while Colby was a serial dater.

And then there was my father. My unexpectedly not-dead father, who also happened to be a career criminal. Nothing about Colby and me said *forever.* And did I mention I was wary of commitment?

There was nothing medium about Colby Jameson, U.S. Marshal. If you looked up badass in the dictionary, there he would be, all smoldering and sexy. Tall, muscular, with intense green eyes and a killer job chasing actual killers. Life with him would not be comfortable and safe. There would always be a hint of danger and uncertainty. But, Colby was the one having all the adventures. I was the one staying behind, keeping the home fires burning.

Sure, we looked like the average couple, living in a small Colonial with a cat and a dog, a fenced backyard, and a vegetable garden. We were settled, at least for the moment. Colby was spending more time in the office now that he was promoted to Senior Inspector, making it home for dinner most nights. We grocery shopped on weekends, completed cute little renovation projects, and divvied up unpleasant household chores.

That's what had me worried — this feeling of ennui, this overwhelming dread that this was all there was. Shuffling paperwork, paying bills, doing all the ordinary, daily tasks that made for a stable life. All while Colby ran fugitive task forces and protected the innocent. I hated to admit it, even to myself, but I missed fighting off killers, counterfeiters, kidnappers, and art thieves.

Sure, pursuing a second master's degree had been stimulating, but the end result wasn't exactly what I had expected. I had hoped for more mystery and felonious activity and less administrative wrangling. I thought I would be traveling to exotic places to chase down priceless works of art stolen by the Nazis and reuniting them with deserving families, or unraveling the mysteries of long-lost jewels suddenly found in an attic or chest of drawers.

Instead, most of my days were spent rifling through old records, making dozens of phone calls to verify authenticity and provenance, and then writing up reports. So many reports. I was drowning in reports.

I found myself a little envious when Colby jetted off in pursuit of a fugitive or spent a late night in a van surveilling a suspect. Despite the danger, there was intense satisfaction in kicking criminals in the balls and then watching Colby cuff them. I missed that.

And then there was my dad. Out there, living a clandestine existence, swooping in when I needed him, all while remaining in the shadows, Mr. Mysterious and Dark. He had the knack for knowing when I was in danger or needed an assist. Then he would provide the precise clue I would need to avert disaster or save a friend. And I was grateful for that, despite my indignation at his ability to know everything about me while revealing nothing of himself. I was, however, beginning to suspect that my thirst for adventure might be genetic.

All of this was why, when Mimi contacted me with her request for assistance, I was ready to jump without much thought or caution.

Mimi and I had spent little time together once we moved away from Boston and our lives diverged. Before that, we had worked tirelessly together, sifting through the chaos precipitated by her former boss's arrest. Trevor Davenport was guilty of smuggling stolen art, assault, and kidnapping. Leaving both of us stunned and soon to be unemployed.

But first, we were tasked with dismantling his ties to the buildings he owned in the South Boston neighborhood where we lived and worked, so they could be sold. We were paid well for our efforts - enough for me to pay for graduate school - but it was emotionally exhausting. It did give us the time needed to process the betrayal we felt from his villainous actions.

After that, we shared a townhome while I returned to grad school and Mimi set about restoring her reputation. Neither project was easy, but we had each other and the men in our lives to get us through. Well, I had Colby. Mimi had an assortment of beaux. Most of them could not understand her drive and passion. They would drift away as she threw herself deeper into her work. And then another would drift in.

Our days together changed after I finished my degree and Colby asked me to move in with him in Virginia. Then Mimi took off for Paris. Frequent phone calls and meeting up when we could, kept our friendship strong. But with my job and her relocation to Los Angeles, it had become more and more difficult. Her call for assistance was a welcome invitation and a potential respite from my personal discontent.

"TJ," she began when I answered the phone. I could tell from the excitement in her voice that this wasn't just a catch up call. "How are things in the heart of democracy?"

"I'm muddling along. I just finished piecing together the history of an Art Deco ruby and diamond necklace. You would love it."

"Oh, yes! What did you find out about it?"

"I used its French hallmark to trace it back to the original owners, pre-WW II," I began. "And was able to determine the patron's family had smuggled it out of France and the museum could accept the donation." Mimi knew as well as I that provenance was important with items from that time period. The Nazis had stolen so many works of art that then made their way into private collections. Museums and art dealers were finally doing the right thing and ascertaining the ownership history before any additional transactions occurred. This was why I proudly proclaimed, "It made me a real hero to the Board."

"You could be a real hero to me, TJ. I need an assist," Mimi said, getting directly to the point, as always.

"What's going on? Trouble with your tech-bro boss?"

Mimi had left Boston behind for the sunny climes of Los Angeles. She had been working with a fancy gallery in the Art District, an area in downtown Los Angeles. Soaking up the art experiences at the Getty Center, the Museum of Contemporary Art, and the Los Angeles County Museum of Art.

There was also plenty of beach time and thrift stores filled with unbelievable treasures. When she first moved, she would call every week to gush about a new find. And then proudly declared that she had entirely furnished her studio apartment with discards from the ridiculously rich. The busier we both found ourselves, the more time passed between calls.

One day she called to tell me that a frequent visitor to the gallery, Tom Meadler, had approached her. Meadler had worked in Silicon Valley, making a fortune in the tech world before cashing out and moving to Los Angeles. He made her an offer she couldn't refuse.

He asked her if she would help him build his personal collection with an eye to one day opening his own gallery. With a mansion in Pacific Palisades and warehouses in Long Beach to be filled, there was a promise of steady work. She jumped at it.

I was a little surprised, considering how our last engagement with an art entrepreneur had ended - with him in jail and Mimi and I unemployed - that she would be eager to take a similar risk again. Perhaps I should take a lesson from that.

"I found something," she began. "Something I need your expertise to verify its authenticity." Mimi was always one to cut to the chase. "It's almost too good to be true, so I'm suspicious and being super cautious before I let Tom purchase it."

"Sounds intriguing. What do you need from me?"

"How would you like to fly out to LA, all expenses paid, for a week or so?"

"Are you kidding?" I looked out the window at the never-ending gloom that had been late winter. "Is it sunny? Is it warm? And I get to see you? I'm in." I should confer with Colby, as couples do, but I needed a change, and this seemed perfect.

Mimi laughed. "Aren't you even interested in what I found?"

"I suppose, but I don't think the answer is going to change my mind. I'm already deciding which bathing suit to pack." Quickly, I scribbled some notes on my desk pad: call my boss, reschedule the cleaning service, and get the suitcases. Mimi interrupted my list-making.

"TJ, are you listening? I had someone contact me this week regarding an original oil painting from an old movie, a film noir classic. No one has seen it in decades, since before the film was released, and I have to determine if it's authentic."

"Oh," I said, a bit deflated. "Mimi, I know absolutely nothing about classic films. Nothing. Nada." Tracing the history of a piece of movie memorabilia was not exactly in my wheelhouse. My movie knowledge started with the great films of the eighties and nineties and continued to the present day. What I knew of classic films was no more than what I gleaned from the few classics I watched on TCM.

"I've learned a lot, so I can help there," Mimi reassured me. "I just need someone who knows how to do this type of research. Tom really wants this piece, and he told me he would pay any expert who could authenticate it. You were the only expert I wanted."

This was important to her, I could tell, and the entire project intrigued me. I was more than willing to do the homework to enhance my knowledge of the genre. The entire enterprise sounded invigorating, exactly what I needed. I was up for the challenge and excited to see Mimi. "I'm willing to help you any way I can, Mimi. Let me talk with Colby while you iron out the travel details."

"Thanks, TJ, you'll never know how much this means to me."

We disconnected with a plan to talk again after I cleared things with my boss. Mimi suggested I invite Colby along, and I hedged a bit. It's not that a California vacation wouldn't be fun for us, but I also thought some time apart could give me the perspective I needed to make some serious decisions.

It turned out I didn't have to worry about making it a solo excursion. When I told Colby of Mimi's offer at dinner, he had no concerns about the trip, but he would not be able to accompany me.

He explained, "I've been asked to head up a major task force, and things are heating up quickly." Although something was off. He was short on details and changed the subject abruptly back to the trip.

I expressed my disappointment, but told him that Mimi and I would have plenty to keep us busy. As we continued to discuss Los Angeles, he was distracted. He obviously had something on his mind. His usual voracious appetite was absent, and he pushed his food around his plate.

"What's going on?" I asked after another monosyllabic response. "Something obviously has you preoccupied."

He put his fork down and looked at me, his face serious. *Uh-oh*, I thought, *here comes the dreaded marriage conversation again*. Or worse.

Even though we had been together for years, in the back of my mind I was always waiting for the explosion. The one that would throw my entire world into chaos again. I tried not to hold my breath waiting for his response.

He hesitated long enough that I silently saw myself with custody of our cat, Stevie, and once again putting my entire life in storage. When he finally spoke, I could not have anticipated the gut-kick.

"Teej, the task force I'm on," he began carefully. "It's a fugitive case. It is an intense one, someone the various agencies have been after for decades. This involves forgery, counterfeiting, and murder, among other crimes."

He picked up his glass and tilted it back and forth, watching the water's movements. I swallowed the urge to grab it from him and slam it onto the table, demanding he get on with whatever was bothering him.

"The Marshals and the FBI are working on this together and..." he paused again, giving me that look again. "And they have called in your father to help with the case."

I stared at him for a long moment. It was a good thing I was sitting down. It was quite the bombshell. Not only that my dad, Thomas Joseph Wilde, ex-con, ex-witness, and current consultant, was coming to D.C., but they all knew how to contact him. That Colby knew how to contact him. No wonder he had difficulty telling me. All these years and he knew.

The most I ever received from my father these days was a card on birthdays or holidays and the occasional encouraging note around life events. My mom, who was dating a very nice guy these days, received periodic deposits into her bank account from him. Despite leaving witness protection years ago, he remained elusive, an enigma, in order to continue to protect his family. His consultant work with law enforcement agencies across the globe kept him at high risk. Or so I was told.

"Have you spoken to him?" I asked once I had processed the news.

"Not yet. He has to be cleared by the FBI first," he explained. "Then he'll be on the team I'm leading."

And there it was. I swallowed hard, grappling with the rush of warring emotions. My father's cryptic help when I was in trouble had morphed into cryptic encouragement at random moments. He always seemed to be aware when I had achieved some milestone or needed a boost. I suspected with aid from my mother.

Yet he had never reached out to meet. Now it appeared that everyone had a relationship with him. My mom, Colby, Colby's boss, and his colleagues in law enforcement, and who knew who else in my life, just not me.

I had no idea what he looked like, beyond an old photo of him holding me as a baby. And I was angry. Angry that no one told me he was a talented artist with a sharp eye for detail, who chose to use those skills for crime over the life of a starving artist. Angry that no one told me he was alive and in witness protection, instead letting me think he was dead for most of my life. Angry that when he left WitSec, he didn't come back to us. Angry that he abandoned his life of crime to become a consultant with law enforcement on high-profile forgery cases, yet remained a mystery in my life.

"I suppose the fact he has resurfaced means something significant is happening that needs his extraordinary gifts," I said flatly, not actually caring. I viciously snuffed out any hopeful thought he might have jumped at the opportunity in order to reconnect.

"Yes, it is an important task force, but I think he does want to meet you. I believe that was part of the appeal of coming on board," Colby said gently. "There is something else." He placed his hand on mine. "The suspect is a man who has openly threatened your father. He's escaped capture at every turn. I think your father would like to eliminate that threat. With it gone, he might feel safer having a normal relationship with you." His hand tightened on mine, reassuring me he was there, even if my dad wasn't.

His words stoked a small ember in my heart that maybe what he was saying was true, that my dad wanted to come out from the shadows and be part of my life. Suddenly I could see us going to a Red Sox game together, eating Fenway Franks and sipping warm beer. Or visiting the Museum of Modern Art in New York together, dissecting paintings and sculptures. Or even experiencing the ordinariness of having dinner together.

Oh yeah, I would have to stomp out that ember, and fast. But it was not going to stay out.

THREE

Welcome to Hollywood! What's your dream?- PRETTY WOMAN

I told Mimi I would be the only one arriving in Los Angeles over the weekend. She didn't ask, and I didn't bother with the details of Colby's absence. We would have plenty of time to deliberate on that topic in person.

"I found you the cutest beachside hotel," she said after she gave me my flight information.

"I'm not staying with you?" That was a surprise. I assumed we would be having many a late night, catching up on life's happenings.

"My studio apartment is so small, you wouldn't be comfortable. I keep thinking I should be looking for something larger, but I have not had the time. Besides, Tom is paying, so you should enjoy the beach view."

"Sounds lovely. Should I rent a car?"

"No, you'll be using one of Tom's. How fancy do you want to be? I've got an electric BMW, a Land Cruiser, or I think the Porsche is back from the shop."

"What, no Maserati?"

"Don't joke. If he wasn't so occupied with his art collection, he'd probably have a garage full of expensive cars.

Wait until you see his mansion, it's...well, you'll just have to see it."

"The EV will be fine, though I'm a bit nervous driving one of his cars," I said. "I'm excited and can't wait to see you Friday."

After we disconnected, I finished downloading some reference books on old Hollywood and vintage Hollywood collectibles to read on the plane.

I packed what I hoped would get me through two weeks away. Taking time off from work was not a problem. My boss, Beverly, believed I deserved a vacation, and it didn't hurt that there was nothing urgent in the pipeline. She was excited that I would have the opportunity to explore the art scene in Los Angeles.

Beverly also mentioned the idea of looking into future acquisitions. There were rumors of an enormous estate going up for auction in Santa Barbara that had an excellent art collection, including a full-sized Rodin. The museum would consider extending my time if that sale materialized.

I talked with our pet sitter, Abby, arranging daily walks for Wyatt and lots of lap time for Stevie. I figured it was best to book her time in case Colby's newest case led to long days or possibly even longer nights. It would be easier for her to transition from dog walker to full-time food-poop-cuddle attendant if needed.

I canceled our fresh vegetable and egg deliveries from the CSA for the foreseeable future. In the event that circumstances extended my stay. I let out a sigh and hoped I had remembered everything. I would double-check with Colby at dinner and see if he could think of anything else.

With everything done, that left me with a boatload of time to think. And mostly what I was thinking about, obsessing about really, was my father. I reflected on when he showed up and disrupted my already upended life.

Stuck in Peoria after an unexpected divorce, seeing a friend murdered, and being stalked by numerous people almost paled in comparison to learning my father was alive. And Colby knew. That put a dent in our budding relationship.

And here we were again, Colby collaborating with my father while I stood on the sidelines, waiting for some kind of connection. I was trying not to be resentful, but failing miserably. I was grateful to be leaving town, if only to get my thoughts in order.

Dog feet scrambling across the kitchen floor meant that Colby was home. I zipped up my toiletry bag and tossed it with the other luggage. I put on a smile and proceeded downstairs, pledging to set aside my fears and doubts. At least for the night.

Colby was unpacking Chinese food while Wyatt wound around his legs, making the task difficult. God bless that man for bringing dinner after what was probably a very busy day.

"Wyatt, are you supposed to be in the kitchen?" I admonished.

He stopped, sat and cocked his head as if to say, "But this is where the good food is."

I raised an eyebrow, and he let out a deep sigh, got up, and walked out. Where he then stood, just beyond the threshold, hoping he could sneak back when we were distracted. I loved that big, furry doofus.

"Smells delicious," I said as I grabbed plates from the cupboard. I set them on the oak table in the breakfast nook.

It was my grandmother's and had traveled with me from Boston to Peoria, back to Boston, and now here. I remembered the first time I saw Colby sitting at it. I was freshly showered, traumatized, and exhausted. Seeing him there was the most comforting sight I had ever seen. It wasn't long after that he lifted me onto it and kissed away all my fears.

I walked behind Colby as he grabbed the last container out of the bag. I wrapped my arms around him and leaned my head against his back, feeling his warmth and strength. He turned around and lifted my face to his, looking deeply into my eyes before kissing me. Gently at first, then hungrily, with purpose, before breaking away.

"If I weren't starving, we would be skipping dinner right now," he said. "But I hope we can continue this later." He waggled his eyebrows at me and gave me that wolf grin.

Damn, the man was fine.

And true to his word, dinner was just the main course. Once the animals had been attended to and the kitchen cleaned up, we made our way to the bedroom. I wisely shut the door behind us, leaving the curious fur babies to live in wonder.

Colby wasted no time, taking me into his arms and kissing me passionately. The man knew how to kiss. Soft and gentle, that evolved into devouring my lips with his, tongue darting, desire conveyed without a word. He pulled away just long enough to pull my shirt over my head before dipping back down to take my mouth in his.

His hands got busy. He unclasped my bra, letting the cups swing back and away. That cool rush of air made my nipples harden with anticipation. He gently lowered the straps down my arms, and gravity did the rest. Meanwhile, his lips had not strayed from mine.

I busied myself with the button on his jeans and then unzipping them, moving the zipper down his hardness. I moved my hand against him, and a moment later he had me on the bed, removing the rest of my clothes. Then he nuzzled against my thighs and kissed his way up to the promised land.

I really should marry the man.

"You'll call me if you need anything, right?" I asked Colby as we drove to the airport.

"Of course."

I looked out the window anxiously. I had one of those Mimi feelings. She had a spooky way of knowing when something was about to happen, good or bad. This felt bad. I was sure it was nothing, but I couldn't assuage my nerves.

"You're awfully quiet over there, Kit-Kat," Colby said as he reached over and squeezed my thigh. "What deep thoughts are you thinking?"

"Nothing really. I just feel..." I searched for the word. "...unsettled."

"Are you worried about LA? My new assignment?"

"I'm not sure, maybe both? I can't remember the last time we were doing separate inquiries in separate locations. It's making me anxious, I guess."

"Well, that's probably because the last time we did that, you ended up in a dark tunnel on a deserted island, among other dangerous things." I'm sure he was thinking about my impromptu trip to Havana.

I smiled at him and then reached over and kissed his cheek. "That's probably it. Flashbacks of you and me separated, and Mimi and me getting into all kinds of mischief."

"Promise me you'll keep the mischief to a minimum this time."

I raised an eyebrow at him. At least he knew better than to ask us to keep out of trouble completely. That would be a fool's request.

We did the long lover's goodbye at the airport. As much as we joked about my uneasiness, I was still leery of this trip, so it was difficult to let Colby go. But go he must, and I had to brave airport security.

Once settled on the plane, I pulled out my tablet, intending to tackle my Hollywood reading list. My seat was first class, aisle, because when I, along with Mimi and a few others, received the reward money from recovering all that stolen art in Boston, I swore to never fly coach again. Best decision I had ever made. Well, besides moving in with Colby.

Instead of reading, I promptly fell asleep. And except for waking for drink and snack services, I slept most of the six-hour flight. I would have thought it unusual, but I hadn't slept well once Colby dropped the dad bomb.

LAX was bustling when we landed, but my bags arrived quickly, and I texted Mimi that I would wait curbside for her. My phone dinged quickly with a reply.

> I have shared my location with you. Traffic is heavy and I don't want you waiting curbside when you can be comfy inside.

When the little dot was about a block away, I headed for the exit. The first thing I noticed when I stepped outside was the scent in the air. Sweet and salty, nothing like Boston or Virginia, it was slightly intoxicating.

Mimi arrived in a sporty cherry-red four-door Porsche. And from the lack of sound, I concluded it was electric. It was a sweet, if expensive, looking set of wheels. She rolled down the passenger window. “Do you need help with your bags?”

I shook my head and tossed them into the hatchback. It smelled new inside. I climbed in and took the travel mug of water Mimi handed me before reaching across the console and hugging her. “Sorry to not greet you properly, but it’s a zoo here and the sooner we get out the better I’ll feel.”

“No worries. Just glad to see you.” It had been too long since we had been together. I looked around the interior. From what I could see, it was fully appointed. “Nice car.”

“I’m glad you like it because it’s yours while you’re here.”

“What?! Mimi, this car looks brand new. And expensive.”

“It is,” she replied. “Tom took delivery a few days ago. He was tired of the other Porsche always being in the shop. And this one gets great range on a charge, so it should be fun to drive.”

I wasn’t sure how I felt about driving a recently purchased, very expensive car. However, I had to admit it would be a kick to drive. So I sat back and relaxed as Mimi maneuvered out of the airport.

I had never been to Los Angeles before and watched wide-eyed as unfamiliar architecture and the wildest fauna rolled by as we traversed the busy roadways. Mimi weaved in and out of lanes, pointing out things she thought I would enjoy, swearing at the occasional driver.

“There’s a traffic alert on the 405, so that’s why the surface streets,” she said as she turned onto Lincoln

Boulevard. "Your hotel isn't far from here. You're going to love it, something right out of a 1960s beach movie."

There were tall palm trees everywhere. I had to admit, seeing them rise above rows of strip malls and apartment buildings was stunning. It was nice that beauty could still surprise me. And there was that sweet smell again, wafting through my open window. "Mimi, what is that intoxicating fragrance?"

"It's great, isn't it? It could be any number of things - pink jasmine is blooming right now, tons of roses, sage, Jeffery Pines, an abundance of lavender, and lots of folks have citrus trees in their yards."

"Well, it's amazing."

"Oh, wait until dark, the night-blooming jasmine will knock you out. And if it rains, we'll drive through Laurel Canyon. The eucalyptus fragrance is irresistible."

As we got closer to Santa Monica, the Pacific Ocean was visible on the horizon. Mimi turned onto Colorado Boulevard and headed west, and the ocean came into full view. It was like a postcard come to life.

"That's Santa Monica Pier," she said as we drove by a long pier that ended with a roller coaster and Ferris wheel. "It's a lot of fun. We'll have to walk over one night because your hotel is two blocks away." Mimi slowed and waited for a car to pull out of a parking space and merge into traffic. She moved into the right lane and then announced, "Here we are," as she turned into a small parking lot and parked near a giant surfboard.

She was right. The hotel was adorable. Two stories with a row of rooms, top and bottom, a small lobby on the north side, with a large gated entrance next to it. Ferns, palms, and three-story tall palm trees surrounded the entire building. All backed by the Pacific Ocean.

"Isn't it lovely? I can't wait to see the inside. All the website photos had a total vintage beach vibe, and I knew you'd love it."

We climbed out of the car and walked across the parking lot. The door to the lobby was propped open, and a genial man greeted us at the front desk. The inside was tiny, filled with a variety of novelty gifts, many with the hotel logo emblazoned on them, and a coffee and tea counter, as well as plenty of snacks. Vintage surfboards adorned the walls.

"Good afternoon. Checking in?" Our host inquired in a thick Brooklyn accent. His nametag said Joe.

Mimi got the accounts settled, and we received instructions on all the available amenities. Then Joe walked us to the gate, showed us the code to unlock it, and bid me to enjoy my stay.

We grabbed my bags from the car, fumbled for a minute with the gate code, and then headed to the back of the building, where we found it was not just one building but several. We climbed up the first set of stairs and walked to the end of the open walkway to the last door.

Outside on the deck was a picnic table with an umbrella. There was a long counter bar along the deck railing with several high-backed bar stools and a fantastic beach view. It would be a great place to sit and watch the sunset.

Mimi opened the door, and we entered another era. The room was large, with a separate living room and bedroom. An overstuffed leather loveseat and a mid-century upholstered chair in denim blue gave the living room a homey touch. The coffee and end tables were rattan, and a large mirror graced one wall, while the other had a coat rack made from an old surfboard. A large built-in wall cabinet held a television and a small refrigerator, and had plenty of drawers for incidentals.

One side of the living room had a proscenium opening into the bedroom. Two floor-to-ceiling louvered-door closets with a small built-in desk and mirror between them were on the wall opposite the bed. A charming white coverlet covered the bed, and an abstract painting of surfboards hung above it. I sensed a theme.

The absolutely vintage bathroom was on the far side of the living room. Sapphire-blue tiles lined the tub and shower walls. A pedestal sink stood on a floor of blue and white hexagon tiles. Only the toilet was modern, as I would expect in a drought-prone state.

"Oh, Mimi, this is beyond adorable," I exclaimed as I dropped my suitcases on the bed.

"It's even better than I expected!" she agreed. "We'll be hanging out here, that's for sure."

"Pizza and evening strolls on the beach," I added. I walked around the room and opened a few of the abundant windows to let the salt air drift in. "I'll need to figure out where the grocery stores are so I can fill up that fridge."

"You'll have no problem navigating around Santa Monica. It's like a small beach town with lots of conveniences."

I sat on the couch and took a moment to soak it all in. Los Angeles, Santa Monica, the beach, this room, and thought how lucky I was to have this opportunity. "So, where should we begin on our quest to authenticate your painting" I asked, not wanting to dive into work, but feeling that I should.

"How about we start by taking today to get settled and catch up? We can start fresh tomorrow." I could get behind that plan. Mimi added, "I need to go pick up my car, and you need to unpack. I'll come by around six and we'll make a dinner plan and then gossip the rest of the night." And with that, she was off to wait for the town car service.

She said that Tom's place was just fifteen minutes up the road in Pacific Palisades. I offered to take her, but she said she had already texted the driver. Once she was gone, I flipped on the television to see if there was local news and settled on a station.

I listened to the local traffic, weather, and crime statistics while I unpacked. I made a grocery list and looked on my phone for the closest store. Mimi was right. There was a large chain store less than five minutes away.

With everything unpacked and the newscaster droning on about regional land use policies, I curled up on the soft leather couch and fell asleep. I awoke to laughter outside my open window and realized the sun was dipping closer to the horizon. Disoriented, I grabbed my phone to check the time.

I had about thirty minutes before Mimi came back. The weather-named meteorologist - that could not be his real name, could it? - gave the same forecast I heard while unpacking. Not waiting for the serious talking head to come back on to repeat the day's headlines, I hit the off button on the remote.

I freshened up in the bathroom, splashing water on my face and running a brush through my curls. After changing my clothes, I ambled out onto the deck to sit at the bar and watch the sunset while I waited for Mimi. I spotted her as she walked past the Birds of Paradise by the stairs, just as the Ferris wheel lit up. I gave her a little wave as she ascended.

There was just a touch of a chill in the westerly breeze as the sun dipped into the ocean. I shivered. I'd have to remember to grab a jacket when we left for dinner.

"You better be hungry because I'm ravenous," Mimi said as she walked up to my door. We both ducked inside so I could grab my bag and a coat.

"The time change has me all out of whack, but I am famished." I closed the door. I could hear the crowds at the pier as we descended the stairs. "And since I napped instead of running errands, can we stop at the store on our way back so I can grab some breakfast essentials and snacks?" Mimi hooked her arm in mine.

"Absolutely," she said. "Where would you like to eat? Santa Monica is filled with great restaurants, and if you want to drive a bit further, there are some exotic places to dine."

"For tonight, I think anywhere nearby would be fine."

"Okay, let's go to my favorite Thai restaurant," she said enthusiastically.

And with that, we were off in Mimi's convertible, top down, zipping through the night streets of Santa Monica. Quickly arriving at our destination.

The restaurant was cozy and dark, filled with magnificent aromas. Our egg roll and spring roll appetizers arrived swiftly, and I had to stop myself from scarfing them down unapologetically. My body had no idea what time it was, but at least it knew it was hungry. While we waited for our main courses, it was time to quiz Mimi on the task before us.

"So tell me more about this painting," I requested between bites of another spring roll.

FOUR

It's a beautiful Saturday morning. What the hell else have we got to do? -THOMAS CROWN AFFAIR

Mimi put down her egg roll and detailed the history of the painting. "Around 1944, they were making this film noir. The director commissioned an oil painting of the leading lady to hang above the mantle in the main apartment set. As soon as it was completed and they did the first test shots, the producer was unhappy. Seems the oil painting did not film well in black and white, so they made other arrangements."

Our food arrived, and we made room for the shared plates of Pad Thai and Cashew Chicken. After we served ourselves, Mimi continued, "There were other problems on the set, including a contentious relationship between the director and the producer. Soon the director was fired and he and the painting left the building, so to speak."

"Wait, so it was never used in the film?"

"Nope, and believe it or not, that fact and the fact it disappeared make it a valuable collector's item."

"That surprises me," I said, perplexed. "I have a lot to learn about movie memorabilia. Do you have a good resource, someone who could help me at least authenticate its age? That would be a good place to start."

"Tom uses a guy in West Hollywood, Edric Lancaster, for his more traditional acquisitions. Very reputable, seems to know his stuff."

"But you don't trust him to authenticate this painting?"

Mimi lowered her voice and leaned across the table. I leaned closer to her. "TJ, there is something about him I just don't trust. I can't put my finger on it, but it's a feeling I can't shake, either."

I sat back and thought about that for a moment. This gave me a better understanding of why Mimi wanted me to fly out to assist her. She was alone in the city, in charge of assembling an extensive collection of very valuable pieces of art, and had to rely on people she had known for little more than a year. I had to admire her fearlessness. I wasn't sure I'd have the same audacity - strange city, big responsibilities - all on my own.

"Where is the painting now?"

"At Tom's. The seller took a small deposit to allow us to have time to have it checked out before committing to purchasing it."

"Really? So this isn't going through an auction house or dealer?"

"No, it's a private sale. Happens a lot here. Items get moved from private collection to private collection. Lots of real estate, foreign, and Silicon Valley money, floating around."

This is a strange new world. I had dealt with pieces acquired through personal troves, but there was always a dealer or executor as an intermediary. Generally, in my work, I never dealt directly with a seller. I imagined it could get tricky if negotiations were involved, or worse, we found the painting to be a replica.

"Tom is out of town for the weekend, on a deep sea fishing trip. Why don't you take a walk on the beach in the morning, grab some breakfast and we can meet around ten at the mansion to check it out. Jump right in. You don't mind working on a Saturday, do you?"

"I'm here to work, boss."

With that out of the way, we concentrated on more important matters as we finished our meal.

I dove right in, hoping Mimi had time for more than just work these days. "Anyone special out here you want to tell me about?"

"Not really. I'm usually too busy to meet anyone, and a lot of the men I meet while I'm working are...how do I put this...all about their possessions. Cars, houses, more cars, boats, latest electronics, you name it, they've bought it." She poured more jasmine tea into our cups. "I'm just not interested in those things." She sighed, sipped some tea, and sat back. "What about you and Colby, have you set a wedding date yet?"

I scoffed. "Let's see. I am crippled by doubts and unable to commit. I'm hoping some time apart will give me perspective."

"Is it Colby? Do you have doubts about him?"

"The only doubts I have are about me and my ability to maintain a stable relationship without it blowing up down the road."

"I understand. But you and Colby are great together. And you've been together for a while now."

"Almost five years," I said, nodding in agreement. It sounded like commitment when I said it aloud. "Despite that, I can't shake the feeling that if I let my guard down and make that final jump, I'm going to be left heartbroken."

Mimi looked at me for a long moment, and I knew she was going to say something wise. "If it all went to hell tomorrow, wouldn't you be heartbroken? I mean, marriage wouldn't make a difference would it?"

"No, it wouldn't. But I didn't say any of this was rational," I replied with a morose laugh.

Mimi picked up the credit card and receipt that the server had placed on the table. She popped them into the business folder she had brought along. "Gotta keep all the receipts for Tom's bookkeeper, so I'm not tempted to put frivolous expenses on his high-limit card." She shut the folder and tucked it into her bag. "Look, nobody says you have to get married. It is the twenty-first century, after all."

"Very true, but I can't seem to convince Colby of that. Who knew my big, bad-assed lawman was so old-fashioned?"

We both laughed at that fact as we put on our jackets and headed to the parking lot. The air had gone from crisp to cold. Mimi left the top up on the car as we detoured to the grocery store before she dropped me off at the hotel.

I climbed the stairs carrying two bags of essentials: bottled water, orange juice, yogurt, milk, fruit, and cereal. I put everything away, threw on my nightshirt, and crawled into bed. Just as I dozed off, I realized I had not talked to Colby since I landed. I completely forgot to text him after I said I had arrived safely. I rolled over and double-checked my phone. Besides a thumbs-up, there was no text from him either.

I pushed aside any concerns about that and tried to sleep. The time change was kicking my butt, and the light from the full moon shining through my window didn't help. I got up and turned the wand on the blind to shut out as much light as possible. In the quiet, I could hear the laughter and music drifting over from the pier. I found it oddly soothing and finally fell asleep to the sound of people having fun.

On Saturday, with my body still trying to adjust to the three-hour time difference, I awoke to darkness. My phone said it was four o'clock. I was tempted to pull the covers over my head and wait for a decent hour to arise. But I thought better of it, got up, threw on my running clothes, and brewed coffee.

I checked out the headlines on my tablet while I waited. Then I filled my mug, curled up on the couch, and opened the book on vintage Hollywood collectibles. Flipping through it, I found that most of the collectibles were clothing, scripts, and a few props. Dorothy's ruby slippers, of which there were several pairs, were highly sought after, and items from musicals were among the pricier objects.

Anything Star Wars related was valuable, but not exactly rare. It appeared that most collectors were extremely interested in paraphernalia from the thirties and forties, especially the black and white classics, and film noir collectibles were the Holy Grail.

According to the book, part of this came from rarity. Studios were not known for keeping props, costumes, or scripts. Especially as changing economic times meant the studios were sold and consolidated. And as property became more valuable, studios were more likely to sell their storage facilities and dump the contents after such a consolidation.

Many of these items would have been lost to history if famed actress Debbie Reynolds had not decided it was important to buy large lots of memorabilia from the studios. Her collections included costumes and props from her films, with an eye to opening her own Hollywood museum before she passed.

The book concluded with a list of online resources where I could continue my education. I was about to dive into a few when I realized the sky was brightening with the dawn. It was time to walk the beach.

I grabbed my jacket and pushed sunglasses onto my head in anticipation of sunrise. Jogging down the steps to the sidewalk, I realized there was a path leading to the beach. It led to a heavy steel gate. When I pushed it open, it revealed a dozen or so concrete steps that ended near the bike path that ran the length of the beach.

There were a few people out and about when I reached the bottom of the steps. Mostly serious runners, keeping a good pace along the asphalt walkway, while a parallel path had a few cyclists and a skilled skateboarder. I crossed over both and continued westward on the long stretch of sand until I was at the water's edge.

The rising sun made the water and sky shades of baby pink and blue. The ocean was mirror-glass smooth, with small waves lapping on the shore. I removed my water shoes and dug my toes into the wet sand, walking toward the now quiet pier, the Ferris wheel frozen in place, waiting.

I strolled at a leisurely pace for about half an hour, watching the tractors, each with a large grate on the back, sweep the sand as the unhoused folks, who had been camping on the beach, got up and moved onto their next location. Seabirds ran in and out of the waves, catching their breakfast, paying little mind to me or the fisherman setting up just ahead. And then a lone dolphin surfaced and followed me as I continued my trek.

I wasn't sure why, but the Pacific felt markedly different from its Atlantic counterpart. The eastern seaboard was powerful, rushed, and even a little angry. But here, the dawn light and calm waters were peaceful. Beckoning me to kick off my shoes and tarry a while. Contemplate the meaning of love and life.

Reluctantly, I knew it was time to return to reality, head to my room and earn my keep. The sun was glaring through the spaces between the buildings as I trudged back to the hotel. I popped my sunglasses over my eyes to deflect the glare and thought about the task ahead. I hoped I was up to it.

An hour later, I had showered and was ready to meet Mimi. Unfortunately, I still had about two hours to wait. Adjusting my internal clock was going to take a few days. My responsible self said I should use the time to continue my research.

Instead, I stuffed a banana into my bag, filled my water bottle, and jogged to the parking lot to see if I could figure out how to operate the Porsche. I thought it would be nice to explore Santa Monica, as long as I had some time to kill. I climbed in and made the necessary adjustments to the seat and mirrors, then set the navigation to downtown.

As I gingerly pressed the pedal, the car zipped out of the parking lot. Impressed, I settled into the sumptuous leather seats and listened as the GPS guided me around the block toward Ocean Avenue. I rolled down the windows and opened the sunroof. My curls tangled as the wind whipped them around my face.

I shoved my sunglasses up onto my head to act as a headband of sorts, and that tamed them a bit. At the stoplight, I turned left so I could drive along the beach. Traffic was light, and I was having difficulty keeping the Porsche at the speed limit. The power was deceptive, with no engine noise, smooth acceleration, combined with the warm breeze and ocean air, my foot was heavy.

My next stop was going to be the farmers' market. A little research made it sound like the place to be on a Saturday morning. I asked the GPS to find parking near there, and it surprised me with a premium spot within walking distance. It didn't hurt that it was still a few minutes before the stalls opened. I sat on a low wall and pulled out my phone.

The time change was messing with my mind. One moment I would think it too early to text Colby, and the next I would remember he was probably not only up, but had already taken Wyatt for his walk. And Stevie was at this moment haunting him while he caught up with the day's news, demanding attention and ear scritches.

Chagrined, I realized I hadn't thought to text him until just now. I attached a few photos from my morning walk and wished him a nice day. For good measure, I included a heart emoji. Top-tier girlfriend, I was not.

I walked the block to the open-air market just as they opened. Tall palms stood over the white-tented stalls that lined the streets, which had been closed to traffic for the occasion. I strolled through the market, enjoying the warm sun and people-watching.

They were diverse, vibrant, and happily spending their Saturday poking through the abundance of fresh produce and craft items. The tables filled with fresh chilies, passion fruit, and a variety of greens beguiled me. There was an entire stall of berries, in every shape, color, and flavor I could imagine. I wanted a pint of each.

I wandered past the carrots, beets, and turnips and held out against tempting the flower stalls. The oranges were irresistible, and I succumbed, struck by both the weight and fragrance as I dropped two into my bag.

Musicians played on every corner, and if I listened carefully, I could pick out a United Nations' worth of languages being spoken. It was invigorating. By the time I'd walked the entire market, eating one of my fresher than fresh oranges, it was time to meet Mimi.

I returned to the Porsche and made my way to Tom's house. As directed, I turned the car onto Ocean Avenue, took a sharp left that led me to the Pacific Coast Highway, PCH to the locals. The short drive north on the PCH was the stuff of Hollywood dreams. Beach and ocean on one side, steep, palm tree dotted hills on the other. And in the distance, the Santa Monica Mountains rose above the landscape and followed the coastline north.

As I turned east onto Chautauqua Boulevard and drove inland, it was evident that Pacific Palisades was not what I had been expecting. It differed little from the Santa Monica neighborhoods I had just left as I wound my way down Sunset Boulevard, through narrow residential streets to a small retail area. That street was bordered on both sides by charming shops that gave the area a small-town feel. As quickly as I had come upon those shops, I was back in residential neighborhoods. The houses appeared unassuming, with quaint Mediterranean bungalows mixed with Spanish Colonials and standout Craftsman homes.

The closer I got to my destination, the newer the homes. Styles remained the same, with each home having a distinct look, from Cape Cod to extreme modernism. These were not suburban tract homes. Still, where I was expecting lofty mansions and vast expanses of manicured lawns, based on Mimi's characterization of Tom's home, these were all two stories on narrow lots. Nothing I would describe as opulent. Boy, was I in for a surprise.

The GPS announced I had reached my destination. If I hadn't recognized Mimi's car in the driveway, I would have been sure I was at the wrong location. The house was a two-story, modern building with Spanish flourishes, most notably the tile roof, which stood in stark contrast to the sharp angles and white stone walls, with dark chocolate brown windows, doors, and trim. It should have been an indecorous disaster, but somehow it worked and stood out from the rather mundane homes around it.

Still, it did not impress me as the residence of a tech millionaire. I spotted Mimi through the chocolate brown lace-like wrought-iron entry gate, as she walked down the long breezeway to greet me. I grabbed my bag and scrambled out of the car, just as she opened the gate, leaning against it to keep it open.

"Good morning! You found it okay?"

"No problems. Cute little British guy was great with the directions." Mimi looked at me curiously. "The GPS. I chose the British male voice. Felt less bossy than the others. I call him Jeeves," I clarified. "I walked over to her and turned to look again at the neighborhood. "This isn't exactly what I was expecting from your description."

Mimi laughed and waved me into the vestibule. It was a covered walkway, with a matching iron gate on the opposite end, opening into the house. "Just wait," was all she said.

I walked through the second gate and into a dream. A grand foyer that was open all the way to the back of the home. Where I could see not only the ocean, but a pool with an infinity edge and an enormous spa. We appeared to be on the second of three levels, with sliding glass walls on each side of the hall, leading into separate wings of the home.

What appeared to be a spacious suburban home from the front expanded into a four-story contemporary mansion, replete with views of the hills and coastline from the patio.

"Takes your breath away, doesn't it?" Mimi remarked as she led me into one of the living areas. "You can see all of Los Angeles from the rooftop deck."

"I'm speechless. I don't think I've ever been in a home like this. A museum, yes, but not..." I was at a loss. I spied the bold colors and cubist style of an original Jacob Lawrence in the alcove at the top of the staircase. I had never seen one outside of the Smithsonian.

Mimi followed my gaze. "Oh, you are in for a treat. Let me show you around before we tackle our real job."

She walked me over to the white floating staircase, bordered by glass railings, and we took the stairs to the lower level. All I could think was, *don't get fingerprints on the glass* and *who has to clean all of this?*

When we reached the bottom, I sucked in my breath to keep from swearing in amazement. Every wall had an original work on it, and several wall alcoves held modern sculptures.

The room was white on white on white, so the focus was on the artwork. I couldn't decide if it was amazing or grotesque. It was something.

There was a Luis Alberto Acuña on one wall. On another, a Pop art piece by Marjorie Strider, a contemporary of Andy Warhol, but in my opinion, her work was edgier. There were several modern Impressionists I wasn't as familiar with, one possibly a Paul Verdell. I'd have to inspect it closer to be sure.

The alcoves held unbelievable sculptures: a horse and rider by Frederic Remington; a Pompon Running Rabbit; and a Marcello Mascherini dancer.

I turned and couldn't believe what I was seeing. "Mimi, that's not an original Tamara de Lempicka, is it?" I asked in awe.

"It is. Trust me, before we're done you are going to want to get up close and personal with a lot of this art," she said, grinning with pride.

I had no way to process what I was seeing. I couldn't imagine the work or the cost of acquiring this eclectic collection. And there was an entire house left to explore.

"Follow me," Mimi said, and I had to peel my eyes off the walls to catch up with her as she wound her way down another flight of stairs and through a small hallway. She opened the big double doors to the home theater room and stepped back so I could get the full view.

"Oh...my...god..."

FIVE

Let's work the problem, people. Let's not make things worse by guessing - APOLLO 13

It was impossible to take everything in as I stepped over the threshold. Reclining whiskey-colored chair pods stood in raked rows on thick, textured carpet. The front row boasted two Art Deco couches with deep seats, upholstered in matching whiskey leather. All leading to a wall-sized screen, bordered by thick crimson velvet drapes at the far end of the room.

Art Deco crystal sconces were spaced evenly along the red velvet walls leading to the screen. Walls trimmed with navy and gold wood millwork and dotted with small alcoves held various treasures. One of which, I swore, was an Oscar. The entire design was a cinephile's fever dream.

Every other inch of the room exhibited film memorabilia. Any open wall space held movie posters, lithographs, and frame after frame of signed photos. I recognized *The Wizard of Oz* and *Breakfast at Tiffany's* the remainder were a mystery to me. Most of the photos were black and white, with a few full-color shots scattered about of people I didn't recognize. The wall next to us held a full-sized circus banner. From my limited knowledge, I knew those were highly collectible.

There were at least ten dress forms draped with antique clothes placed eerily in and around the seating rows. Even if they weren't from films or red carpet events, they were all stunning. A suit of armor stood in the far corner, guarding the screen. There were shelves full of a mélange of artifacts, many appearing to be mundane objects. However, I had to assume they were movie-related. Ashtrays, matches, cigarette cases and martini glasses mingled with jewelry, a couple of daggers and a vintage pair of binoculars on the shelf closest to me.

I stepped around a large box of scripts on the floor. The title page of the one on top said *Casablanca,* covered in notes and signatures, and a prominent coffee ring. I curbed my impulse to search through the box to see what other treasures it held. I turned my attention to several long utility tables that sat behind the back row of recliners. Packed with even more items, as was the floor beneath, I couldn't process it all.

"Mimi, did you acquire all of this for Tom?"

"Oh, no!" she exclaimed. "This is his hobby. He scours the internet, goes to shows and estate sales, picking up things that pique his interest." She walked over to a door and opened it, pulling out a very large wooden painting case.

To my eye, it looked historical. She set the box on the only empty spot on one of the long tables, carefully flipped the clasp, and opened the cover. Then she began to lift the painting from the box, struggling with its bulk. I steadied the container as she maneuvered the ungainly canvas out of its confines and set it on an empty easel.

It was huge. I'm not sure what I was expecting, but it was at least twice the size I thought a portrait should be. I gave Mimi a quizzical look.

"It's not your imagination," she said. "She is extremely large. The canvas had to be to match the set design. I'll screen the movie for you, so you can see what they eventually used and how big the living room set was - the windows and drapery look like they belong in a castle instead of an uptown New York apartment."

"Well, she certainly has presence," I noted as I stepped back to take in the image.

She was beautiful, with dark hair cascading to her shoulders, wearing a black, sleeveless dress that accentuated her alabaster skin. She was sitting, looking over her bare left shoulder, her right shoulder draped in a sheer wrap, maybe chiffon. Her eyes had a dreamy quality.

The background and her dress below her waist melted into an impressionistic, fully shadowed lower third. It was all meant to draw you into her face. All meant to elicit a femme fatale countenance.

I would say it succeeded, and I wondered how much the final image matched this abandoned one. Notably, it was unsigned. Which, I guess, made sense. The actual artist couldn't sign it if it was to be attributed to a fictional creator in the film.

I stepped closer to it to examine the brushwork. It was undeniably oil on canvas. The brushstrokes were delicate, which was interesting on such a large piece. I grabbed the pair of white gloves Mimi had laid out for me and slipped them on before running my fingers over the paint.

There were tiny cracks, as I would expect in an older painting that had not had any manner of restoration. The colors were crisp, and I noticed minimal dirt or smoke haze. It was amazing how many art pieces were covered in cigarette smoke residue.

"Has it been cleaned?" I asked.

"The seller said it's exactly as he found it."

"Hmmm..." I tipped it forward to observe the backing. Definitely looked old and somewhat fragile with the passage of time. It would have to be removed eventually by whoever was going to authenticate its age. I rested it back on the easel and looked closely at the frame. "What's with the frame?"

Baffled by what I was seeing, I tilted it toward the light to get a better look. "It looks gilded, but there is some type of coating on it to dull the finish."

"My guess is they had to spray something on it to keep the gold from reflecting the stage lights."

That seemed reasonable because I had no other context for this type of alteration. I felt like a neophyte who still had much to learn about filmmaking before I could make an educated assessment of its authenticity. I had many more questions about the painting itself, but they would have to be answered by an expert who could safely remove the backing and the frame. Then we could examine the entire piece thoroughly. Incompetent forgers would forget about unexposed areas of the canvas, and that was often their undoing. The unadorned canvas would have its own story to tell.

"Let's see that movie," I said as I removed the gloves.

"Should I pop some popcorn?" Mimi asked with a laugh.

“I think I’m good for now, I really do want to see the set, see if the dimensions look right for this painting.” I was laser-focused, feeling out of my depth, and afraid I would miss something.

Mimi swiped through what looked like a tablet, pressed a few icons, then the lights dimmed and the credits rolled on the screen.

“Are there any photos of the original painting…before they replaced it?” I asked as a series of actors’ names I had never heard of scrolled across the screen.

“Only a couple of screenshots from the set. Nothing with the quality that would help you with identification.”

I sighed and focused on the screen.

The movie opened on an opulent apartment, and soon various characters assembled by the fireplace with the replacement painting hanging above it. I looked carefully at the dimensions of the painting in the film. It seemed reasonable that the original oil canvas we were examining was a similar size.

I could see what Mimi had meant about its dimensions. It had to be oversized to work on screen. Not only on the set itself, but for it to have the impact needed as a central character in the film.

Mimi paused the movie as it panned to the woman in the painting, and the canvas filled the screen. I looked from the woman on the screen to the woman on the canvas.

“So tell me why this painting wasn’t used in the film.” I was looking from the screen to the canvas and back again.

This was like playing one of the *Spot the Difference* games, where you look at two seemingly identical cartoons and figure out what makes them different. There were subtle discrepancies between the portraits. Her hair was softer and fuller in the film. Her face was still the central focus, but there was a steelier look in her eyes, and most importantly, the entire piece was flatter. The monochrome colors were muted, with little depth or dimension. I wasn't sure if that was a trick of filming in black and white or if it was created that way, but it was a significant alteration from the one we were examining.

"Once they did their first test shots of the original," Mimi explained, "the director did not like how the oils looked in black and white. From the limited history I could find, he said the entire aesthetic was too harsh."

I looked at the canvas on the easel, and I had to agree with the director's point of view.

"So this one," I gestured toward the screen, "isn't an oil painting?" That would explain the lack of depth.

"Nope, they took a photo of the lead actress, enlarged it, and then the art department painted over it to make it resemble an oil portrait. I think it is the reason her facial features are so expressive, too. All in all, it worked well to convey the mood of the mystery."

I tried not to be overwhelmed by all I did not know at this point. I knew from experience we would have to take this a step at a time. And the first step would be to verify its age.

"So this expert, will he come here or are we transporting this possibly priceless piece of movie history to him?"

"Edric is on his way, should be here shortly, with all his various tools of the trade. By the time he's done, we should have a solid idea if it's old enough to require further investigation."

I looked at Mimi for a minute, realizing I had missed something very important in all the excitement of the trip. She did not return my gaze. "Mimi," I said as I raised an eyebrow, "Why didn't you have him authenticate its age *before* you asked me to fly out here?"

She rearranged a few items on the table, stalling. Finally, she took a deep breath and answered. "TJ, something isn't right about all of this. I can't quite explain it. I told you I don't trust Edric. There is just something off about him, besides his general pretentiousness. You'll see." She rearranged a few more items that didn't need to be rearranged. "And then, it just all of this, the art trades...." Her voice trailed off.

I waited, to let her find her way to what she wanted to say. Mimi was seldom at a loss for words, so I knew this was important. Then a low, melodic chime resonated from somewhere deep within the house.

"That has to be Edric," she said before quickly exiting to greet him.

"We are not done talking about this," I called after her.

While I waited for them to return, I took the opportunity to examine Tom's collection more closely. What was deemed collectible intrigued me. But then, that could be said of any art, past or present.

A black desk phone captured my attention. It had to be from the thirties or forties, based on the Art Deco styling. I picked up the handset and was startled by the heft. I had to guess the entire telephone was Bakelite. Bakelite was the first commercially available synthetic plastic, highly collectible, especially the jewelry, which was often dyed in muted colors and hand-carved. It was also quite heavy.

I was curious why this phone was so important. Perhaps it sat on the desk of a hard-boiled film noir detective, like Sam Spade in *The Maltese Falcon*. Or it was on a nightstand in the bedroom of the endearing characters Nick and Nora in *The Thin Man.*

Struck by a burst of whimsy, I couldn't resist the urge to dial a number and listen to the satisfying sounds of the rotary mechanism returning to its starting position. Then, feeling guilty, not knowing its true value, I gently replaced the headset before I was discovered. I quashed the urge to spin the dial again before I walked away.

Another shelf caught my eye. It contained an enormous, and might I editorialize, hideous diamond necklace on a black velvet display easel. I walked over to get a closer look, trying to imagine, indelicately, just how large a woman's décolletage would have to be to wear it stylishly.

"That is from *Philadelphia Story*," Mimi said as she reentered the room. "It was a running joke throughout the film. Luckily, it's costume or it would be in a museum for the diamonds alone."

A diminutive man followed her into the room. He couldn't have been more than five-foot-three, and I swore he was doing his best to emulate Truman Capote in style. He wore a blue and white popover seersucker Oxford with crisp jeans. His wispy blond hair was topped with a jaunty diamond-crown straw fedora, and the final touch, a tweed scarf, fell from his neck. He looked more like he was heading to a Vogue shoot instead of determining the age of a painting on a sunny Saturday morning.

"TJ, this is Edric Lancaster," Mimi said as she placed a hand on his shoulder. He put down the large valise he was carrying and reached for my hand. I could see the Louis Vinton logo on the well-worn leather. Even his supplies had impeccable taste.

"TJ, very nice to meet you. From all Mimi has said, it is clear she holds your skills in great regard." His voice and grip were professional, but I could see the disdain in his eyes.

How dare Mimi bring in an outsider, they said. *How dare she question my authority,* they exclaimed as he shook my hand. This was going to be an interesting evaluation. "Let's get down to business," he said as he released my hand, grabbed the bag, and walked over to the painting.

"Here she is. Would it be better if we moved into one of the sitting rooms, where there is more natural light?" Mimi asked, looking at me for reassurance.

"Yes, yes, that would be ideal," Edric replied as he pivoted and stepped out into the hallway, fully expecting us to follow his lead.

Mimi quickly put on gloves and picked up the canvas. It tipped precariously, and I grabbed a glove and used it to help her steady the behemoth. Once she had it balanced properly, I followed her out the door, carrying the easel. We wove our way down the hall to one of the exterior rooms. It had expansive floor-to-ceiling windows on perpendicular sides, giving ample natural light to better examine the painting.

It was sparsely furnished, so I placed the easel in the center of the room. Mimi put our lady on it and stepped back. Edric set his case on a large table that sat in front of one bank of windows and opened it. From one slot, he pulled a pair of gold loupe glasses and popped them on his head. Then from another pocket, he produced an exquisite pair of white gloves and put them on before stepping over to the easel. He left the loupe glasses on his forehead, preferring to examine the painting with the naked eye first.

Running a gloved finger around the gilded frame first, he then tipped the canvas in several directions before moving it to the table and setting it flat. Finally, he flipped down the loupes and continued to examine it through the thick lenses. Mimi looked as if she were about to climb out of her skin. I was familiar with the process and the often quirky characters that treated it with all the seriousness of a surgeon.

"Hmmm..." was all Edric said before walking to his equipment bag and pulling out a large cloth, a flat brush, and a few tools. He spread the cloth over the table and placed the painting face down on the cloth. He brushed the back to remove any debris and then ran his hand over it. "The owner is aware I'm going to have to remove the backing, correct?" Mimi nodded. "It is extremely fragile and will be destroyed in the process." He looked at her for confirmation that she understood this, and she nodded again. "Okay, let's begin."

Edric carefully pulled up the lower corner, and I watched as pieces flaked off. Once he had it completely removed, it revealed the wood stretcher attached to the canvas. It was a light wood, with mitered corners, indicative of an American frame. This was a good sign, but I continued to temper my expectations.

Edric continued his inspection, making a few 'hmmmms' and an enthusiastic "aaahhh!" at one point. I was confident Mimi had stopped breathing as she awaited his analysis. Edric grabbed a flat, butter knife-looking tool from his bag and began working on extracting the canvas from its frame.

It was delicate work because years of heat, cold, and humidity could warp even the best canvas and make it difficult to remove. It was important not to damage the painting or the frame because original frames were often as valuable as the work they encased.

After a few moments of struggle, Edric successfully separated the canvas from its bonds. He lifted the frame from the table and handed it to Mimi. I quickly slipped my gloves back on and stepped closer to her.

The inside edges revealed brilliant gilding, untouched by whatever had been used to dull the exposed frame. The unstained wood looked old and showed signs of exposure to years of unregulated temperatures and humidity. I would be interested to hear Edric's evaluation of the frame's age.

Mimi set the frame on the table, and we both peered over Edric's shoulder as he stood the portrait up and inspected the edges. Small, black nails held the fabric to the edges, which I felt was a good sign. Those would have been used around the time the work was created. Although I knew there were counterfeiters who would pull the small tacks from old, worthless paintings to use in forgeries.

Finally, he flipped the painting over and laid it flat on the table. As the light illuminated the paint, Mimi and I gasped at what we saw on the outer edge of the canvas.

SIX

You know what you're getting into. It's gonna be rough -
TO HAVE AND HAVE NOT

There, on the right stile of the canvas was a signature, date, and description of the work. It was in a delicate script that I thought matched the brush strokes on the portrait. The writing was black on the already dark background, so it was difficult to read. Edric pulled out a small light from his Mary Poppins satchel and shone it over the script. We all leaned in to get a better look. It was signed, *Fiona V. Limon 1942 for the film*.

I squinted at the writing. The name of the film wasn't there. I looked again, resisting the urge to reach over and run my fingers across the canvas. I thought the title of the film must be hidden under dirt or lost in the dark paint. But it wasn't, at least not that could be seen with the naked eye.

"Is there a reason she didn't write the name of the film?" I asked, again feeling out of my element of expertise.

"Could be any number of reasons," Edric replied thoughtfully. "Most likely, they hadn't settled on a final name for the film."

"That would make sense," Mimi agreed. "The movie was based on a book. From what I read, there were several iterations before they finally settled on using the title of the book. It had been a best seller in its day and they rightly assumed it would be a big draw."

I was a little disappointed. If one of the original film title iterations had been printed on the edge, it would have been a stroke of luck. The likelihood of it being a forgery would have dimmed. However, with the artist's name and a signature, we were off to a good start.

If Edric determined it was old enough to be the original, then I had a place to begin my research. Edric was scraping some paint from the previously hidden edge of the work into a glass vial. He pushed up his loop glasses, held the vial up to the light and shook it before putting it in his satchel.

"Well, ladies, I'll do a bit of chemical analysis, but from all indications here, this painting looks to be from the time period of the original." He began to pack up his various tools. "Without further research, I cannot say definitively if it is the authentic painting, commissioned for the film. If you like, I can take the painting to my gallery to do further study."

"Thank you for that," Mimi said graciously. "I'll talk to Tom about it, since while it's here it's his responsibility."

Edric snapped his case shut, nodding. "You know how to find me." I was slightly disappointed he never pulled out a ridiculously large plant, coat rack, or floor lamp from it.

"Edric, have you any experience with Limon's works?" I asked. Hoping he could direct me to another of her paintings.

"Never heard of her before," he said flatly.

With that, Mimi led him through the maze leading to the front door. "Please bill Tom for your services and if it's okay, I'll contact you if we need further assistance on this project."

The walk down the long hall was icy. As we reached the entryway, she reassured him of his value. "When Tom returns, he has several other works he wants your expertise on," she said as she opened the door. "I'll be in touch later this week about them. And again, thank you for your help on this one, it was invaluable."

Edric appeared somewhat mollified and strutted to his vehicle, assured we recognized his worth. As he backed out of the drive, Mimi shut the door and turned to me. "Welcome to LA." She seemed exhausted by it all.

As we wound our way back to our lady-in-waiting, I was making a list in my head of our next steps. Now, being relatively certain of its age and with the benefit of an artist's name, I felt on more solid ground. I was ready to begin the hunt.

"What next?" Mimi asked as we rejoined the guest of honor.

"Let me get a few photos." I pulled out my cell and snapped open the lens cover.

"Fancy, looks like it could survive the apocalypse."

"Colby always wants me to be ready for any disaster. It's in his nature." I turned on the macro lens and snapped close-ups of the brushstrokes in several areas. Then I returned to normal mode and took photos of the signature, the tacks, and then the entire painting. Once I was done, I backed the photos up to the cloud and pocketed the phone. "Let's get her back to her safe place."

Mimi and I donned gloves, then gently secured the painting to the frame and carried it to the movie room. Once she was re-boxed and back in the locked closet, we decided it was time for lunch.

Mimi led me upstairs to the pristine kitchen at the back of the house. It included a dining alcove and a sitting area. The entire space opened to the patio and infinity pool. I could have fit my entire first floor in it. Mimi pulled packaged salads, sliced fruit, and sparkling water from the massive refrigerator. I rummaged through a few drawers and grabbed utensils and napkins - cloth, of course - and we made ourselves comfortable outside by the pool.

The weather was perfect. The sun was warm, a light breeze blew in from the ocean, and it seemed like everything was in bloom in the immaculate yard that surrounded the patio. Raised planters sported the orange and midnight-blue flowers of the Bird of Paradise plants that mingled with hot pink azaleas. Bougainvillea climbed over an Asian-inspired pergola that led into a shaded area filled with Elephant Ears and Coral Bells. Beyond the stone wall that edged the patio, was a wild and steep hillside. Sitting back in my chair, I relaxed in the surrounding beauty. I could get used to this.

I was going to miss these salads. I opened the container and dumped the contents onto cute melamine plates covered in pink flamingos and palm leaves. Cherry tomatoes of every color, three kinds of greens, red and orange sliced peppers, topped off with sliced avocado spilled across the plate. I sprinkled the container of feta cheese over it all and then drizzled everything with dressing. I was three bites in when I noticed Mimi.

She sat staring off into the distance, absently stabbing some lettuce. She twirled it with her fork, looking as if she had no interest in eating. Turning her attention to me, she asked, "What's next?"

"We are going to have to do a bit of research on who Fiona Limon was and what other paintings she has done. Hopefully, she had a professional reputation and wasn't just one of many generic studio artists. If I can compare this painting to another of hers, especially seeing a signature, that would be a great start." I explained and then took a bite of the salad. "Oh, my, how is this better than any salad I've ever had?"

"One of the many perks of Southern California - the produce," Mimi replied with little enthusiasm. She still hadn't touched her lunch.

"Wow." I grabbed a large strawberry from the mixed fruit container and ascended to heaven with my first bite. Once I recovered from that, I plotted our next move. "If we can be relatively assured it's her work, the next step is to try and find a record of her being paid to create it."

"I have a very good connection at the Getty Center who might be able to help us with their archives, or point us in the right direction," she explained as she pushed her salad aside. "I've been trying to cultivate a contact at the Academy Museum - it's essentially the Hollywood movie museum - but it's been difficult. I suppose I don't blame them for being cautious, I'm sure they get some looney tunes in there."

"Are you going to tell me what's wrong?" I asked, gesturing at her untouched salad with my fork.

Mimi didn't reply, but looked out over the hillside toward the ocean and sighed. I waited.

"Teej," she began tentatively. "It's possible I'm uneasy because of what happened in Boston. One creepy, criminal boss, and now I'm hyperaware of anything suspicious." She paused and looked out at the ocean again, absently twirling her fork.

"If it helps, I trust your instincts."

"The problem is, I'm not sure I do." She set her fork down forcefully, got up, and walked over to the glass railing. It separated the patio from a rather intimidating drop-off.

She turned back to me, leaned against the railing, and crossed her arms. "Something is not right. The art sales, Tom's trips, Edric's entire demeanor - it all sets off my radar." She shook her head and returned to the table.

"Everything is well documented. I have paperwork on every item I've helped procure. I've met sellers and buyers. All above board." She sat down and looked at me with those gold-rimmed eyes, which were deeply concerned. "But something is not right. And I hate feeling that and I hate even more saying it. And I hate that I dragged you out here to reassure me. All of this because Trevor is a convicted felon."

I sat back with my drink and absently swirled the ice with my finger. Things were beginning to come into focus, and I felt a little foolish that I hadn't picked up on it faster. Of course, I understood everything Mimi was feeling. And I understood why she didn't trust her instincts.

Trust was hard to come by when your former murderous boss is sitting behind bars in a federal prison for kidnapping, assault, and art theft. Neither of us saw that coming and spent a great deal of time extricating ourselves from the aftermath.

"You may not trust your instincts, but I do. And if you feel something is amiss, I'm happy to examine anything you need to either validate you or reassure you." I sipped my water, ashamed that I was excited to have a little intrigue mixed in with the provenance research.

"Thanks. It's probably nothing, but I can't shake my suspicions."

"We'll dig down on it and see if there is anything there," I assured her.

With that reassurance, Mimi found her appetite again, and we finished our lunch.

"I'll call my friend at the Getty on Monday and see if he can see us. He knows everything about Hollywood and the LA art scene. I'm sure he would be happy to help. Especially if he knows what we are looking at, can't imagine he wouldn't be extremely interested."

"Exactly how valuable would this painting be, if it turns out to be authentic?"

"At auction, I would think several million. I mean, until now, I don't think anyone believed it still existed." Mimi said as her phone buzzed. She flipped it over and looked at the message.

"If that's true, then we should be judicious with who we involve."

"Worried about unscrupulous parties?" she asked as she quickly typed a text.

"More concerned about driving up the asking price and having your seller find a more lucrative offer," I elaborated.

"There's that," Mimi agreed, and appeared unconcerned. I had to wonder just how much money Tom had. "That text was Tom. He'll be home tomorrow night late and would like to meet you on Monday." She quoted the text, "Thought we could all have dinner here."

"That sounds like a plan." I was eager to meet her boss, to get a sense of him.

Mimi stacked our plates, and we returned to the kitchen. After cleaning up, Mimi made sure the floor-to-ceiling patio doors were locked, then we made the long walk to the front door. Getting my steps in would be a cinch in this house.

"Are you okay on your own tonight?" she asked as we walked down the hall. "I have a butt-load of paperwork to catch up on. The least favorite part of my job but if I get it done, we could spend all day tomorrow playing. I'm thinking beach and the Pier."

"That sounds amazing. And I'll be fine tonight, I still need to catch up on sleep and maybe reset my internal clock to California time." Besides, I was hoping for a long phone call with Colby, since he had yet to return any of my morning texts.

Mimi set the alarm and locked the door behind us. "Good, then I won't feel bad abandoning you on your first full day here. You call me if you need anything or a good restaurant recommendation," she said and then hugged me before getting into her car.

Once settled in my driver's seat, I set the GPS to take me back to the hotel. I was tempted to drive up the coast, at least to Malibu, to clear my head, but exhaustion dictated otherwise. With luck, after a quick nap, I would be up for cruising the Pacific Coast Highway like some cute girl in a Beach Boys song. I thought I might have to look for a charging station, but I had barely moved the needle on the battery, so I could worry about that later.

After parking in the lot, I climbed the stairs to my room. I fought the urge to crawl onto the couch and take a quick nap. Instead, I refilled my water bottle and called Colby. It rolled straight to voicemail, so I sent him a simple text: call me.

I could no longer fight the urge to sleep, and after a brief nap, I felt human again. I decided it was time to start researching Fiona Limon. Still no message from Colby.

An internet search turned up little about Ms. Limon. She was known for painting portraits of the stars, a few socialites, and the occasional politician. After she married a prominent producer in her mid-thirties, she dropped off the radar completely. Probably stayed home, had babies, and lived the nineteen-fifties dream. I jotted down the names of her subjects. Maybe, with some luck, we could track down one or more of the more prominent ones.

Then I set my sights on the film. I thought it might help if I understood its significance in both the era and the world of modern collectors. For a movie I had never heard of, there was a plethora of information.

Based on a pre-WWII best-selling novel, the adaptation was put on hold several times. First delayed by the war, and then by various recasts, firings, and tensions on the set, it finally made it to the movie theaters just before the D-Day invasion. It was a hit with audiences and critics.

Largely forgotten as the decades wore on, cable classic movie channels revived it, and once again audiences were wowed by it, and a cult following was born. The mysterious, never-seen original portrait of the leading lady became the white whale for collectors. Long thought to have been destroyed in one of the many studio sales and consolidations, there wasn't much hope of it being found. Despite that, there were several chat threads dedicated to following any lead or sighting.

I found out the mock oil painting used in the film sold at auction a decade ago for one point two million. I was beginning to understand the Hollywood collectibles market. Film noir and classic hits from the late thirties and the forties were valuable. Not just because of the interest in those films, but because of the rarity of surviving items.

More modern works found their significance in the movie's popularity, say Star Wars, The Mummy, or Pulp Fiction, or with the cult classic fan base, such as The Rocky Horror Picture Show, Blade Runner, and even the 1960s Batman television show. Rarity still determined valuation, but even a few of the more common items could get pricey based on desirability. It wasn't all that different from my day job. What I needed to do was to set aside my preconceptions of what I believed art to be.

Feeling slightly more confident in my abilities in this realm, I realized I was suddenly hungry, very hungry. And annoyed. Colby still hadn't returned my call or any of my texts. Couldn't do much about Colby, but I could grab a bite to eat. There was a cute Mexican restaurant about half a block from the hotel, so I walked over there and grabbed a to-go order.

Back at the hotel, I sat on the deck and ate dinner while watching the sunset over the ocean. The sky lit up in pastel orange and blue hues as the sun dipped behind the distant mountain range that curved dramatically west enough to capture the waning fireball. Across the way, at the Pier, the roller coaster and the Ferris wheel lit up. The echoes of happy people carried by the ocean breeze made me inexplicably happy.

I realized that for the first time since separating from my ex-husband and moving to my apartment in Peoria, I was on my own. No Mimi in the apartment across the hall or sharing a townhouse. No Colby at the table or sitting next to me on the couch watching a movie. No Stevie on my lap or Wyatt nudging my hand to pet his head.

I was an alien in a strange land of palm trees and orange groves, movie history, and celebrity sightings. I was soaking it all in. With those dark days in Illinois behind me, I couldn't help but marvel at how far I had come. I wasn't sure if it was the warm ocean breeze coupled with the intoxicating smell of the night-blooming jasmine, but I felt content. Life was good.

My phone buzzed, and I flipped it over to see Colby's face looking back at me. I eagerly pressed the accept the video call icon.

"Hi, stranger!" I said with unabashed joy. He looked a little disheveled and had a few days' growth on his face. I knew work must be hectic, but I found that rough look sexy as hell.

"Hello, beautiful," he replied. "I am so sorry I've been out of touch all day."

"The new case keeping you busy?"

"Very. But before I give you those details, I want to hear how things are going in LA. Did you determine if the painting is the real deal?"

I laughed. "Yes, I walked in with my magical art authentication powers and quickly ascertained it is indeed the Holy Grail. The client is quite impressed with me."

"Smartass," he said with genuine warmth in his voice. "Seriously, how was your first day?"

"It was good. The painting shows promise. I got to wander around an honest-to-goodness modern Hollywood mansion. Replete with a hillside view of the ocean and I'm driving around in a car that is worth more than my yearly salary. About the only LA thing I didn't do today was drive up the coast and watch surfers shooting the curls."

"A real California girl in just a few hours," he teased.

"Yup. How are things going with you?" I chose to avoid any questions about my father and instead asked the most important one. "Do Stevie and Wyatt miss me?"

"About that...

SEVEN

I guess you're the kind of a gal they don't forget-
THE MAN WHO KNEW TOO MUCH

I held my breath, worried that something had happened to one of them.

"I'm not in Virginia at the moment," he said, and I began to breathe again.

"You aren't? Did your case take you out of state?" I knew from experience it could be anywhere. A U.S. Marshal's jurisdiction is wherever the criminals abscond.

"You're not going to believe this," he said and gave me that dazzling smile that still melted me after all this time. "I'm in California. Down in San Diego."

"I guess the fates will not allow us to roam around the world separately," I joked. I was sure it was just some weird coincidence that we would end up in the same, very, very large state. Nevertheless, the hair on my arms stood up.

"I guess not," Colby agreed. "We suspect our fugitive lives here, so doing a bit of surveillance. If our intel is correct, I don't expect this to take long. He's no spring chicken, if you get my meaning, and he's been living his best life here for quite some time under an alias. He's a vibrant member of the community. Not hiding at all."

"Is my dad there with you?" I asked, trying not to wince at the thought of their partnership.

"He'll arrive tomorrow. He received all his clearances and then stopped in Denver to follow up on a lead before flying here. There is a business there that may be laundering funds for our fugitive, so he is going to investigate. We want to make sure we get all the tentacles of this particular cephalopod. He's been busy during his time on the run."

"This guy sounds very dangerous. You be very careful, okay?" Colby was very good at what he did, so I tried not to worry when he was away on a job. Something about this one, this career criminal, put me on edge. And now I had to worry about my father, too. "I guess tell Dad I said hi when he arrives." I could not keep the sarcasm from slipping out.

"I will. I'm sorry that this case is dredging up old wounds," he said softly. I shrugged, and he wisely changed the subject. "Anything else exciting happening there in the land of angels?"

"It's beautiful here. I start each morning on the beach. Today I was joined by a dolphin. It was magical. I wish you were here to experience it with me," I said and meant it. That felt good. "I can't wait to explore more. Mimi and I are taking tomorrow to bop around and have some fun before the hard work begins."

There was a knock on a door somewhere in his room. Colby turned away and said, "Come in," before he returned his attention to me. "Babe, I'm going to have to get back to work, but I wanted to check in and give you an update."

"I'm glad you did, I've been missing you." It wasn't technically a lie. When I thought of him, I did miss him and wished he was here to run around with Mimi and me. The problem was, I wasn't thinking of him all that much. To be fair, there had been a lot going on since my arrival.

To my surprise, a tall, exotic-looking woman came up behind Colby. She had silky dark hair that fell perfectly below her shoulders. She placed her neatly manicured hand on his shoulder and leaned into the frame.

Her dark almond eyes were beautifully lined, and I suspected that was all the makeup she wore, not that she needed any at all. She wore a tight navy blue scooped-neck tee. Her proximity to Colby mostly obscured the FBI emblem on the upper right shoulder. The only word to describe her was stunning. And she seemed extremely familiar with Colby, as she placed her face close to his.

"Well hello!" she exclaimed when she saw me. "You must be TJ. Colby has told me all about you."

Well, that's nice, I thought, *since I have no fucking idea who you are and get your lithe body away from him*. That green-eyed monster came out of nowhere, I swear. I trusted Colby implicitly.

"Uh, TJ," Colby looked uncomfortable...or was it guilt? "This is Ailani, she and I have worked on cases together before. She's with the FBI."

Oh, dude, you've more than worked with her. I could see it all over both of them.

"I'll meet you downstairs," Ailani said. "TJ it was nice to finally meet you." And then she was gone.

"Time to clock in," Colby joked. "Listen, I'm going to be kind of tough to reach while I'm on this case. I'll check in when I can. But text me if anything urgent comes up, I'll make the time to respond. Check in with Abby, would you? I barely had time before I flew out here."

"Sure thing," I replied. I guess we weren't going to discuss the slinky brunette who just waltzed into my nightmares. "I've got plenty to keep me busy, so don't worry too much about being incommunicado. It'll just give us lots to discuss when we get home."

"Well, promise me you'll call if you have any issues," he pressed.

"Of course, but I don't expect to run into trouble this trip, unless it's with the fashion police for my lack of style. I am going to struggle to fit in with this art crowd."

"You look mighty fine to me, Kit-Kat."

I smiled at the endearment. We ended with I love yous and then he was gone. I stared at the dark screen for a moment, trying to push away the irrational thoughts about my dad and Ailani.

Damn, even her name was exotic. I wanted to call Mimi, to confer with my best friend about it all, but it was late and I didn't want to bother her. There would be plenty of time tomorrow to dissect my love life and my father drama.

Instead, I grabbed a sparkling water from the refrigerator and sat outside to listen to the sounds of happiness drift over from the pier. Squeals of laughter and tinny music from the boardwalk combined with the mechanical sounds of the roller coaster flying over the tracks were the rhythm of the night.

Down by the bike path, someone was rapping as they walked along the beach, fading away the further they traveled. Only to be replaced by young girls laughing and talking as they walked toward the Pier. All those lovely sounds and the cool breeze off the ocean helped me relax. I sipped my tonic and let my mind wander far from Colby, my dad, and the incomprehensible world of movie collectibles. I slept peacefully once I crawled into bed.

The next morning, I was once again awake before dawn. I enjoyed a cup of coffee on the patio and then took another sunrise walk on the beach. An entire pod of dolphins surprised me, playing in the surf as the sun turned the water a rosy pink. They accompanied me for the remainder of my stroll. I took that as a good sign.

After that, I showered, styled my hair, and did the makeup thing. I looked in the mirror and thought, this is as good as it gets, LA. While I waited for Mimi, I took a yogurt and a banana outside. Sitting at the table, I jotted a few notes of the things I wanted to discuss with her. Something was nagging at me regarding the painting. I needed more information about where they found it and how the owner knew to contact Mimi and Tom. I'm sure it was all on the up and up. There was just a knowledge gap.

Understanding how the work was acquired would help in authenticating it. Provenance was important, even with items like this. I was hoping Mimi could arrange a meeting with the owner, and they could walk me through what they knew. Best-case scenario, it was handed down from family member to family member. An ancestry tree was the easiest to follow and verify.

My phone buzzed. The message from Mimi said she was on her way. I gathered up my trash and headed inside to finish getting ready for the day.

Mimi rapped on my door just as I popped extra sunscreen into my bag. I pulled it open and directed her to come in as I ran into the bedroom to retrieve my sunglasses and a hot pink scrunchi. I had opted for white walking shorts, a pink tee, and sandals.

Mimi looked completely put together in khaki pedal pushers, an orange polka-dot top that totally complemented her red hair, and cute little white tennis shoes. A brown leather crossbody bag completed her look. I felt dull in comparison.

"Where are we off to first?" I asked. Then I double-checked that I had my keycard before I locked the door.

"I thought we could start with a drive up the coast to Malibu and Zuma. Then a little shopping in Venice, before we finish with dinner and rides on Santa Monica pier."

"That sounds amazing," I replied as I jogged down the stairs with her. "Should we take Tom's car? It's super sporty." I handed her the keys.

"It is a kick to drive," she agreed.

We climbed in, and Mimi pulled out, turning right on the boulevard and expertly making a U-turn at the next intersection. The day was beautiful. Bright sunny skies, warm sun and an ocean breeze made for a pleasant drive up the coast. I opened the sunroof, and we both settled into the ride, enjoying the views. There wasn't much point in attempting to talk with the windows down and the wind whipping in through the sunroof. That was fine. It was just great to be in the same place and hanging out together.

As we drove through Malibu, she pointed out all the luxury homes and a couple of hot spots to eat. We continued further, and then Mimi turned left into a parking lot. The signage said Zuma Beach.

She paid the parking fee and pulled into a slot. The beach stretched for miles and was sparsely occupied, which surprised me. Just a few souls sunning themselves and several families spread out under big umbrellas, their kids splashing in the waves.

"I expected it to be busier." I noted.

"Sometimes it is," she explained. "Especially in the summer, but there are not a lot of amenities out here, so tourists don't frequent it. It is mostly locals. Its real claim to fame is the surfers. The waves are impressive, and in the early mornings, there are quite a few enthusiasts welcoming the dawn."

We exited the car and walked along the perfectly groomed sand. It was impressive to watch crews rake the beaches in the morning while I walked, keeping everything pristine.

"This is a quiet stroll most days," Mimi remarked. "I come out here when the LA-ness of things get to me."

I slipped off my sandals as we neared the water's edge, enjoying the feeling of wet sand between my toes. The tide was out, and the water lapped gently against the shoreline. "Is that Catalina out there?" I asked, having observed it from Santa Monica Beach, too.

"Yes. It's very pretty there. If we get lucky and finish up early with this authentication, we should go for the day. There's a ferry or we could take a helicopter," Mimi said.

"That would be great fun," I agreed. We turned to walk back to the car just as a pod of dolphins surfaced off the water's edge. "That is the second time I've seen dolphins today," I said with a touch of awe. "I'm surprised how close they swim to the shore."

"They like to play with swimmers and surfers," she replied and snapped a quick photo when they surfaced again. "How's

Colby doing? You haven't said much about him this trip. Is he super busy with his new assignment?"

"You are not going to believe this," I said, surprised at myself for not telling her sooner. My mind was undeniably elsewhere. "He's in San Diego...with my dad. Or at least my dad will be joining him shortly."

"Oh, boy. That has to be interesting for you. Is your dad still playing at being the mysterious stranger?"

"Psssh...yeah. I don't know why I expect anything else, but I am both annoyed and disappointed with this development," I said, tamping down the anger bubbling below the surface. "And I'm trying not to take it out on Colby."

"I'd be pissed," Mimi said fiercely. "If my parents ghosted me, there would be hell to pay."

"I guess I'm just used to it," I said, shaking my head. How the hell could I be used to it? Or okay with being used to it? Mimi was right. I should be good and angry about this. "Speaking of your family how is everyone?"

"Mom and Dad are in Botswana on a safari. Mom always wanted to go, so Dad surprised her with a trip for a Christmas gift. Jamie and Audrey are back in New Zealand for the next six months. Audrey is doing some research project. When they come back, he'll go back to work for the DA in Boston, but get this, he wants to go into politics. He's definitely the higher achiever in the family." She seemed wistful as she talked about her brother's accomplishments. "Oh, and I guess I'm going to be an aunty by Thanksgiving!"

"Wow, they didn't waste any time," I laughed. Colby and I had just attended their wedding last summer on Martha's Vineyard.

"No they didn't. But Jamie has always wanted to be a dad of a basketball team."

"That seems like a lot of pressure on Audrey," I said with a laugh.

"I think the plan is to foster once they are settled back in Boston."

"Wow, well now I'm feeling inadequate," I said, happy for their amazing future.

Back in the car, we drove down the coast. We passed all the now familiar sights in Santa Monica and continued a few minutes more south until we reached Venice. Mimi drove around a few blocks until she found a parking spot.

"Let's grab lunch at one of the cute shacks near the beach and then we can hit the shops. There are a couple of cute vintage clothing stores, tons of touristy stuff, and a nice antiques store down the block over there." She pointed east before we turned and walked to the boardwalk.

We had a tasty lunch of grilled fish and fresh produce that included more luscious strawberries. While we ate, I filled Mimi in on Ailani and my frustrations with Colby's need to wed.

"You're crazy if you think for a moment Colby is anything but faithful to you. He's head-over-heels in love with you."

"I'm sure you're right, but you didn't see her. I mean I might cheat on me with her," I laughed as I stabbed some peppers with my fork. "I'm more worried that my inability to commit is the real issue."

"I'm sure he not only understands why you are reluctant but is happy to be engaged and living your best lives together." She patted my hand, which felt both reassuring and a bit of a rebuke.

"I'm sure you're right. I have no idea why I've been so emotionally erratic lately. I think I'm having a mid-life crisis." Mimi laughed at that, and I ignored her. "I'm just feeling dissatisfied all around. I suppose mostly my job." I sipped my iced tea and shook my head. "I have no idea what I'm whining about, Mimi. Look at me. I'm in LA, researching an exciting vintage Hollywood artifact. I need to get it together."

"It's okay, Teej, I think it's common for us to have these questions about our lives. I mean, do I really want to spend the rest of my life catering to acquisitive tech millionaires? Or even living this far away from the rest of my family? I'm having fun here, but I'm going to be an Auntie soon and I don't want to miss that joy."

"Well, here's to questioning all our life choices," I said, raising my glass to clink with hers.

After lunch, we partook in a few hours of retail therapy to assuage our discontent. The shops throughout Venice were cute and fun, but nothing caught my eye enough to persuade me to get out my wallet. That was until I saw a boxy 1950s pink gingham jacket that had to come home with me.

We collapsed into the very hot Porsche, and Mimi turned on the air with alacrity, as we sweltered in the dark interior.

"This car would be much better with butter cream seats," I opined.

"Agreed. You still up for Santa Monica Pier?"

"Do they have ice cream?"

"You bet they do," Mimi replied and then pulled out of the parking space, while another car waited to take her place. We were quickly cruising back to the hotel. "Let's park here and walk over," Mimi said when we arrived.

"Sounds good to me," I agreed. "Let's run upstairs first, I want to change into my running shoes and grab more water."

Once we had prepped, we descended to the concrete path that led to the pier. Ten minutes later, I was a kid again. Music blared, people screamed as the roller coaster clattered down steep drops, and others screamed as they plunged down a ninety-foot tower overlooking the bay. The Ferris wheel offered a quieter experience for the less daring.

Kids ran from all corners, dodging street performers and couples holding hands, while parents called after them. Food cart vendors, burger shacks, and restaurants filled the air with irresistible smells. Cotton candy, ice cream, and sausages with peppers and onions all beckoned. It was sensory overload in a good way.

We made our way through the crowds and explored the entire pier, riding a few rides and eating too much food. By nine, we were exhausted and headed to my hotel.

"What's the plan for tomorrow?" I asked as we walked slowly back.

"Tom wants to meet for dinner, but I haven't heard from him yet to confirm a time. I did contact my friend at the Getty and he said to stop by whenever and we could confab. He is extremely interested in seeing the photos and hearing more about the painting." Mimi's phone rang, and she pulled it out of her crossbody bag. "Speak of the devil." She slid the talk button. "Hi, Tom."

EIGHT

You have a great talent for creating difficult situations - REAR WINDOW

After a brief conversation, Mimi disconnected and pocketed her phone. “Tom would like to meet for coffee and pastries tomorrow around ten, instead of waiting until dinner. I told him that would be okay.”

“Definitely,” I replied. I was anxious to meet him, wanting to get a sense of the situation. Specifically, if I were to find out this painting wasn’t authentic, how much trouble would that cause for Mimi? It would be helpful if I could also determine what about him was making her uneasy.

I walked Mimi to her car, and we said our goodbyes before I returned to my room, exhausted by the day’s events. Sleep was immediate after I crawled into bed, and I had a good, dreamless eight hours. I once again woke before sunrise and despite a restful night, I felt anything but rested. I must be getting too old for all this traveling and partying. Was I the same woman who flew to Havana for the night on a whim and followed Colby to Costa Rica for a weekend of wilderness trekking?

I dragged myself out of bed, showered, drank some OJ, and took a banana out on the deck to eat as the sun rose. I made coffee and turned on my laptop. Before meeting Tom

Meadler today, I wanted more information about him. Surprisingly, I found little information and absolutely no social media footprint. It seemed odd, but it could be that he valued his privacy. Still, something felt off. Unfortunately, it was a feeling, not anything concrete.

I searched for the financials on his property and found it was owned by a corporation, so I dug a little deeper into that entity. Property records showed warehouses in Long Beach, another house in Santa Barbara, and a building in West Hollywood. I was about to do a map search on all those locations when my phone buzzed. It was a text from Colby.

> Wanted you to know your father has landed safely and we start working together today. He looks well. Asked how you are doing. Should I tell him you are in LA?

I stared at the text. I read it again. Did I want him to tell him I was in Los Angeles? Hell, he probably had that information already. He had witchy ways of keeping track of me over the years. Always providing mysterious assistance or words of encouragement when I needed it most. I sipped my coffee and read the text a final time before replying.

> Sure

It was terse, but I was feeling terse. A normal father would text me himself. Or at least stay dead.

It was time to get ready for my meeting, so I saved my searches, closed my laptop, tucked it into the desk drawer, and tried to do something with my curls. I put on black slacks, topped with my fuchsia silk tank, and then slipped on my new vintage pink jacket. My silver hoops with rhinestones were the only earrings I packed, so I added those. I wished for a scarf or retro sunglasses to complete the look, but this would have to do.

Checking the times, I decided that even though it was early, I would leave now. Didn't want to be late to my first client meeting. If I arrived before Mimi, I could circle the block until she materialized. I threw my purse, a notepad and pens into my leather satchel and made my way to the parking lot.

Traffic was steady, but nothing outrageous, so I arrived at Tom's house and watched as Mimi pulled in ahead of me. We parked and walked to the big metal gate. Mimi rang the bell and Tom buzzed us in. We walked through the maze until we reached the kitchen. I was sure I'd never be able to navigate this place without GPS.

The man at the counter, surrounded by a bounty of breakfast items, surprised me. Framed by the light pouring in from the wall of sliding glass doors, he seemed rather nondescript. Average height, tousled light brown hair, gray eyes, and soft features, I wasn't sure I could have picked him out in a line-up. Dressed in expensive jeans and a black t-shirt, he stood up as we entered. I noticed he was barefoot and his feet were perfectly manicured. I glanced at the hand holding an exquisite white coffee mug. It, too, was perfectly manicured. I thought of my own neglected nails and was a bit envious.

"Good morning, Mimi. And you must be TJ, Mimi has sung your praises." He held out a hand to me. I grasped it. It was soft, but his grip was firm as we shook. He gestured to the counter. "Fresh coffee and fresh bagels. The bagel truck was in the neighborhood this morning, so we got lucky."

I had no idea what a bagel truck was, but the spread was amazing. There must have been two dozen bagels of various flavors and a dozen schmears and toppings. Mimi and I both prepared a bagel, and she poured two cups of coffee before we joined Tom at the dining table.

"So," Tom began once we had settled, "what have we found out so far?"

"The painting looks to be the appropriate age," Mimi replied. "The frame is period and the canvas appears to be genuine." Tom looked excited by this. "We also found the artist's signature and the title of the painting on the edge of the canvas. With that, we can continue to explore and validate its authenticity."

"But, it's looking good, isn't it?" He looked like a kid spotting his gifts under the tree.

Damn, I suspected he would not take it well if we found out the painting was a fake. I looked at Mimi, but she was focused on Tom.

"It's a start, Tom. I will feel better if we can find another work by the same artist - "

"That will help?" Tom cut her off excitedly. "What will you be looking for?" He could not hide his eagerness.

I jumped in. "With another of her works, I can compare the brush style and her signature, among other things. And I'm hoping we can talk to the seller to verify how he obtained this piece. That will be an important indication of its authenticity."

Tom nodded. "I feel like I'm in expert hands here." He looked over at Mimi and beamed. "Mimi would never let me invest in something until she had thoroughly vetted it." His phone buzzed. He picked it up and furrowed his brow. "Please excuse me, I have to take this." He crossed the room as he spoke in hushed tones. He stepped outside and closed the sliding door before walking to the stone wall. He faced the ocean and gesticulated sharply as he spoke.

Mimi didn't seem to notice. Instead, she smiled at me. More like beamed. "I think you've won him over," she said. I nodded, but was more interested in what appeared to be a heated discussion out on the patio. I raised an eyebrow and nodded in Tom's direction. She shrugged.

A moment later, Tom rejoined us. "I'm sorry ladies. I'm going to have to cut this meeting short. Something has come up." He picked up our bagel plates and handed them to us before ushering us toward the door. "Wouldn't want you to go hungry. Let's meet tonight for dinner, I'll have Chef Ritchie make something decadent. Let's say, seven-thirty." And with that, he veered down the other hallway, leaving us to find our way out, and didn't even wait for a confirmation on dinner.

Outside, standing next to our vehicles, Mimi shook her head and looked toward the house. "I'm sorry, TJ, I have no idea what that was about."

I lifted my plate. "Hey, we got bagels out of it. I'm not too worried, I assume an eccentric client comes with the job."

"I guess," Mimi sighed. "But that was odd, even for him."

We made a quick adjustment to our day. Mimi followed me back to the hotel where she parked her car, and I handed her the keys to the Porsche. I settled into the passenger seat, and we drove up to the Getty.

The Getty Center sits high on a hill, just off the 405 freeway near Brentwood. I had done a quick search on it and was looking forward to seeing their collection if we had time.

It housed thousands of pieces from Medieval to Modern art and was an architectural wonder. There was a conservation center and a research institute on the campus. Not to mention rotating exhibits and a majestic courtyard that overlooked the surrounding valley. And, if that were not enough, there was the Getty Villa a few miles up the Pacific Coast Highway from my hotel, which had spectacular gardens along with more art. I hoped we might have time before I flew home to explore that.

Once we merged onto the 405, traffic slowed but was steady, so Mimi chose to stay the course and not exit onto the surface roads. I was glad she was driving because that allowed me to take in the scenery. Green hills and clear blue skies contrasted with high walls on both sides, creating a canyon-like effect. If it weren't for all the traffic, it would almost be peaceful.

"What is that?" I asked Mimi in awe as I pointed at a tall, cylindrical building just before the Getty exit.

"Oh, that's a hotel, the Hotel Angeleno. Been there forever. Really stands out, doesn't it?" She maneuvered over and took the exit to the Getty Center.

We wove our way through a lovely hill-lined driveway and into the parking garage. Then we took the escalator to the tram, which was an experience unto itself. The train rode quietly along tree-lined tracks, climbing almost a mile up to the museum.

The four-minute ride provided spectacular views of the Santa Monica Mountains, the neighborhoods below, and the elegant garden entrance of the Center. No expense had been spared for a museum that was always free to the public. Funded entirely by the J. Paul Getty Trust.

The J. Paul Getty Trust was the largest art trust in the world. Oil tycoon J. Paul Getty left the bulk of his fortune to his trust when he died in the nineteen seventies. The envy of any art collector, his bequest has financed two museum locations, as well as a plethora of visual arts educational programs, scientific research and training, and decades of grants for art, architecture, and archeology studies.

The Getty Research Institute housed over nine hundred thousand books and publications, along with millions of photographs of architecture and art. It was a museum curator's dream to have the resources the Getty had. I was on a mission, but was still a little disappointed we wouldn't have time to explore the grounds.

We made our way to the main entrance. If the center was imposing from the highway, it was magnificent up close. The curving white stone blended seamlessly with the Santa Monica Mountains, reminiscent of the Guggenheim Museum in New York City.

The gardens, with their fountains and sculptured hedges, were inviting, and I wanted to sit by the water and soak it all in. But we were on a mission, so I followed Mimi inside where she explained to the person at the information desk that she was there to see Darrius Siemek. The smartly dressed woman smiled warmly at us, made a brief call, and then told us Darrius would be right down.

A very tall, very handsome man appeared, and Mimi exclaimed, "Darrius! Thanks for helping us with this." She and Darrius hugged, and then Mimi turned to me. "Darrius, this is

TJ, she is an art curator for a museum in Arlington. Virginia. And she's here to assist me in authenticating this painting."

"TJ," he said as he reached out a hand. "It's great to meet you. I think we have similar jobs, though mine is geared more to finding interesting traveling exhibits to showcase."

He shook my hand enthusiastically. "I bet that is a bit more exciting than mine," I said with admiration. I suspected his job was much more exhilarating.

"Hey, I'm not the one examining the holy grail of Hollywood memorabilia. Let's go up to my office, I can't wait to hear more about this."

His office was opulent. Beginning with the floor-to-ceiling windows, there was marble everywhere. Heavy wooden shelves lined the walls, filled with books and art pieces. Metal and glass office furniture, two wingback leather chairs, and a matching couch were arranged around what must have been an Adrian Pearsall teardrop coffee table. I had to stop myself from gasping at the beauty.

Darrius must have seen my expression, though, because he said, "Yup, this is what you get when your museum is a trust fund baby." I couldn't disagree. The advantages of being the product of an unlimited trust fund were evident.

"Impressive," I said, thinking of my cramped, one-window office back in Virginia.

"I can't wait to see what you have," he said enthusiastically as he motioned us to the couch. I pulled out my phone and realized the screen was going to be ridiculously small for all three of us to crowd around.

"Here," Darrius said, reading my mind and handing me a USB cord. "We can plug it into the big screen." And with the flick of a button, one bookshelf slid open to reveal a large, flat screen.

That will do, I thought.

Once we had everything set up, I displayed the images of our Lady on the screen. Darrius walked over to get a better look. Mimi and I joined him. He scanned the images closely, occasionally drawing a finger over sections that intrigued him. Mimi explained what we had found on Saturday as we dismantled the frame.

"It sure looks legit," Darrius said as he peered closely at the photo of Limon's signature. He turned back to us. "So what you need, I'm assuming, is something to compare it to, correct?" I nodded enthusiastically. "I might be able to help with that."

From his desk, he picked up a file folder and brought it to us. He set it on the coffee table. Mimi and I sat beside him as he flipped the folder open to reveal a short list of names, along with phone numbers and addresses. "This is a list of the five known portraits Ms. Limon did before she quit working to raise her family. They are all of famous actresses of the time, so collectors love them. I tracked down the owners for you."

"That's phenomenal. How did you manage that?" Mimi asked.

"It is amazing the responses you receive when you say, I'm from the Getty Center," he laughed.

"I bet," I agreed, thinking how I have to explain where my museum is to most people and how they always sounded disappointed I wasn't with the Smithsonian.

"Do you think they'll talk with us?" Mimi seemed concerned as she scanned the list.

"I told them you would be contacting them," Darrius explained. "And that they would be assisting in verifying a very sought-after art piece that had been missing for decades. That was enough to secure their cooperation. Everyone loves a good mystery and they are all avid Limon collectors."

"Darrius, this is invaluable," Mimi enthused. "Thank you for doing this for us. I owe you."

"I was happy to do it, and you can repay me with all the details once you have established if it is authentic or not."

"Every juicy tidbit, I promise," Mimi replied.

He escorted us to the lobby, and we said our farewells. As much as I wanted to explore the museum and the glorious gardens, I was now more excited to begin our quest to find our elusive artist's other works.

"Let's grab lunch," Mimi said as we rode the tram back to the car, reading my mind. "How do you feel about Oaxacan?" she asked as we walked to the car. I blinked at her. Mimi smiled and unlocked the Porsche. "It's a regional Mexican cuisine. There are a couple of really excellent restaurants around. One isn't far from here."

"I've never even heard of it, but I am game for anything new."

"You'll love it. It's a region of Mexico renowned for its flavors, especially the masa tortillas. Out of this world. And mole, it came from that region."

"Yum," I said and realized I was famished. I should probably carry nuts or something with me since my body was refusing to adhere to local time and demanding food and sleep at odd hours.

The restaurant, like most things in Los Angeles, was located in a strip mall, and from the exterior, I wasn't expecting much. Stepping inside, however, transported us to another country. Decorated with Saltillo floors, warm brick walls, and colorful orange, rust, blue, and white décor that matched the tiered skirt and embroidered blouse of our hostess. She seated us at a table that looked to have been hand-carved from an ancient tree and buffed to a soft shine.

I was so enamored with the atmosphere that I almost ignored our poor hostess as she tried to hand me a menu. "It's so beautiful in here," I said to her after Mimi nudged me and I reached for the menu she held out.

I had no idea what to order, so I followed Mimi's lead and ordered Chilaquiles con Pollo. The server brought iced tea and lemons to the table while we waited. Mimi pulled out the list of names, and we pored over them, trying to decide who to approach first.

"I have to tell you, I'm a little intimidated looking at a few of these addresses."

"Really?" I was surprised. Mimi was never one to succumb to insecurities when it came to others' wealth or prestige. We had both worked long enough in the art world not to be flustered by affluence or the trappings that came with it.

"It shouldn't matter, but two of the addresses are in neighborhoods so ritzy, you and I are going to look like the help."

Our food arrived, and we tabled the discussion until we had at least sampled the delights before us. Steaming plates filled with crispy corn tortilla pieces in a spicy tomato sauce, sprinkled with cheese, onion, sour cream, green salsa, and shredded chicken were placed before us, and I couldn't wait to dig in. The meal was heavenly, with flavors both familiar and exotic melding together for a flavor feast.

Satiated, we were ready to tackle our list. Mimi paid the tab, and we jumped into the car. She made the first call, and I held a notepad, ready to jot down any instructions or directions.

"Hi, is this Joslyn Ellis?"

"Yes, it is," said a delicate voice with a breathy quality.

"My name is Mimi Webster, I'm a colleague of Darrius Siemek over at the Getty Center."

"Oh, yes dear, he said you'd be calling. I am happy to help you in any way I can." Her voice quivered a bit. I wasn't sure if it was from excitement or age. "When would you like to look at our Fiona Limon?"

NINE

Good morning! We meet under the most artistic circumstances -
HOW TO STEAL A MILLION

After looking at the map on my phone, Mimi told Joslyn Ellis we would be there in about thirty minutes. I was almost giddy with anticipation. I didn't think it was possible that we would move this quickly on finding one of Limon's other paintings.

Mimi disconnected and started the car. She put the address into the navigation system, and we were on our way.

"Joslyn lives in Brentwood, it's not that far from here," she explained.

"Is it an exclusive area?"

"Pretty much. People love it because it's close to the ocean, the hills, and the homes have more privacy than some of the other expensive real estate."

"I can't believe how excited I am about seeing another one of Limon's works. I'm enjoying running around solving our little mystery like a couple of girl detectives," I effused.

"Honestly, this is the most fun I've had since I moved here." Mimi agreed. "Our own little film Noir adventure. All we need is a rainy afternoon to set the mood."

I looked up at the crystal-blue sky. No clouds or even haze to disrupt this quintessential Southern California afternoon. I'm sure the Beach Boys had a song about it.

Mimi turned off Sunset Boulevard onto a tree-lined street marked with a NO OUTLET sign. She continued to drive until the GPS told us we had reached our destination. Mimi double-checked the address and then pulled up to the thick wooden gate. Finding a moat on the other side would not have surprised me.

She rang the buzzer, and a deep voice responded. After confirming we had an appointment, the voice allowed the gate to open, and we proceeded down the long, lush driveway, lined with trees in bloom with purple blossoms.

"What are those trees?" I asked in awe of their beauty.

"Jacaranda trees, they're originally from Brazil, but there are entire neighborhoods lined with them. Breathtaking when they are all in bloom."

A single-story Spanish-style ranch home greeted us as we continued. The outside was stone, stucco, and thick timbers. Every inch of the property was covered in greenery: vines, flowers, bushes, and trees. Stunning was not a strong enough adjective.

There was a multi-car garage and stables to our left. To the right of the home, a trellised walkway covered in what I guessed was wisteria, though it wasn't in bloom. Mimi pulled into a small parkway just before the garage.

We exited the car, and I had to keep reminding myself not to let my mouth fall open in awe. There was nothing ostentatious about it. It had a simple, quiet elegance. So the woman who greeted us at the door was not a surprise.

She was as elegant as the home. Dressed impeccably in white linen pants and a white silk blouse, topped with a cream cashmere cardigan that complemented her perfectly coiffed silver hair. She smiled at us warmly.

"Hi, Mrs. Ellis, I'm Mimi. We spoke on the phone," Mimi said as she held out her hand.

"Oh, darlings, call me Joslyn." She enveloped Mimi's outstretched hand with both of hers. "Come in. I had Maria prepare us a light snack." She turned her attention to me. "And you are TJ, correct? Darrius said you worked at a museum in Virginia?"

"Yes, I do. I'm responsible for their acquisitions."

"That sounds fascinating. I have always loved art. Had my life been different, I might have become an artist."

We followed her through the house, and I couldn't help but think our host was perfectly color-coordinated with the cream and white interior. Every room had vaulted ceilings with dark timber beams and floor-to-ceiling windows that opened onto a lush courtyard. From what I could see, the ranch-style home was horseshoe-shaped, with one section sporting a second level and a balcony.

Joslyn led us to a sunroom that overlooked the pool. Every corner was filled with exotic plants. I spotted a banana tree, a fiddle-leaf fig, and several small palms. In the center of the room, between the floral sofa and matching overstuffed chair, was a portrait of a woman propped on an easel. On the coffee table in front of the sofa, there was a pitcher of iced tea and a plate of shortbread cookies.

"I had my husband bring the painting in here," Joslyn explained. "It's usually hanging in the library, but the light is so much better in this room." She indicated we should sit on the sofa, so we did.

I was conflicted. As much as I wanted to dive immediately into my examination of the artwork, I also wanted to learn more about our host. I suspected she had a fascinating life story.

Joslyn poured three glasses of tea and offered us lemon and sugar. I snagged a lemon wedge and declined the sweetener.

"TJ, tell me about your job, I bet it is exciting," she said as she sat in the upholstered chair.

I swept aside my current discontent with my career. Instead, I told her about a few of my more interesting acquisitions. I described how I helped return Indigenous clay pots to their rightful home and traced the provenance of a small woodcut by Albrecht Dürer, so it could be returned to the descendants after the Nazis looted it during WWII.

"Most of my days are providing documentation on potential acquisitions," I explained. "But I will admit there are a few pieces where authenticating their provenance is an adventure." I looked over at the painting. "Kind of like this assignment. I'm learning so much. I knew nothing about cinematic collectibles before I started this project. Can I ask how you acquired this one?"

"Actually, we have always had it." She stood up and walked over to the portrait, and I followed. "This is my mother. She was an actress, famous in her day. Worked and played with...and loved...quite a few leading men." She ran her hand over the frame lovingly. "Until she met my father and quit Hollywood for a family. She would share stories of her wild adventures with my sister and me when my dad wasn't around." She smiled at the memory.

"He was a lawyer, worked with the studios and the talent, so even though Mother no longer acted, our home was always filled with glamorous people." She tenderly touched the face on the painting, and it was obvious she adored her mother. "Fiona was often at our house. She and mother were friends, both having given up their careers for family." She looked at us, a little wistfully, I thought. "I suppose that sounds quaint to your generation."

"You'd be surprised," I replied honestly. "I followed my now ex-husband across the country for his job, leaving behind my career aspirations. So I do understand." I smiled at her and added, "The things we do for love."

She nodded and laughed. "I followed my husband around the world. He started as a politician and then ended up as a diplomat, first picked by that dashing John F. Kennedy. So I understand completely."

Finally, I could no longer suppress my curiosity. "Is it okay if I take a closer look?" I asked, and she bid me to do whatever I needed.

She and Mimi continued to chat about Fiona and her career. I listened intently while I examined the signature and the brushstrokes on the portrait in front of me. Joslyn's life was fascinating.

She had traveled the world, rubbed elbows with people I could only dream of, including dining with the Queen and meeting Castro. "He never put down that blasted cigar," she said. She met and supported a litany of artists, many names I recognized and envied her interactions with them.

I presumed there were some pretty pricey pieces of art throughout the house. It also sounded like she had a deep desire to follow in Fiona's footsteps and study art in Paris. *Life takes us all in wild directions,* I thought.

I opened my phone and pulled up the photos of the film portrait. The signatures were identical and the brushstrokes sure looked identical to me. I was getting excited because, on first inspection, it appeared we might have an authentic work.

"Did you ever see this painting?" I asked as I showed her my phone. She took it and sat back on the sofa. She pulled glasses from her cardigan pocket and looked closer at the screen.

"I remember this one. It was in the studio at her house." She paused and looked up at us. "She still painted and occasionally did commissioned pieces, but when she did this one, she was supporting herself with her work. If I remember the story correctly - I was maybe six or seven at the time when I heard it - she was hired by the director to paint the lead actress as the film character. Then the director was fired, the producer decided to direct the film himself, and her painting was lost in the shuffle." Joslyn handed the phone back to me. "She really loved that work and was disappointed when they decided not to use it, especially after the film became a big hit. I think she always wondered what might have happened to her career if it had been used in the film."

"Any idea what happened to it?"

She shook her head. "They let her keep it, even though I think technically the studio owned it. I only saw it that once, decades later. I don't know what happened to it after that."

Standing by the painting, I remained impassive. Not wanting to jump to conclusions. However, in my opinion, unless the painting sitting in Tom's closet was some sort of expert forgery of a painting no one had seen in eighty-plus years, it was genuine.

"What's the verdict?" Joslyn asked.

"The evidence is pointing toward authentic," I said cautiously.

"I can see you are being judicious. But if you do decide it's the real thing, I would love to be able to view it."

"Absolutely," Mimi exclaimed. "You have been so very helpful with all of this, I'll do what I can to make sure you get that chance."

We talked for a while longer before taking our leave. I was sorry to say goodbye. She had a life story I would love to explore more. Unlike me, I bet she rarely had moments of restlessness.

In the car, as we drove to the gate and waited for it to clunk its way open, Mimi and I could barely contain our excitement.

"It's real, isn't it?" Mimi almost squealed.

"I have very little evidence stating otherwise," I said, still cautious.

"What's our next step?" Mimi pulled out past the gate and stopped as it slid shut behind us.

"I think getting the results of Edric's tests on the paint chips. If they are age appropriate, that's another mark in our favor. But I really want to talk with the owner to understand how they came to possess it. That's going to be important. We don't want to authenticate it only to find out it was acquired illegitimately."

"You mean stolen," Mimi said.

"Yes. Given my day job, I'm always on the lookout for stolen goods, no matter when they were stolen." I said, thinking of how careful museums were finally being toward Nazi contraband and Indigenous treasures taken from sacred areas.

We were quiet as we drove back to my hotel. I was making mental lists of how to proceed, and Mimi was concentrating on the heavy traffic. We pulled into my parking lot, and as Mimi got out and transferred her belongings to her car, her phone rang.

"Oh, good, this is Edric, maybe he has some answers for us." She hit accept on her phone and then said, "Hi, Edric." She paused for a moment, then covered the phone and said to me, "I'll see you tonight at Tom's."

As I gathered everything I needed from my car, Mimi listened to Edric. When she spoke, her tone was sharp. "What can I do for you Edric?"

A car drove by, blaring its bass. Reflexively, I looked over to see a black Lexus with darkly tinted windows whiz past. I ducked back into my car to grab my sunglasses as Mimi continued her conversation.

"All right, Edric I'll check it out, I'm sure it is in my files," she said as she rolled her eyes at me, sounding exasperated. I gave her a sympathetic look as she climbed into the driver's seat. She waved and then pulled out into the heavy afternoon traffic. It appeared she was still dealing with Edric as she drove away.

I returned to my room, filled my water bottle, and sat out on the patio. Relaxing to the sounds of the ocean, I reflected on the day. Joslyn was fascinating, and I could have chatted with her for hours. I suspected she had many stories to tell and that her life had been anything but ordinary.

My phone buzzed, and I flipped it over to see a text from our pet sitter. I opened it to see that Abby had sent me a photo. It was Stevie and Wyatt curled up together on the couch, and it reminded me of how much I missed them. I sent a note of thanks, glad we had such a gem to look after the crew.

No word from Colby, but that didn't surprise me. This task force sounded like a big operation with a lot of moving parts, and his focus would be on that. That was a good thing. Best way not to get shot.

I did wonder, though, about my dad and how they were getting along. As weird as my relationship with my father was, I was trying to imagine how Colby was coping with working with his fiancé's absent parent. I'm sure the word odd barely covered their partnership.

Back inside, even though I could have used a nap, it didn't seem like a good idea since I needed to leave for Tom's shortly. Instead, I changed my clothes, refreshed my makeup, and tousled my curls.

My phone buzzed again, this time with a message from Mimi.

> I might be a bit late. Something is going on with Edric, and I want to check it out before I see Tom tonight. In case he has questions. It's suspicious and I'm concerned. Talk then

It seemed innocuous enough, but I read it twice because I felt like I was missing something important. Deciding I was being paranoid, I returned to prepping for the evening meeting. I jotted down a few notes to discuss with Tom, laying out what we knew and what we still needed to ascertain. I had to tamp down any assumptions he might make regarding a purchase at this stage.

My default for most of this had been to let Mimi take the lead. I was, after all, just the consultant. But if she needed backup, I wanted to be ready with the facts. Once I finished those notes, I did a quick search on Joslyn. She was indeed a very accomplished woman and led an extremely diverse life.

The alarm on my phone pinged to remind me it was time to depart for dinner. Joslyn stalking would have to be continued at a later date.

Traffic was heavy as I drove to dinner, and it came to a complete standstill when my GPS said I was still several miles away. Fearing I would be late, I called Mimi.

Her phone went straight to voicemail, which I thought was odd, but maybe she was on another call. Once the beep sounded, I left a message that said I might be a few minutes late. After I disconnected, I tapped impatiently on the steering wheel. I was no stranger to traffic delays, but I did not want to be tardy for this meeting.

I was excited to share our findings with Tom and to get another look at our lady-in-waiting now that I had examined an authentic Fiona Limon. But I was also anxious. I couldn't put my finger on why. Perhaps it was Colby being out of touch, or the fact Mimi hadn't returned my call, which was definitely out of character for her.

Then I had a horrifying thought. What if the delay was an accident? What if it was Mimi? Which I realized was a completely irrational thought because she was coming from the east, not the south. "Calm the fuck down," I said to no one, impatient with myself.

This business with my dad and Colby was obviously weighing on me more than I wanted to admit. That was the only explanation for the irrational pit of anxiety in my stomach. Traffic finally began to crawl again, and within moments, we were once again zipping along. My GPS alerted me to my turnoff. I looked at the dashboard clock. I would only be about five minutes late. Perfectly respectable.

As I wound my way through Pacific Palisades to Tom's mansion, the street was impossibly quiet. I pulled into the driveway and Mimi's car was not there.

"Call Mimi," I said to my car once again, and her phone rang. And rang. And rang. And rang until her voicemail engaged. I didn't leave a message this time. Choosing to stay in the car, I would sit and wait. I was sure she'd call me or arrive shortly.

When fifteen minutes passed and still no Mimi, I tried her phone one more time, and again, straight to voicemail. I looked around. It was getting dark, and the trees were casting long shadows on the drive. I wondered what to do next. The only logical action was to go to the damn door and ring the doorbell. Although I had no idea what Tom and I would discuss while we waited for Mimi to arrive.

"Dammit, Mimi, where are you?" I said to no one again.

I screwed up my courage, headed to the gate, and pressed the call button. Then I looked down and my breath caught. The gate was unlatched and slightly ajar. Okay, TJ, don't jump to conclusions. It was possible that Tom left it open so that you could let yourself in.

Sure, and ice cream had no calories if you ate it fast. I pulled out my phone and dialed Mimi one last time, knowing she wouldn't answer. I clicked off but held my phone close as I pushed the gate open and walked through the long corridor to the interior gate. It was wide open.

"Hey, Tom?" I called down the hall. "It's TJ. The door was open so I'm letting myself in." Didn't want to get cleaved by some knife-wielding chef I had unwittingly startled, or interrupt an early evening tryst.

I made my way slowly, trying to remember how to get to the kitchen. The lights must have been on a timer or sensor because as the sun moved behind the trees, creating long shadows on the walls, they flickered on throughout the house. I called out again, but the house was tomb-quiet.

I somehow managed to wend my way to the kitchen and dining area. I could see into the kitchen now, and my heart pounded as I walked toward it. Still no Tom. No Mimi. And thankfully, there appeared to be no armed intruders, either.

It was eerily empty. I glanced over to the sitting area, which looked out onto the pool patio, and suppressed a scream.

TEN

I may be old-fashioned, but I thought murder was against the law - STRANGERS ON A TRAIN

I took another step, keeping an iron grip on my phone. My hand was shaking and my breathing ragged. I closed my eyes, trying to make sense of what I was seeing. When I opened them, he was still there.

Tom Meadler, lying face down in front of the wingback chair, blood pooled in the carpet around his head. It had seeped into the textured white wool Berber, following its deep-carved grooves, making a lurid, abstract design.

His face was angled to one side, his eyes open, staring blankly at the lights sparkling across the pool outside. There was no need to check his vitals. He was most certainly dead.

Mimi's prophetic words echoed in my head. She had a feeling. She knew something was not right with Tom, with his art sales. I castigated myself for not taking her concerns more seriously. I took one last look around the room. Then I turned away from Tom, knowing there was nothing I could do for him.

I retraced my steps to the front door. My first call was to 911, where I reported the crime and gave them the address. My next call was to Mimi. When she still did not answer, dark thoughts flooded my mind. My final call was to Colby, where, despite my best efforts to remain calm, ended up being a frantic plea on his voicemail for a callback. Why was no one fucking answering their phones?!

I looked around, suddenly aware of my surroundings. Twilight was giving way to full darkness. The street was still eerily quiet. Lights were flickering on all along the block, yet I still felt vulnerable.

I got into my car...Tom's car. Tom, who was no longer among the living, who was lying alone in that cavernous house. I swallowed hard, trying not to be sick. How could I continue to drive his car? But how could I not? I had no other transportation. Until I could locate Mimi, I had no clue what we would do next, about anything.

I moved the car to the street to make room for the emergency vehicles I knew would soon arrive. And then I waited. I waited to hear sirens, to see flashing lights. I waited for the cavalry to arrive so that I would not feel so alone and lost. I waited for someone, anyone, to appear, who could take charge of this nightmare. After an eternity passed, I finally heard the first sirens in the distance, and they became louder as the police drew closer.

I inhaled deeply, stepped out of the car, and leaned against it for support as first one patrol car pulled up and then another. Three officers, dressed in black wool shirts, ballistic vests, with radios clipped to their shoulders, exited the vehicles. They looked calm and professional, so I tried to match their demeanor, but my whole body shook when I stepped away from the car. I inhaled again and tried to regain my composure.

One officer walked over to me quickly, probably worried I was going to vomit or faint. He reached out and grabbed my elbow. I noticed the sergeant's stripes on his sleeve.

"Are you the one who found the deceased?" he asked. His nameplate read: LOPEZ.

"Yes, I am. I'm TJ Wilde," I replied as I stepped back and steadied myself against the car. "I was supposed to have a meeting with Tom...Mr. Meadler...tonight with another colleague. When I arrived, the gate and the front door," I nodded toward the entrance, "were unlocked and open." I took another deep breath before I could continue, remembering the long, quiet walk through the house. Sergeant Lopez waited patiently. "I rang the intercom. When no one answered, I entered, thinking that he may have left them open for us."

"And where did you find him?"

"Just off the kitchen, there is a sitting area. He is on the floor between the wingback chair and the coffee table." I closed my eyes. "Blood all around him."

"Did you touch anything?"

"Just the front door. But Mimi - that's my colleague - and I were here over the weekend, and this morning, working on a project for Tom...Mr. Meadler."

The advantage of being engaged to a cop, you have a good idea of what the police need from a witness. Give them the facts, leave the emotion out of it, and say nothing to incriminate yourself. I rose to the task. I knew they would need to eliminate our prints at some point, but for now, they were assessing the scene.

He looked over to the other officers and indicated they should go inside. He was definitely in charge. "Will you be okay here while we look around?" I nodded yes. "Okay, wait here and we will get your statement once we examine the scene." He left me to join his team.

I opened the driver's door of the car and sat sideways on the seat, my feet firmly planted on concrete, ready to join the police when needed. Eventually, they would begin looking at a motive, and I could think of a few million in artwork alone that would provide it. I wished I'd examined the scene long enough to figure out how he had been killed.

If he had been hit, he could have surprised an intruder or possibly been killed during a heated argument. If he had been shot, that might mean premeditation. That could mean a vendetta or some kind of deal gone wrong.

It was all speculation, and yet, a missing Mimi had ugly scenarios swirling through my panicked mind. I willed Colby to call me. If I couldn't locate Mimi, at least let me hear Colby's reassuring voice before I had to talk with the authorities again. I did not get my wish as I watched Sergeant Lopez walk out of the house, talking on his phone and heading straight for me.

"You doing okay?" he asked as he pocketed his phone.

"Not really," I said as I stood. "How else can I help you? I don't know much, but I can tell you what I do."

"Let's start with your meeting. You were meeting the deceased and others here?"

"My colleague, Mimi Webster, and I were scheduled to have dinner and discuss a painting," I paused as I remembered what Tom had said at breakfast. "Dinner!" I'm sure Lopez wondered why food had me so excited. "At our meeting this morning, Tom said he would have the chef prepare something special for dinner. I don't remember seeing anything prepped in the kitchen. Where's the chef?" Suddenly I dreaded there were more bodies in the enormous house. And where the hell was Mimi? "And I can't reach my friend," my voice caught, and I fought back tears. "My colleague - Mimi - I've been calling her," I checked the clock on my phone, "for at least an hour."

"Let's not jump to conclusions. The other officers are searching the house now, and so far they have found no indication of any other victims." He paused a moment and patted my arm, waiting to see, I suppose, if I was going to lose my shit. When I didn't, he continued with his questions. "You said you were meeting to discuss a painting?"

"Yes," I replied and then explained to him about our business with Tom, what Mimi's job was, and how our morning meeting had ended abruptly. I kept it vague, only the basic facts, mostly because that's all I knew. Anything else would have been conjecture. I did tell him it appeared there was good news about the art we were evaluating.

"Would you be able to tell if any of his art was missing?"

I shook my head. "I have walked through the house all of three times. Some pieces caught my eye, and of course, the painting we were examining, but Mimi would do a better job of discussing an inventory."

"And when was the last time you saw your friend?"

I didn't like the way he asked that, and I looked at him sharply, trying to read his expression. He returned my gaze with cop face. I knew it well. I would not determine his motive from that cool demeanor. "We had an afternoon meeting with a collector and after that, she dropped me off at my hotel. We arranged to meet back here at seven-thirty."

"Are you aware of what she was going to do between then and now?"

I searched my memory. Adrenaline had made my brain fuzzy. Was she going home to freshen up or to get some work done? No! The phone call from Edric. Was she meeting with Edric or just another call? "I believe she was meeting with an art dealer regarding another acquisition. Nothing to do with tonight's dinner."

He nodded, and I assumed we would circle back to that, but more vehicles pulled up, including a white van with LAPD emblazoned on the side. The crime unit, I surmised.

He walked over to the new crew and directed them on where to go and what to do. The occupants of the van opened the back and pulled out an impressive amount of equipment. Soon they all disappeared into the house, dressed from head to toe in the prerequisite forensic gear: coveralls, booties, and gloves. Each one of them carried black equipment boxes.

I looked at my phone. It was devoid of any messages or voicemails. Suddenly, I was very, very tired. I sat down again, resting my head on the open door, wishing I was home in Virginia, snuggled on the couch with my critters. A gentle voice brought me back to my current reality.

"Are you okay?" she asked, placing a gloved hand on my arm. "Here, do me a favor and drink this." She handed me a bottle of water. I took it and realized from the lettering on her uniform that she was with the coroner.

"Thank you," I said and opened the bottle. She then followed the forensic team into the house. As I took a sip, my phone buzzed. I almost dropped the water in my scramble to answer the call. It was Colby, and I felt my heart clench as I heard his voice.

"Honey, what's going on?" his voice filled with concern.

"Colby," I whispered as I adjusted myself into the car and closed the door. "Mimi's boss is dead. He's been murdered and I can't find Mimi anywhere." I choked back tears, so relieved he was on the line.

"Wait, slow down. Mimi is missing? Do you think she's been hurt, too?"

"I don't know what to think," I said, trying to keep the panic out of my voice. "I've been calling and texting her for the past hour without a response."

"Take a breath and walk me through what's happening."

I did just that, grateful to have my big, bad lawman nearby. If things went sideways, I knew he would drop everything to be with me.

When I finished, he said, "Let me make a few calls and see if I can't get you an ally there. At least until I can get to you." I could feel the love across the miles.

Feeling much better and much braver now, I reassured him I would be okay. And I promised him I would keep him abreast of any developments. I reiterated that my priority was finding Mimi.

"Don't do anything rash," he cautioned me. At least he didn't say stupid. I told him I would be careful. We disconnected as Sergeant Lopez rapped on my window.

He stepped back as I opened the door and exited. "Did you reach your friend?" he asked, pointing at the phone in my hand.

"No, that was my fiancé. He's a U.S. Marshal, so I wanted to make sure he knew what was happening. And that our friend Mimi was unaccounted for," my voice was casual, but my meaning was clear. I was not to be ignored, and Mimi was a potential victim here, not a suspect.

"Good to know," he said with unyielding cop face. "If you give Officer Lin here your contact information, We can let you go home for the night. We'll want you to talk to a detective tomorrow. And I'm afraid you may have to extend your stay, if you were planning on leaving in the next few days."

As if. I wouldn't dream of leaving until I knew exactly what happened here tonight. The sergeant left, and a young officer took his place. She asked me to write down my contact information in her notebook. I had to look up the exact address of the hotel, as my current stress level made it impossible to recall it. Once she had the information, she told me I was free to return to the hotel and reiterated the "don't leave town" bit.

No worries there. Despite being released, I sat in the car for another thirty minutes. I needed to collect my thoughts. I also wanted to watch the team work in case they found something revealing. And I was hoping against hope that Mimi would miraculously show up, even though I knew she wouldn't.

Time to go find her.

My first step would be to drive to her apartment. I hadn't been there yet. It was on the east side of Santa Monica, and it made more sense to meet at my hotel, since it was on the same side of town as Tom's place. It was a rather quick drive from my hotel to his house.

We had planned on having dinner and an evening of catching up at her place tonight, before Tom changed our scheduled meeting. I pulled Mimi's contact information up on my phone and tapped her address into the GPS. I followed it zombie-like as the disembodied voice led me through turns and down a cul-de-sac, ending at a gate that protected a lot of identical buildings, each dotted with lights in various windows.

Well, this would be a challenge. Without Mimi around to buzz me in, I wasn't sure what to do next. I pulled up to the gate. Next to the speaker was a number pad, where you would dial in your code or call your friend to buzz open the gate. Next to that was a small brass plaque. It instructed me to dial 011 to speak with the manager. I wasn't sure what I would say, but that was what I was going to do.

My phone rang through the Bluetooth in the car, startling me from my plotting. It was Colby. I braced myself for bad news.

"Tell me something good," I said when I answered.

"It is somewhat good news," he began. "I had locals check all the hospitals. No one matching her description has been admitted. And no deaths either."

"That is good news." For now, but I would take it.

"Are you still at the crime scene?"

"No, they released me," I said, avoiding detailing my current whereabouts.

"Are you back at the hotel?"

"On my way, I need to grab something to eat. Not that I feel much like eating, but should at least have something in the fridge in case I find my appetite."

He remained silent, long enough for me to understand he knew I was obfuscating, but he didn't push it. Instead, he just said, "I'll keep doing what I can on this end. Call me when you are settled in your room."

"Will do," I replied, ignoring the implied "it had better be soon" in his voice. "Love you."

"Love you, too."

We disconnected, and I rolled down my window. I had decided what I would say to whoever answered my call. I dialed the manager's number and waited. After two rings, a quiet voice came over the speaker. I double-checked the time to make sure I hadn't woken someone from a sound sleep. It was nine-thirty. It felt much, much later.

"Hello, how may I help you?" a sweet voice asked.

"Good evening. My name is TJ Wilde. I'm a friend of one of your tenants, Mimi Webster. She's had an emergency and it would be very helpful if I could get into her apartment to get her emergency contact information." I closed my eyes. I hated lying. Although I supposed it wasn't much of a lie. I just hoped the manager believed me.

"All right, I will let you in. Come to the leasing office. It's on the ground floor, first building on your left." With that, the gate swung open, and I followed her directions.

I pulled into a parking spot with a sign that said: VISITORS. I got out and watched a spry older woman, in shorts and a t-shirt declaring the wearer as a *Cat Granny*, walk across the parking lot toward me. The manager, I assumed.

"Well, good evening," she said. "That is one fine piece of machinery."

"Thanks, it's a loaner. But I agree. It's a sweet ride."

She unlocked the office door and switched on the light. "Come on in and tell me what's going on with Mimi. She's a lovely girl. I hope it's nothing serious."

I entered the cramped office that consisted of several tall filing cabinets, a large desk, and three chairs. She pointed to a chair for me as she walked around the desk and sat down behind it.

I sized her up and made a quick decision. "She's missing, I'm afraid. We've notified the police and I'm hoping to find her contacts so I can start calling around to see if I can locate her." I pulled out my wallet. "Here's my business card and my driver's license, to reassure you I'm legitimate. I'm terribly worried. She's my best friend and she missed our dinner meeting tonight. She'd never do that without calling." I decided leaning into gaining her sympathy was the quickest way to get what I needed. Seemed like a safe bet with a Cat Granny.

The manager took my business card and license, gave them a thorough examination, and handed the license back. "I can see you're worried. Let's go up to her apartment and see what we can find."

I breathed a sigh of relief. It pays to be honest. We walked through the complex, a maze of identical stucco two-story buildings with exterior stairs and mini balconies in front of every second-floor door. There was a noticeable chill in the air, and I shivered against the strengthening wind.

"Looks like we are going to get some weather," Cat Granny said when she stopped in front of Mimi's building. We climbed the stairs to the second-level deck and walked to the end unit. Ms. Cat Granny put her master key in the lock and turned it. She pushed open the door and flipped on the overhead light.

ELEVEN

I'm going crazy. I'm standing here solidly on my own two hands and going crazy - PHILADELPHIA STORY

I was relieved to see that the apartment looked untouched. No one had ransacked it, and Mimi wasn't lying dead on the floor. Believe me, after seeing Tom, that thought had crossed my mind more than once in the passing hours.

The studio was larger than I expected. High ceilings and large windows gave it an open feeling. There was a spacious kitchen alcove with an island dividing it from the living area. That area was large enough to hold a loveseat, an entertainment center, and a desk.

To the side of the living and kitchen areas was another alcove that held a full-sized bed behind a very stylish silk screen. A small hallway led to a huge walk-in closet and a full bath. Nothing screamed luxury or historic. It had a classic utilitarian nineties vibe to it.

Mimi had made the most of the space. She had lined the walls with shelves made of wood and metal. There were labeled baskets and clear containers on each shelf. Her small desk sat under the window in the living area, surrounded by more shelves. Those were filled with reference books and stylish linen filing boxes, all neatly labeled for her financial and business documents.

Everything was neat and clean. Her bed was made, dishes were stacked neatly in the dish drainer, and there was unopened mail on the island. Everything looked as if she would walk in any minute, as if nothing had happened. I wish I believed that were true.

Examining the closet next, it was the first place that looked in any way disheveled. Her laundry basket was overflowing. There were clothes scattered on the floor, the drawers of the small dresser were open, and her shoes were tossed everywhere. Not the work of a nefarious intruder, just a woman who hated doing laundry.

Nothing in the apartment looked suspicious. No cut-and-paste notes saying she had been kidnapped, so I returned to her desk. I wasn't sure what I was looking for, but I couldn't let the opportunity slip away. I doubted I could convince the manager to let me in again, at least not without a police escort.

There was a small wooden standing file on her desk, filled with neatly labeled hanging files. There were different colored files for each subject that needed to be tracked. I flipped through the papers in each folder, looking for anything that might hint at where she could be. They were primarily filled with acquisitions Tom wanted her to explore, as well as notes on contacts and prices. There were some bills that needed to be paid and receipts she needed to turn in for reimbursement. Nothing seemed suspicious or out of the ordinary for Mimi's job.

There were a few printouts of upcoming auctions tossed haphazardly on the desk, and on top of that pile was a receipt. The logo looked familiar. I picked it up to examine it.

It took me a moment, but I remembered where I had seen it before.

It had been on the tools inside Edric's case. Lancaster Gallery was in simple, crisp silver block letters at the top of the receipt. The itemized list was in smaller, black block typeface, all on premium white stock.

Very expensive and classy, as I would expect from Edric, I thought as I read over the items. It all looked straightforward. A cleaning and restoration of an acrylic on wood, by an artist I didn't immediately recognize. Dated a month ago, it was marked paid in full.

I dug out my phone and snapped a photo of it. I wasn't sure why, but if Mimi had pulled it out, it might mean something. That could be why Edric wanted to meet with her.

I saw little else on her desk that would help me locate her. I took one last look around and told the manager that I had found what I needed. She made sure all the lights were off and locked the door behind us. As we walked back to the office, I thanked her for allowing me into the apartment.

I also felt it necessary to warn her. "If she doesn't show up by tomorrow, the police may be by to look around, too, so don't be surprised."

"Oh, my, it sounds serious," she said with genuine concern.

"I'm afraid it might be if we don't locate her soon." I tried not to allow the panic to well up again. We said good night, and I drove out of the lot and through the electronic gate, unsure where I should go next. I didn't know Los Angeles or Mimi's life well enough to know where to search.

My phone rang as I pulled out onto the street. It was Colby again.

"Checking up on me?" I asked when I accepted the call.

"No, should I be?" he replied. I remained silent. "I wanted keep to you in the loop, I talked to the Assistant Director and explained the situation. He's authorized me to drive to LA tomorrow. I should be there by lunch."

"That's not necessary," I protested. "I don't want you compromising your job for this."

"I won't be. There are actually a few leads I want to follow up on in the area. I'll get there, we'll locate Mimi, I'll run down a few known associates on my case, and maybe we can even figure out what happened to Tom. We might even have time for some hot sex. Then I'll be back in San Diego before anyone can miss me." His optimism and humor worked. I felt lighter, and I knew having him here would buoy me while I searched for Mimi.

"All right," I acquiesced. "But just so we are clear, I am perfectly capable of taking care of myself." There was a need to assert my independence, and I tried to ignore the weight of the ring on my finger.

"I have no doubts you can handle this on your own, but a little extra support never hurts. I will call you when I'm on my way. Text me the address of your hotel."

We said our goodnights, and I was grateful he didn't ask me where I was or what I was doing before he disconnected.

I was both ravenous and exhausted. The night's events were taking a toll. I found a drive-thru and grabbed a burger and fries before making my way back to the hotel. Climbing the stairs to my room, my legs felt like lead weights. I ate my burger and picked at my fries, only eating out of necessity. I tasted nothing.

Locating the remote, I turned on the television and found the local news. I was desperate for information on Tom's death and if there was anything new. Other than a brief mention of a homicide in the prestigious neighborhood, his murder was barely a blip in the broadcast. I guess not enough car chases were involved to warrant an extensive story.

With that cheery thought, I readied for bed, turned the notification volume on my phone fully up in case Mimi called or texted, and was asleep moments after my head hit the pillow.

I was startled awake a few hours later. Groggy and confused, I reached for my phone, irrationally thinking it might be a message. A boom so strong it shook the windows brought me back to reality. Having never experienced an earthquake, I worried briefly that's what was happening.

Several flashes of light lit the room, followed by more thunder, and I finally realized it was a thunderstorm. A pretty intense one, from the sound of it. I threw back the covers, got up, and checked the windows. The rain was heavy, and I couldn't see the room across the deck from me. Once I was sure the rain wasn't coming in any of the windows, I crawled back into bed and slept soundly.

When I awoke again, it was still raining, though the light show had subsided. I checked my phone. It was four-thirty. It was disappointing, but I was not surprised that there were no missed texts. More sleep was warranted, but the images of Tom and my concern for Mimi inundated my brain. I gave up and made coffee instead.

I glanced out the window. It was still raining and pitch-black. The lights from the city could not penetrate the rain and fog. The day was dawning, dark and dreary. I felt desolate and alone, even as I tried to remind myself that Colby was on the way. Finding Mimi was my priority.

I poured a cup of coffee, sat on the couch, and turned on the television to stave off the isolation. The meteorologist was gushing about the rain as if it were a Midwestern blizzard, complete with traffic delays. She warned of flash floods and landslides, which left me wondering if this was an overreaction to a little rain or a legitimate threat.

I dialed Mimi's number, knowing she would not answer, but reassured when it rang several times before rolling over to voicemail. At least it was still active, not dead somewhere. Hopefully, that meant Mimi wasn't dead somewhere, either. If it hadn't been turned off or if the battery wasn't dead, Colby could track it.

Track it!

I could track it. How could I have forgotten? I scrolled through my phone to find the app we had used at the airport. I had rarely used it, so it was no surprise that I didn't remember it was on my phone. But there it was, and there was Mimi. Just a few miles away and moving slowly. I was so excited I almost screamed until I remembered where I was.

I dressed in moments, teeth brushed and hair scooped up in a hair tie. I grabbed my jacket and wished for rain gear, even a ball cap, but I had none of that. My sneakers would be woefully inadequate in the river of rain, but I didn't care. I knew where Mimi was.

I filled my jacket pocket with necessities: keys, wallet, phone, and was about to leave when reality hit me. It wasn't even five yet, still pitch dark out, and while I was a strong, independent woman who could take care of herself, rushing out into a city I didn't know before dawn wasn't a smart move.

It took all my willpower to remain in my room for another hour. I forced myself to eat. Then I sat in the comfy chair and willed myself to find my center. That place where calm and clear thinking could guide me, so that once I did venture out, I wouldn't do anything stupid.

Our trusty meteorologist, a buxom blonde who definitely knew her stuff, dashed any hopes of an early clearing. No chipper banter between the anchors as she tossed to the traffic guru, who solemnly detailed the various alerts and accidents. It was apocalyptic and matched my already dour mood.

I texted Colby to let him in on my plan. I knew he would disapprove, but I also didn't want to wander off into who knows where without someone knowing what was happening. Finally, after what felt like hours, the sky began to lighten. Nothing a sane person would consider daylight, but it felt less intimidating than the pre-dawn gloom.

I slipped on my jacket, my essentials already tucked into my pockets. That way I wouldn't have to carry my bag into the rain. I opened the door and braced myself against the onslaught, then ran down to the car.

By the time I'd slipped into the driver's seat, I was soaked. This wasn't a gentle, steady rain. It was a deluge. But I would not let it deter me from my mission.

I put my phone on the passenger seat and felt a surge of optimism as I turned onto the deserted street in the direction of the little red blinking dot. A helpful green arrow assured me I was traveling in the right direction, and it inched closer to the blinking dot as I proceeded to Venice.

My wipers could barely keep up with the water pouring down, but the sky continued to lighten as the invisible sun climbed higher in the sky. I drove slowly, even though I wanted to speed through the empty streets. The risk of hydroplaning in the outrageously expensive car of a dead man kept my foot light on the pedal. Even with my caution, the green arrow and the red dot met up quickly in the parking lot off the fishing pier.

A thick fog enveloped the beach. The ocean had disappeared as it was impossible to see more than a few yards in front of me. I looked around. There were no other cars to be seen, no people either.

I had hoped at least to find Mimi's car. The steady rain picked up in intensity, coming down in sheets now. The wind blew it first in one direction and then another. I dreaded getting out of the car, but I had no choice. I would not find Mimi sitting here, but the heated seats were difficult to leave.

Finally, I turned off the car and cracked open the door. Rain poured in, and I fought the urge to pull it quickly shut and wait out the downpour. I forced myself out into the torrent of wind and rain. It only took moments before it drenched me.

I looked at my phone. The dot was still pulsing and moving in a small circle. The map showed she was over the sand berm just beyond the parking lot. I made my way to the hill of sand, and that moved me closer to the dot.

I picked up my pace, fighting the blowing sand and rain. Without proper protection, it felt like a thousand needles piercing my face. I didn't care. All that mattered was Mimi.

The berm felt insurmountable. Meant to protect the area from further erosion, it stretched from north of the dock to quite a way up the beach. That soft sand would have been a challenge to climb, even on the best day, which this was not. I had to find another way.

I looked south toward the dock, where the sand was level, and decided that even though that would take me away from the blinking dot, it would be quicker. Jogging across the parking lot, I hurdled over the low wall constructed of lashed-together logs, and then made my way toward the dock.

Without the dune barrier, I was exposed to the open ocean. Sheets of rain and surf spray slapped me in the face. It was difficult to keep my footing on the slick sand as a sudden, powerful gust of wind buffeted me. But I pressed forward and ducked under the dock, trudging the short distance to the ocean side of the dune.

Water rushed around my feet as the ocean swelled aggressively inland. I didn't bother trying to dodge the waves. Fuck it. My shoes couldn't get any wetter, so I slogged through the heavy sand and seawater. Another wind gust sent stinging sand into my eyes. I ducked my head, impatiently pushing my dripping locks from my eyes, cursing the lie of Sunny California.

I turned my back away from the onslaught so I could look at my phone, grateful Colby had insisted on a military-grade, waterproof, shockproof model. It was holding up to the deluge better than I. Of course, I'd never admit that to him. Keep him guessing, that was my relationship motto.

The little red dot was still blinking, and I attempted to regain my bearings. The fog made it difficult to figure out what might be ahead or where Mimi could find shelter. A beach cottage? A condo? A cute little beachside cafe? I had no idea what was out there, as the beach, ocean, and clouds became one just feet from me. The only thing I could do was to keep moving and hope I would stumble upon her.

That thought gave me chills. I didn't want to trip over her. I wanted to find her sipping hot tea in a comfy cafe booth, not lying injured, or worse, somewhere on the beach. Head down, I pushed forward, but when I looked at my phone to judge my progress, the dot was gone.

No! I almost shrieked aloud with frustration and fear. Not that anyone would have heard me over the storm. I shook the phone in some irrational attempt to coax the dot back. Panic ripped through me. My only lifeline to Mimi was gone.

I stopped and looked around in all directions. There was nothing to see but a gray wall of misery surrounding me. I walked back to the dock, not even bothering to dodge the enormous waves crashing inches from my drenched shoes. I scrambled up the sand berm, powered by fear and adrenaline, hoping it would offer me a better vantage. When that proved useless, I slid down it to the walkway and followed that to the ramp leading to the pier.

I fought headwinds as I walked to the end of the long landing. Hoping against hope, I would see something up or down the beach. Willing the clouds to part and the fog to lift, if only for a moment, long enough for me to see something, anything that would indicate where Mimi might be.

Dammit, Mimi, where are you? I worried her battery had died, cutting her off from any help. Or worse, someone had turned it off, seeing me, even though I could not see them, and suspecting I was tracking Mimi's phone. Suddenly, I wished Colby were here. I felt abandoned and bleak. All the hope I had when I set out this morning had evaporated.

Colby would have more resources. He wouldn't have run out without a plan. Hell, it probably wouldn't have dared rain on him.

Defeated, I retraced my steps to the car. I hesitated only a moment before folding my sandy, dripping body into the immaculate vehicle. What did it matter? Tom was dead, so he wouldn't care. Still, I had a moment of guilt as sand fell from my pant legs onto the floor.

I fought the urge to slam my head against the steering wheel, instead firing up the car and turning on the heated seats. Shivering uncontrollably, I was unsure if it was out of cold or fear. I flipped on the wipers and looked out at the beach.

Nothing was visible beyond the parking lot, not even the immense berm. If anything, the fog was gaining strength, along with the rain. The wind had picked up to almost gale-force. I didn't want to leave, to leave Mimi wherever she might be out there alone, but I had no idea what else I could do.

Reluctantly, I drove out of the parking lot and turned toward the hotel. When I reached the first stoplight, I realized I was sobbing. How had this grand adventure turned into such a nightmare?

TWELVE

Snap out of it! - MOONSTRUCK

I cried for a few more blocks before willing myself to get a grip and regain my composure. I needed a clear head to work through Mimi's disappearance. By the time I pulled into my parking place, a budding plan had formed.

My phone chimed over the car speakers, startling me from my preoccupation. I was relieved to see Colby's name light up the screen.

"Hi, honey," I tried to sound upbeat and not as discouraged as I felt. "Are you on the road?"

"Hi, Kit-Kat. I am about forty-five minutes away, as long as the traffic doesn't snarl. They really don't like rain here."

That made me smile. "Don't seem to," I agreed. "The morning talking heads have been discussing it like it is the end times. Are you hungry? Should I grab us some breakfast?"

"I'm good. There was one of those plentiful buffets at our morning briefing. I could use more coffee, though."

"Coffee, I have plenty of," I replied. Relieved that he would be here and that we would find Mimi together.

"No luck locating Mimi?" he asked.

"I'll fill you in when you get here, but tracking her was a bust."

"Don't worry, we'll find her," he said with confidence.

I felt better already. Assured that with Colby's assistance, we would locate her by the end of the day. We disconnected, and I headed upstairs to shower and brew a fresh pot of coffee.

I did the hair and makeup thing, even though I was sure the weather would render both futile in record time. But I hadn't seen Colby for a few days, and now that I knew I was competing with the likes of Ailani, I wanted to make an effort. Besides, I knew he would worry if I looked like several miles of bad road, which was precisely how I felt.

My phone buzzed as I hung this morning's soaking clothes on the shower rod. It was Colby. He was in the parking lot, and I needed to run downstairs and escort him to my room.

I draped my still-drenched jacket over my head instead of actually putting it on and dashed into the rain to greet the badass lawman. Who was the love of my life. He stood at the locked gate, waiting for me, looking solid and unflappable. The antithesis of my condition - fragile with a side of dread.

Of course, he was fully decked out in waterproof gear. He had a pack slung over his shoulder, and even from a distance, I could see he was armed and dangerous. He was the most beautiful sight I had ever seen.

A wave of relief, love, and desire washed over me. I fumbled with the gate latch, and when it finally clicked and he stepped through, I threw my arms around him.

"I'm so glad to see you," I mumbled into his neck. "I thought I could handle this on my own."

"Of course you could," he whispered as he held me close. Then he pulled away, just enough so that he could kiss me. It was a sweet, reassuring kiss, but it was enough to buttress me against the past day of terror. He tucked a wet curl behind my ear and then brushed the rain from my cheek. "But I'll always be around for the assist." It sounded sexier than I'm sure he meant it.

I reluctantly pulled away from his embrace and adjusted my jacket over my head again. I grabbed his hand and practically dragged him up the stairs. Partly to get out of the rain, mostly to get him alone for a proper welcome before we got down to the important work of the day. I scanned my key and opened the door. We quickly stepped inside and I closed the door against the sudden gust of wind and rain threatening to swamp us.

"Wow," he said as he set his bag down. "This is great."

"It is, isn't it," I agreed. "I keep expecting Gidget or the Beach Boys to show up any minute."

Colby stripped off his wet jacket and hung it on the surfboard coat rack. "We should throw a towel under that," he laughed as he watched the water pour onto the floor.

He looked good in his U.S. Marshal's navy t-shirt, with the Marshals' insignia emblazoned over his left pec. The insignia was impressive, consisting of a white, five-pointed badge on a blue background with an eagle overlaid on it. In one talon, the eagle held an olive branch. In the other, thirteen arrows. Notably, the eagle looks to the branch. The thirteen original stars, and the words Justice, Integrity, Service, encircled the eagle. A gold ring and the words Department of Justice and United States Marshal Service then circumscribed them. The short sleeves struggled to contain his biceps, while the rest of the shirt was neatly tucked into his black cargo pants, outlining his trim, muscular chest.

In the bathroom to grab a towel, I noticed my dripping attire had already soaked the bathmat. This would have to remedy that before we left. I tossed my jacket over the shower rod. It was useless to me now. Then I threw a towel underneath it all before I rejoined Colby. While he pulled various items from his pack, I threw another towel under his coat. At this rate, we would need fresh towels before the end of the day.

"Here," he handed me a black raincoat, "I thought you might need this. I doubt you packed for monsoon season."

"Isn't that the truth? Everything I had on this morning is drenched." I sighed before filling him in on my morning adventures. "I was able to track Mimi's phone to Venice Beach. But it stopped pinging before I could locate her and the fog was so thick -" my voice broke as I choked back tears. Colby put his arms around me and pulled me into his chest, holding me tight. "It was raining. I got wet."

"I'm glad you thought to text me your plans before you adventured out. Although I wish you would have waited for me," he said gently, clearly concerned. He kissed the top of my head and held me tighter.

His warmth, the sound of his heartbeat, and the strength of his arms allowed all the tension of the past twenty-four hours to ebb away. I was so grateful he was here, so grateful he understood me. Tears welled up again, this time in relief that backup had arrived. I pushed them back and reluctantly pulled away from him. As much as I wanted to remain wrapped in his arms, I knew time was not on our side. We needed a plan.

"I am too worried about Mimi to remain static. The longer she's gone, the worse I fear the outcome," I told him, voicing for the first time my darkest thoughts. "I need to do something, I can't just wait here." I felt desperation rising.

"Give me the details about what's happening and what avenues you've explored since Meadler turned up dead." Colby's voice was deep and placid, as if he were asking about my sightseeing adventures. It had the desired effect, and I was able to push back the fear.

He walked over to the counter and poured himself a cup of coffee. "Do you want a cup?" I shook my head. I was already vibrating. More caffeine would be a bad idea.

"There's milk in the little fridge," I instructed. He pulled out the milk and added a bit to his mug. He leaned against the counter, sipped the coffee, and waited for details.

"After the police released me," I began. "I couldn't wait for them to look for Mimi. It was clear they believed her disappearance is proof she's their main suspect right now." I sat on the couch, tucking my legs and pulling the blanket around me. I realized I was still chilled to the bone, even with dry clothes. Colby sat next to me, an obelisk of reassurance. "It seemed only logical to begin my search at her apartment."

He nodded. "That's what I would have done."

"No, you would have remembered you had a tracking app on your phone and were sharing locations with her," I replied ruefully. "Anyway, I drove over to her complex and convinced the manager to let me into her apartment, where absolutely nothing looked out of place. Other than a few receipts sitting on her desk, it was neat as a pin." I didn't bother to mention the mess in the closet since that was the status quo for my friend.

"If needed, do you think the manager would let us in again?"

"Probably, especially if you flashed your badge at her. She's as worried as I am about Mimi."

"And your adventures this morning?"

"I woke up and finally remembered we had shared our locations while I was waiting at the airport. I wasn't sure if it was still active, but when I opened the app, there she was, just down the road. But when I got there, the phone stopped pinging. I hope that doesn't mean her battery is dead." I winced at the word. And fought hard against the tears that threatened to derail me again.

"Do you think someone saw you? Realized you were trying to locate her?"

"I'm not sure. The area was deserted, and the fog thick. They would have had to been close to see me, and I probably would have seen them. There is really nowhere to hide there." I tried to remember anything beyond rain and fog, but if there were any lifeguard stations or buildings, I didn't see them - couldn't see them.

"And tell me about yesterday, before Mimi ended up missing."

I relayed the details of our morning at Tom's, including the abrupt way he rushed us out while promising a nice dinner that evening to make up for cutting our meeting short.

"There was no sign of his chef or any meal prep when ..." I hesitated, remembering Tom's body in the otherwise immaculate kitchen area. "...I found Tom. It appeared that whoever murdered him did it before he made any other plans for the day."

"I'm working my contacts to get the autopsy report. At least get us a time of death."

I nodded and continued to narrate the day, telling him about the Getty and meeting Joslyn Ellis. "I'm almost positive that the painting is authentic. Not that it matters now, to Tom anyway. The owner might be interested."

"Do you know who the owner is?"

"I don't, but I'm sure Mimi does. Unless Tom inexplicably kept it from her."

"Would he do that?" Colby asked.

"Well, she said she did find him troubling at times," I explained.

"In what way?" Concern flooded Colby's eyes. Mimi had been a part of his life as long as he knew me, and I knew he cared deeply for her. I think, like me, he was surprised that her LA experience had been awash in drama.

"I'm not sure," I replied. "We didn't have a chance yet to delve into it. She kind of brushed it off as being overly sensitive due to what happened in Boston with our old boss." I fought back that dark thought that we might never be able to discuss it...or anything again.

"Well, that may be true," Colby agreed. "But I've always thought she had good instincts."

"I agree, I would trust her vibes about something over anyone's." I added, "That was our day. We were supposed to meet up at Tom's at seven-thirty. And you know the rest."

"What time did you split up?" Colby asked.

"Just after we met with Joslyn, around four-thirty, I think. My internal body clock is a mess right now and I don't remember exactly what time I got back. But late enough, I didn't get the nap I desperately needed."

"Are you aware of what Mimi did in that time period?"

"Yes, she was meeting with Edric, the art dealer, and then she sent me a text that something felt off, so she might be running late while she checked on it." I pulled out my phone and opened the text, letting Colby read it for himself.

"Has anyone interviewed Edric yet?" he asked, handing my phone back.

"I truly have no idea, but the officer in charge seemed less than interested, and I haven't spoken with any of the detectives yet." I thought that was odd, but maybe Los Angeles police did things differently. "You don't think I'm a suspect, do you?"

"I doubt it. They would have brought you in by now to answer questions. You gave them what they needed and didn't set off any alarm bells. They have bigger leads to run down, and they know where you are."

"I'm sure it didn't hurt that I threw around the information that my fiancé was a U.S. Marshal," I said with a smile. Then I sobered and added, "Nothing seems like a priority to them."

"A lot of crime and limited resources." Colby explained, knowing well the dilemma of law enforcement. "Yesterday alone, they had a big dollar smash and grab at a high-end jeweler, a possible gang shooting not far from the Promenade, and a home invasion in Brentwood. I'm sure they are waiting to see if they have any DNA or other physical evidence before chasing around after potential suspects in Meadler's murder."

"Well, Mimi and I have both left our fingerprints and DNA around Tom's."

"I'm sure, but you know the drill. They'll ask for your prints to exclude them, and unless they find them on the body or a murder weapon, neither of you will be at the top of their list."

Colby was doing his best to reassure me, but I couldn't shake the feeling that as long as Mimi was missing, they weren't looking very hard for other suspects. "Colby, I think they believe Mimi had something to do with Tom's murder."

He wrapped his hand around mine and squeezed it reassuringly. "Tell me more about this Edric guy."

"Beyond what Mimi told me and my brief meeting with him, I don't have much other information. He seemed ... prickly, when I met him. But Mimi knew exactly how to handle him." I tried to remember everything she had told me about him. "She said he did most of the evaluations on Tom's acquisitions. He seemed very offended that I was injected into this project," I explained, remembering his cool demeanor and terse answers to my questions. "But Mimi worked her magic to smooth things over."

"So Mimi worked with him frequently?" Colby asked.

"It seemed so. He also did any cleanings or minor repairs that were needed. I believe they sent any items that needed extensive restoration to an actual restorer, or Edric had one on call."

"And that was the last place you knew for sure where Mimi was going?"

"Yes," I replied. "And I don't know if the last text I received was before or after her meeting," I paused, suddenly thinking that could mean Edric was the last person to see her.

"We should pay him a visit. What do you think?" Colby didn't wait for a reply. He walked into the bathroom and rinsed out his mug before placing it back on the tray by the coffeepot.

"That would be a good place to start after we revisit where I lost Mimi's phone signal."

Colby looked out the window at the rain and fog, but didn't protest. Instead, he nodded and took his jacket from the hook. I followed suit, grateful to have actual rain gear against the continued onslaught.

"Do you have an address for Edric's studio?"

"I don't," I replied as I grabbed my bag. "But I have the name, so it shouldn't be difficult to find." We stepped out, and I pulled the door tight behind me. We were once again pelted with wind and rain. I resisted the urge to swear at the clouds.

We dashed down the stairs and out to the parking lot. I chuckled when I watched him beep a big black Silverado to life. His rental was almost identical to the one we had at home. The man did love his big trucks. At least it was electric. I slid into my seat and buckled up as Colby did the same.

"Lead the way," he said as he pulled the beast out of the narrow parking spot, and I directed him to turn right.

"It's not far, just a couple of miles from here, at Venice Beach." I had little hope that our luck would be any better than when I ventured out on my own.

The windshield wipers could barely keep up with the sheeting rain. At least the fog had lifted somewhat, and we could see a few blocks ahead. I was lucky to be in love with a man who was willing to indulge me, without judgment, and without questioning my motives. I could depend on him, and I knew that with him by my side, we would find Mimi.

"Turn right here," I directed him when we arrived at the beach lot. It was as desolate now as it had been at dawn.

"This is where you tracked her signal?" Colby asked as he pulled into a parking spot.

"Yes," I said, trying not to sound dejected as I looked at my phone. I was checking the tracking app on the off chance her phone had started transmitting again. It hadn't.

Colby reached over and wrapped his hand around mine. "We are going to find her, Teej. I have someone trying to get a location on her phone now. They'll see if they can trace her movements last night and get a last known location before it went quiet. If it turns back on, they'll know immediately. I promise." He looked out at the downpour before asking, "Do you want to get out and search?"

"Without some direction, I don't know what good that will do," I replied, miserable and discouraged by our options. I leaned across the cavernous compartment and put my head on his shoulder, needing him close for a moment before we continued our search.

He wrapped his arm around me and pulled me into his chest, holding me tight. There was no need for words. We were at that point in our relationship - a comfortable understanding of what was important.

I reached up and kissed him before moving back to my side of the truck. Having looked up the address of Edric's studio on the drive over, I told Colby, "I have the address for the Lancaster Gallery - that's Edric's studio. It's about thirty minutes from here. Over in West Hollywood." I read it off my phone and Colby programmed it into the navigation.

We drove surface streets after the GPS warned of long backups on the freeway. The rain eased the further we traveled from the coast. It was still a soaker, but at least the wipers could keep up now. Before long, the imperious voice told us we had arrived at our destination.

The gallery was a standalone building with parking in the back. As Colby maneuvered the narrow drive between two buildings, I gasped when the parking lot came into view. What I saw took my breath away.

THIRTEEN

Why can't we spend a normal day together?- TWISTER

There were two cars in the lot, and one of them was Mimi's convertible. I fought the urge to jump out of the still-moving vehicle. I grabbed Colby's arm and squeezed. "That's Mimi's," I whispered, almost afraid that if I spooked it, the car would disappear. I couldn't believe it was here. I willed myself not to think of all the unimaginable scenarios that would lead to her car being in that spot.

Colby pulled up beside it. "Do you recognize the other car?"

"I think it might be Edric's. I only got a glimpse of it when he came to consult with us on Saturday." My heart raced, and it was difficult to catch my breath.

"I want you to stay in the truck while I check out her car, okay?" He was asking, not ordering, and I understood his concerns, so I sat tight. For the moment, but at the first sign of trouble, I would be out in a flash.

Colby unholstered his gun, holding it at his side as he disembarked. He left his door open and walked over to Mimi's car. I watched anxiously as he inspected it. He looked inside the windows and then tried the doors.

The driver's side door was unlocked. As he pulled it open, I was out of the truck and making my way to him. I was terrified of what he might find. Praying it wasn't Mimi. My heart clenched when Colby popped the trunk.

When it was clear her car was completely uninhabited, I resumed breathing. I returned to the truck and climbed in while Colby examined the other vehicle. The locked doors limited him to looking in the windows through cupped hands. He stood up and shook his head in answer to my inquisitive look. Then he walked around the parking lot, surveying the surroundings before returning to me. I opened the passenger door, prepared to join him.

"How are you doing?" Colby asked.

"I'm okay," I lied. "We should go inside, right?" It was a statement, not a question. I dreaded what might await us. Unable to fathom a good scenario for Mimi's car to be abandoned and unlocked, I was still anxious to continue our search.

I slid out of the truck. He caught me and rubbed my arms before pulling me in close. I briefly rested my head on his shoulder, wishing I could stay there, where life felt normal and safe. Instead, I pulled back. "We should get this over with."

Colby nodded, and I shut the passenger door, following him to the back entrance. He stopped and turned to me. "Why don't you stay out here," Colby cautioned.

"Oh, hell no," I said as I crossed the lot, leaving him behind. I'm sure he knew it was fruitless to argue. He caught up to me and resigned himself to at least keeping me behind him as I ignored his request.

When we reached the door, Colby motioned me to stop and remain behind him. He brought his gun to eye level as he pushed down on the thumb latch. He turned back to me and mouthed, "Unlocked."

I stepped around him and indicated that I would open the door while he covered me. I pulled my sleeve down over my hand, closed my eyes, and pulled the handle. When the door swung open, the overwhelming smell of death greeted us. It took all my willpower not to vomit.

My eyes welled with tears, and my knees buckled. I leaned against the door for support, welcoming the icy rain on my face. I stole a look at Colby and I could see the concern etched on his face. He stepped over the threshold, and I steadied myself to follow him.

"Stay here, please," he pleaded. I knew he was trying to protect me. But if Mimi was in there, there was no protection, just harsh, cold, heartbreaking reality. I shook my head.

I thought I saw fear flash across his face before that unreadable, professional cop demeanor reappeared. He grabbed his flashlight, holding it and his weapon at shoulder level before crossing the threshold. The hallway was dark, the only illumination coming from the open door and Colby's torch. He nodded toward the wall, and I searched for a light switch.

Just inside the door was a panel of toggles. I flipped them all with a swipe of my still-covered hand. Light flooded the room. It was actually a small vestibule used for storage. An arched opening on the opposite wall led to the rest of the gallery. Colby holstered his flashlight and crept toward the opening, keeping his gun level.

I followed close behind. The archway led to an expansive showroom filled with natural light, despite the gray day.

There was a small office to the right, just beyond the door. The gallery itself was an open space, partitioned with six-foot tan wall panels, laid out in what appeared to be a random pattern. Although I suspected Edric had an artistic design in mind. Floor-to-ceiling windows banked the far wall facing the street.

Art was everywhere. Paintings, sculptures, and massive mobiles occupied the majority of the space. In one section, vases, pottery, and small sculptures filled rows of shelving. On the back wall, next to the office, there were two large drafting tables. One flat and the other at a tilt, covered in what must have been Edric's cleaning and repair supplies.

The smell of death was overwhelming now. I was desperate to find the source, unable to even comprehend that it might be my best friend. There were two gallery-facing walls that comprised the office, with four large windows that looked out into the gallery. All four had the blinds pulled and louvers shut.

The door was ajar. Colby looked back at me before he pushed it all the way open and stepped inside. I waited a moment and then followed. I assumed that if he had found Mimi in there, he would have already stepped out and pushed me away.

He had pulled out his flashlight, as the room was dim, but I didn't need it to see the figure lying behind the desk with papers strewn about, blood seeping into many of them. I knew immediately who had met an untimely end.

"Is that Edric?" Colby asked as he flashed the light on the face. Unseeing eyes stared up at us.

I couldn't believe what I was seeing. It was Edric, but his face was almost unrecognizable. He had been badly beaten.

His hands were bloody and raw. And two bullet holes pierced his perfectly pleated designer shirt.

Trying hard to catch my breath and steady myself, I could no longer fight the waves of nausea. I ran out the back door and threw up in the low shrubs that bordered the wall. Colby was beside me immediately as I braced myself with one arm against the concrete wall. He was grabbing my other arm, trying to pull me closer to him. I pushed him away, not to reject him, but I needed air. I needed all the air, all the rain-soaked, cool air. He stayed close, even though I turned away. When I felt I could breathe again, I faced him and put my hands on his chest.

"Find Mimi," I implored him, ignoring the concern in his eyes.

He objected. "I don't want to leave you here now there's been a murder." He looked around, assessing the situation, and I resisted the urge to physically push him into action. "Can you handle standing just inside the door?" he asked, and I nodded, and he led me back to the gallery. I stepped inside while he held the door. He moved past me, stopping long enough to cup my face in his hand. "Stay here, leave the door open, but if you see anything at all, close and lock it. Okay?"

I nodded against his hand, afraid that if I spoke or moved suddenly, I'd break down completely. Or worse, throw up again. I needed to stay strong and upright so Colby could focus on finding Mimi and securing the scene. I steeled myself and nodded again to reassure him I would be okay. He waited a moment, until he was sure I was, then disappeared into the showroom.

Once he was gone, I leaned on the doorframe, looking outside at the unrelenting rain. I was on high alert for any activity. Listening for any sounds of a threat to Colby, while staring at the abandoned cars in the parking lot. I wanted to will Mimi's car away. I wanted it to be anywhere but here at this horrific scene. I wanted Colby to come back to me and say it was all a mistake; there was no sign of Mimi, and there was no sign she had ever been here.

It was a fantasy, of course, but that was all my mind could handle. I choked back tears. How had I ever wished away my quiet life with my unremarkable job? All I wanted now was to be home, curled up on the couch beside Colby, with a drooling pup and purring cat competing for my lap.

"She's not here," Colby whispered into my ear when he returned. He put his hands on my shoulders. I leaned back against him and cried with relief as he wrapped his arms around me.

Once I pulled myself together, I told him I was okay. "I want to go back inside," I explained. "To see if I can find any evidence of how we locate Mimi."

"I can do that. You don't need to deal with the crime scene again."

"I'm fine," I assured him. "I've just been so worried about Mimi, seeing Edric like that, I was sure that..." I couldn't finish that thought, but I didn't need to with Colby. "But I'm fine now."

"It's been a while since you've had to deal with something like this. I'm worried for you."

"You mean dead bodies?" I asked. "Oh, please, I'm an old hand at these crises," I scoffed. This was not my first dead body, nor my first crime scene. Hell, it wasn't even my first one this trip. "Get me some gloves."

Colby sighed deeply, but did as I asked. He jogged back to the truck and grabbed his kit. He grabbed gloves for both of us out of the black bag and handed me a pair. "While I was inside, I called the Chief and Ailani to fill them in on what I've run into here. I'll let them contact LAPD. That will give us time to look things over before anyone arrives."

He was skirting protocol, and I knew it was for me. I was grateful. He handed me a jar of menthol, and I rubbed a dab under my nose.

I steeled myself again for what was next. Searching a dead man's office was not how I thought I would be spending my California days, but I would not rest if we couldn't examine the crime scene. I needed to find out if there was anything at all relating to Mimi on site. We re-entered the building, and this time, I was prepared for what lay ahead.

"Let's start with the office,′ He said as he crossed the foyer. "I can do it if you're not up for it."

"It'll be fine," I told him. "I might be the only one to recognize if something relates to Mimi." I was thinking about the receipts she had left on her workstation in her apartment.

We re-entered the office. Colby had opened the blinds, so the room was no longer dimly lit. This time, I prepared myself and willed myself to look away from the corpse.

Instead, I focused on the desk, scanning the scattered papers and pens that appeared displaced during a struggle. One Edric clearly lost. Nothing jumped out as a reason for his current situation. There were bills of lading, estimates for repairs, and two certificates of authenticity.

Curious, I eased them around until I could see the entirety of the documents without displacing them. Didn't want to contaminate the crime scene. Surprisingly, one certificate had Tom's name on it. It listed a large piece titled: REVENGE. I took out my phone and snapped a photo so I could read it better without disturbing the papers. Colby stood behind me and peered over my shoulder, interested in what I had found.

"Did you find something -" He stopped and reached past me. He picked up the other certificate. "Oh, boy." He put it back on the desk and pulled out his phone. I thought he was going to take a photo. Instead, he made a call. "Hey, boss, I'm still at that homicide in LA, and there is evidence here that this might be connected to our guy." He listened for a moment and replied, "I will take care of it. Agent Kekoa is on her way. I'll have her secure the scene and tell the LAPD that this is a federal case for now." He disconnected. "You're not going to believe this."

"Oh, I suspect I am," I replied.

"The name on this," he pointed at the paper on the desk, "is our fugitive, one of his aliases." He picked it up again and reexamined it, probably still not believing our cases had somehow crossed.

"He's a really bad guy?" I asked, knowing the answer but hoping I was wrong. Hoping it was just a white-collar crime deal.

"A very bad guy."

"Capable of doing...this?" I waved my hand toward the body.

"Unfortunately," Colby confirmed.

I sucked in my breath, not wanting to ask the next question, but needing Colby to be honest with me. "Do you think he could have hurt Mimi?"

Colby didn't answer. Instead, he wrapped his arms around me and pulled me in close. Once again, I pushed him away, not because I didn't find comfort in his embrace, but because I was terrified of falling apart. It took everything I had not to collapse into a heap on the floor. That would not help Mimi. I needed to keep a clear head. And Colby comforting me meant this was bad. Really bad.

"I'm not ready to think the worst," I said with determination. "We need to keep looking until your agent friend arrives." I wasn't thrilled to hand over Mimi's last known location to Colby's old flame. But I was grateful they had a working relationship, which meant she probably would not blow off my concerns for my friend.

I continued to look through the office for anything that might suggest Mimi's whereabouts. I opened the desk drawers and rifled through the items. In the center drawer, there was a set of keys. I picked them up and showed them to Colby.

"Hey, look at these. One of them looks like they belong to the car in the lot." He took them from me. "Wait," I said and pulled out my phone again. "Let me get a photo of all of them before they end up in some evidence bag." I placed them on the desk and snapped close-ups of the five keys on the ring. "Okay, all yours. Are you going to look in the car?"

"I am. It's not protocol, but we are dealing with a missing person. So technically, I'm acting on any information that may lead us to her. You wait here."

It wasn't a request, and I would have objected, but I didn't really want to go out in the rain again, anyway. Unless there was a note on the front seat with Mimi's location on it, I doubted there would be anything useful in Edric's car. Based on his general appearance, today notwithstanding, I imagined the car was immaculate, without even a scrap of trash on the floor.

I continued inspecting the area. There was a small bathroom off the office. I slid the pocket door completely open and turned on the light. It was in shambles, but not because of a fight. The small medicine cabinet over the sink was open, and the contents spilled all over the vanity and into the sink. Towels were strewn about, a small table was knocked over, and the throw rug was crumpled in the corner.

I examined the items from the medicine cabinet. There were your typical toiletries: toothpaste, mouthwash, aspirin, and what looked like an expensive bottle of spray cologne. The contents of two prescription bottles were scattered in and around the sink. I examined them. One was Adderall, which seemed on brand for Mr. Perfect. The other was Halcion, which I had a vague memory of being a powerful tranquilizer. That seemed dramatic. I guess in LA, you could find a doctor to write you a prescription for anything you wanted.

It also made me wonder how much time Edric spent here. Did he ever go home? Did he spend his days going from high as a kite to stoned like a zombie?

I hoped they were all for personal use and that he wasn't using any of it for illicit purposes. I didn't see any Rohypnol or Ketamine lying around, so that was good. Although drugging the wrong person might explain his current situation. I took photos of the two prescriptions. I knew this was going to be my only chance, and I wasn't sure what might be important later.

Once I had garnered all I could from the office and bathroom, I made my way across the showroom to the restoration area. I heard the door scrape open and assumed Colby had finished his examination of Edric's car. I was looking closely at a small oil-on-canvas portrait when he joined me.

"Anything of interest in the car?" I asked.

"That vehicle looked like it had been professionally detailed," he replied.

"I suspect it always looks like that," I said, unsurprised by Colby's discovery.

"What's got your interest there, Kit-Kat?"

I had picked up the canvas and was holding it up to the light, tipping it back and forth. Something about it wasn't right.

"Look at this painting," I said as I tipped it so he could see it. "It's made to appear old, but it has obviously been painted recently. The paint is fresh."

Colby reached out and lightly touched it. "Seems dry."

As he still had gloves on, I assumed he meant his finger had left no mark in the thick oils. "It is dry to the touch," I agreed. "But it's not cured. Oils can take months to cure. With little effort, this paint could be scraped or marred. Cured oils are actually remarkably hardy and difficult to damage."

I looked around. I didn't see any signs of a drying box or other equipment for hastening the process. But if you wanted to keep what you were doing secret, it wouldn't be out in the open.

"Are there any other rooms we might have missed?"

Colby looked around. "Doesn't appear so, but we can take one more look before the agents get here. What are you thinking?"

"I'm thinking this is odd," I said as I gingerly returned the canvas to the table. "Why would Edric paint this to look old? I mean, I guess he could be experimenting, testing techniques for restoration, but a complete portrait is..."

"Odd." Colby finished my thought.

"Yes. It is odd."

"Well, let's look around," Colby said as he strode back to the hallway.

FOURTEEN

Not only are you a cheat, you're a gutless cheat as well -
THE STING

I followed him through to the rear entrance. We hadn't given the foyer much more than a glance on our way to the central area of the building. Now, however, it was time to have a closer look. There was more to this building than expected, and I wanted the chance to explore every corner of it before the wave of agents arrived to interrupt us.

The room was wide, short, and windowless. Even with the overhead light, it was dimly lit. There was an empty wall-mounted coat rack by the door. On the outside wall there was a bank of lockers and two floor-to-ceiling bookshelves. Next to the threshold that led to the gallery, there was a door. The remainder of the room was bare. No storage boxes, no cleaning supplies, only a spotless, neutral tile floor and light gray walls.

Colby drew his weapon and nodded for me to open the solitary door. I turned the knob and pulled it slowly. It felt overly dramatic, considering we had been in the building for almost twenty minutes. There had been no signs of life anywhere, but I knew better than to argue with Colby when he was in cop mode. It was a good thing he had that weapon in hand, otherwise, the vacuum and broom would have had the drop on us.

Colby holstered his gun and leaned into the tiny broom closet, pushing on the walls. Searching, I assumed, for some hidden door. I stood in the middle of the room and scanned it again. Something felt off.

Slowly walking the perimeter, I tried to figure out what felt wrong with the room. Colby watched, his head slightly tilted and a quizzical look on his face. It would have been adorable if we weren't surrounded by death and crime. I returned to the center and gave Colby a triumphant look. He smiled as he closed the closet door. He saw it, too.

"Are you seeing what I'm seeing?" I asked him as I slowly twirled around, arms outstretched.

"This room is not as wide as the building," Colby replied.

"So," I began as I walked over to the lockers, "if I were going to hide a secret room, where would it be? The lockers?" I opened all three doors.

The first locker revealed shelves full of art supplies. Office supplies filled the second, and the third was empty. I pushed on the back of each locker, hoping something would move or slide open. The metal bent outward and hit the wall. When I removed my hand, it returned to its original shape, with a loud clank that echoed through the tomb-quiet building. Nothing but a solid wall behind each unit.

"That leaves the bookcases," Colby said as he walked over to inspect them.

They occupied much of the wall next to the lockers. Each case was solid wood and looked heavy. Sparsely filled with mostly empty shelves, we each took one and began our inventory. There was a shelf crammed with Architectural

Digest magazines, and above that, a few other shelves with a smattering of books. The bottom shelves held woven baskets. Nothing screamed secret entry. Colby grunted as he tried to move one of the bookcases away from the wall. It didn't budge.

"Earthquakes," I surmised. I bent down and examined the surrounding floor. "Those heavy pieces get bolted to the wall. We do the same thing at the museum for general safety."

I was surveying the bookcase closest to the lockers. "Hand me your flashlight." Colby did as I asked. I shone the light at the base and squinted, seeing nothing helpful. Then I did my best to look between the bookcase and the lockers. Nothing stood out.

At the other bookcase, I had better luck when I repeated the process. "I think there is a track here, behind this case and along this wall. It's the same color as the wall." Excited, I stood up and handed him the flashlight.

While he looked at what I had discovered, I inspected the narrow space between the two bookcases. Hoping to move the one with the track away from the other bookcase, I pushed my full weight against it, assuming it would slide along the wall away from its mate. It didn't budge. It was disappointing, but I was undeterred.

I rejoined Colby and ran my hand along the outside edge of the case. I didn't bother to push on there because, unless it was a magic door, there was nowhere for it to slide. The other bookcase and lockers stood in its way.

I wasn't sure what I was looking for, but I was convinced that the bookcase was a ruse. Colby caught on and began searching along the upper lip above my head. I slid my hand down the outside edge and then the edge between the two cases. Nothing budged. No secret latches or springs to trigger movement.

It was then that I saw it. At my eye level, on one shelf, there was a book I was very familiar with: *The Thefts of the Mona Lisa.* It was a must-read for any college art history class. I looked at the other books around it. A few on art history, a couple of fine art books, and an extensive art reference book I recognized from my library.

No, an art theft tome would be too obvious. I reached in and pulled the book out. To my disappointment, it did not trigger some secret latch that swung the bookshelf open, like in a Scooby-Doo cartoon.

Instead, behind the book was a small silver handle. I grabbed it and turned it to one side. There was a click, and the entire bookcase slid across the wall, revealing a narrow doorway to a large room.

"A secret room behind a bookcase, how very Hollywood," Colby quipped. He bowed and waved his arm toward the opening. "After you," he said.

The room was filled floor-to-ceiling. Paint and brushes covered several metal-shelving units. Art canvases leaned against the walls and shelves, and in the center was a large drafting table and an easel. Wooden frames leaned against every vertical surface and were littered across the floor. In the far corner was a drying box. All very incriminating.

"This is interesting," Colby mused as he walked around.

"It's more than interesting," I replied. "This looks like a pretty sophisticated counterfeiting operation."

"You think our dead guy was talented enough to forge artwork?"

"I don't. He might be capable of recreating up-and-coming artists, but not any well-known pieces. Perhaps he knew someone that talented and compensates them well? That's not an unusual arrangement."

"Do you think Mimi figured this out? Could that be why she was meeting with Edric?" Colby asked as he picked up a small canvas of a horse in a field backed by a cloudy sky.

"You're not suggesting she killed Edric because she discovered art theft, are you?" I stammered, shocked at the idea.

"No. Never," he hastened to reassure me. He put the canvas down and walked over to me. "Whoever did that to Edric was punishing him before they killed him. It could have been a disgruntled employee, a powerful client, or a pissed off ex. But I'm sure it wasn't a petite redhead, even on her worst day."

Exhaling in relief, I could only hope the rest of law enforcement saw it that way. Regardless, this discovery made me even more worried. Had Mimi seen something, and then someone felt the need to get rid of her? I closed my eyes to shut out the bad thoughts. It didn't work.

"I don't think Mimi would have come here alone if she knew what Edric had been doing. Something else brought her here." Trying to avoid thinking about what she might have stumbled on when she arrived, I walked over to one of the finished canvases. "I wonder how many forged works Edric has out there?" Picking it up, I examined it to distract myself from the dark thoughts that threatened to overtake me. "If this was a sophisticated operation, if Edric found a talented forger, there is one expert who could find their identity."

"Your dad."

"I'm betting he could. If this entire operation links back to your big fish - maybe they were all in it together. It would have been lucrative. A buyer would present Edric with a painting to authenticate and maybe provide some restoration on it. Then Edric and his team would create a forgery. They would return the forgery to the buyer. After that, they would sell the original work at market value to an unsuspecting collector." My mind whirred with criminal possibilities.

Colby reached over and kissed the top of my head. "I love it when you think like a felon," he laughed.

"Pull out all the finished canvases," I said as I opened the camera on my phone. I wanted to get photos of each since I assumed we would be barred from the gallery while the FBI investigated.

Colby did as I asked, and I took several pictures of the ten finished works. "We should recheck the office. I want to find any receipts for Tom's art. There was paperwork strewn on Mimi's desk, with the gallery's logo on it," I explained. I didn't wait for him before scurrying back to the office.

I steadfastly ignored Edric's moldering remains. There were two wood-grain lateral filing cabinets under the windows. I had given them a cursory look before, but now I was more serious in my probe. I flipped through the alphabetical files, looking for Meadler.

Colby joined me and began searching the other cabinet. We worked quickly and silently, not knowing when Ailani and her agents would interrupt us.

"Found it!" Colby proclaimed as he pulled out a thick hanging folder. He handed it to me and then pulled out another. "It looks like they did a lot of business together."

We set them on the desk, and I opened them. I rifled through the paperwork quickly. The dates went back years. I focused on the more recent invoices and photographed them as quickly as I could flip them over. Once I had finished, Colby put them back and closed the drawer.

"Anything else we should look at before company arrives?" he asked.

"The drafting tables in the showroom," I replied. Now that I knew we were dealing with criminal activity, I wanted a closer look.

Colby's phone buzzed. While he checked it, I walked over and re-examined the items on the two drafting tables. Everything looked legit, which made sense, being out in the open in the gallery. But I had wanted to make sure.

"We need to get out to the parking lot," Colby said as he put his phone in his pocket. "That was Ailani. She was giving us a five-minute warning."

"You think she knew we were snooping around?" I asked, startled that she would caution us to leave.

"I'm sure she did because she would have done the same thing."

We hustled ourselves out the door, making sure along the way that we had left nothing incriminating. The rain had slowed, and I swore there was a hint of blue off to the west. We settled into the truck and waited.

"Did you text my dad and tell him we have a forger question for him?"

"I did, he's very interested. I'll give him all the details tonight." Colby replied.

It was a weird moment as we discussed this, as if seeking my father's guidance was an ordinary occurrence. And just like clockwork, within five minutes, a swarm of black SUVs pulled into the lot. I was relieved when they didn't block the truck. Once we had answered their questions, I planned to continue my search for Mimi.

I waited in the truck while Colby conferred with the FBI agents. The rain had ramped up again. It was discouraging to note that even rain-soaked, Ailani looked completely put together in her FBI-issued jacket and ball cap. She and Colby stood close as they spoke while a younger, clearly junior agent, held an umbrella over them.

In the background, agents were assembling white awnings to cover both cars. No one had entered the studio yet. I assumed they were waiting for a signal from Ailani. She was obviously in charge, as more than one agent approached her with a question while she and Colby spoke.

After a few minutes, Colby sprinted back to the truck and climbed in, dripping with water. "Once they are set up, Ailani would like us to walk her through the crime scene." He watched my face cloud and added, "I know you want to get back out and look for Mimi, and we will." He squeezed my hand. "We are still waiting on the trace on her phone, it shouldn't be long and that will help."

I swallowed my anxiety and continued to watch the agents secure the scene. Teams were going through both vehicles while the remainder of the agents finally entered the building. Less than five minutes passed before Ailani walked over, tapped on the driver's side window, and waved for us to follow her inside. I jumped out and jogged over to the entrance, Colby close on my heels.

"Thanks for being willing to go through this. It can't be easy for you," Ailani began once we were back inside. "Colby

- Deputy Jameson - gave me the basics, but I wanted to confirm the events of this morning. Any context you could add would be helpful."

I detailed discovering Tom's body for her and the assembled agents, then the search for Mimi and how it led us here. And how we found her car unlocked and then the back door unlocked as well.

"Did you touch anything when you entered?" one of the random men in black asked.

"I used my sleeve on anything I might have touched," I explained. I figured I would leave out the later use of gloves. Let Colby give them that information if he felt it relevant. "We didn't waste much time looking around because..." I hesitated and took a deep breath before I continued. "It was obvious someone had died and I needed to find out if it was Mimi. So we made our way to the office."

"What made you think that?" Random Guy asked inconceivably.

I swallowed the smart-ass remark I wanted to snarl at Random Guy, but still rolled my eyes at Colby. He put his hand on my shoulder, moving closer, probably to restrain me if I went for Random Guy's jugular. I was hungry, and my patience was wearing thin.

"It was obvious when we entered," Colby repeated flatly.

"Steve, why don't you go see how the techs are doing with the vehicles. I'm very interested in finding out if there is anything in Ms. Webster's car that might help us locate her." She didn't wait for a response from him, instead turning back to me. "You knew Mr. Lancaster?"

"Not really. I met him on Saturday. It was a brief meeting to discuss a portrait at Tom Meadler's home."

"Was Mr. Meadler there?"

"No, he was out of town. It was just Edric, Mimi, and me. Edric evaluated the age of the portrait for us. This was to determine if we should continue to research its authenticity for Tom...Mr. Meadler." I explained. That meeting felt like a lifetime ago. I was having difficulty processing that it was less than seventy-two hours prior.

"You found Mr. Meadler's body, correct?" she asked me. "This was your second body in two days?" She looked at Colby. She seemed to think that was improbable. To his credit, Colby returned her incredulous look with unreadable cop stare.

"Unfortunately, yes," I replied matter-of-factly, and I wondered if she took my calm demeanor as guilt. With luck, Colby had already explained to her that I was no stranger to trouble.

"So, when you found Lancaster, did anything stand out to you?"

"You mean besides the secret room filled with artwork?" I wasn't trying to be snarky. It was just frustrating, and I was anxious to get back to looking for my best friend. "I'm sorry. I'm just overwhelmed by all that's happened."

"Understandable," she said, and somehow I knew she understood. I wanted to really dislike her, but I couldn't. It made sense why she was part of Colby's inner circle. "I think I've got what I need for now. I may contact you both once we have finished here."

"You know where to find me," I replied. "I'm happy to answer any questions. Once we locate Mimi, she can give you much more information on Edric's business than I can."

I didn't look at anyone because I knew what they were thinking. Locating Mimi and finding her alive appeared unlikely, given the deaths we had already encountered.

"Anything we uncover here that can help in that, I'll inform Colby immediately."

"Thank you," I said, suddenly very, very tired.

We dashed to the truck, Colby holding my door open while I climbed in. He ran over to the driver's side, hopped in, started it up, and then turned to me. "What's the plan?"

I thought for a moment. We needed to regroup, and I needed lunch. "Let's hit a drive-thru and plan our next steps while we eat," I said, reaching over to the dashboard screen to search for nearby food in the navigation system.

I found one that was a few blocks away and looked up the menu on my phone. "This looks good," I handed him my phone to show him the menu for a nearby place called Astro Burger.

"I agree," he said as he set the navigation to direct us there.

I sat back in the comfortable heated seat and willed myself not to fall asleep while we sped down Melrose Avenue. It would have been a brief nap because we arrived quickly, and the GPS instructed Colby to turn and turn again until we were in the drive-thru. We made our selections and then waited.

"So, I'm assuming that the FBI will have already sent agents to Edric's home?" I held out hope that Mimi might be there, though I was still unsure why or how Edric would have abducted her.

"Yes, once you confirmed his identity, they sent a couple of agents to his address and began the process of obtaining a warrant to enter."

"They have to wait for a warrant?" I swallowed my panic, pushing away images of Mimi, alone and in trouble, locked in a dark basement.

"Maybe," Colby replied thoughtfully. "They could claim exigent circumstance, believing Mimi might be there, and in danger, or they could have someone who has access to the house let them in. There is a lot of gray area when a homeowner dies outside their home."

The restaurant window slid open. Colby grabbed the bags and drinks, then thanked the server. He passed the food over to me, powered his window up to avoid getting soaked, and set the navigation for a small park near us.

Colby drove down an empty, tree-lined street, past several apartment complexes and small bungalows. A few blocks more and a small park appeared. He pulled up next to the curb and parked.

"They'll let us know, right? If they make entry, Ailani will call you?" I asked anxiously.

"She will call as soon as she knows anything," he said as he grabbed a bag and pulled out items. "Even if it's bad news, she knows how important this is to us."

I nodded and distributed everything from the bag on my lap. Colby's phone buzzed. Ailani's name flashed on the dashboard screen, and he pressed accept.

"Any news, Ailani?" he said by way of greeting.

"We were able to make entry into Mr. Lancaster's home."

FIFTEEN

I must say, for a charming, intelligent girl, you certainly surrounded yourself with a remarkable collection of dopes - LAURA

I held my breath and stared straight ahead. Watching as the rain sheeted on the truck windshield.

"There was no sign of Ms. Webster. Nothing to suggest she had ever been there. The agents have just started their search, so if they find anything relevant, you'll be my first call," Ailani continued.

I began to breathe again and fought back tears - of relief or frustration? Probably both.

"Have them look for any storage units or rental properties," Colby instructed, and that jump-started my brain.

"Ailani," I began, not sure, or even caring, what the protocol might be in this situation. "Can you see if he has any property near Venice Beach?"

"According to TJ's tracking app, that's the last place Mimi's phone pinged," Colby explained. "If he caused her disappearance and he has property there, it could help us locate her."

"Will do, I'll get the agents on it."

"Thanks for the update," Colby replied before disconnecting. He unwrapped his burger, reached over and squeezed my hand briefly, before biting into it.

I had opted for a club sandwich and a salad, although Colby's fries smelled amazing. I unwrapped the club and wondered how I would even tackle the thick layers of turkey, chicken, and bacon, not to mention all the lettuce and tomato goodness. Good thing Colby and I had been together forever, because this was going to get messy and unattractive. I dove in and realized this was anything but fast food. While I chewed, my mind pondered the next logical steps we needed to take to locate Mimi.

"I think we should go back to Mimi's apartment," I said between bites.

"I agree. Now that we are sure Edric was into something shady, I would like to have a good look around, and see if there is any indication Mimi was aware of it," he replied. I nodded as I snatched a couple of his fries.

"I definitely wasn't looking for anything like that when I was there under the watchful eye of the manager, so I was surreptitious with my search." I opened my salad and sighed with happiness when I saw all the fresh produce. "I told her not to be surprised if the police showed up, so I think your badge will get us in the door."

We finished our food in silence. Colby then used the truck's voice control to add Mimi's address to the navigation, and we were on our way. It was a short drive with minimal traffic.

When we arrived at the complex gate, Colby buzzed the manager. I leaned over to the driver's window to remind her of my identity and introduced Colby. Once he explained who he was and told her how dire the situation had become, she opened the gate immediately. I could hear the concern in her voice as she told us to come to her office.

She was waiting for us in front of her door, seemingly unfazed by the drizzle. She walked over, and Colby opened the window. He showed her his badge and ID, and she handed him the key.

"This is so concerning. Mimi is such a nice woman," she said. She stooped down to pick up a cat that was winding around her legs and snuggled it close to her face. "Tigger, how did you escape again?" To Colby, she advised, "I have a repair to supervise, but I trust you'll lock up and drop the key in the drop box on your way out?" She juggled the very docile orange tabby to her shoulder, dug a card from her pocket, and gave it to him. "If you need me, just call and I'll make my way over. I hope you find Mimi soon."

And then she was off, I presumed, to get Tigger back to his home before solving whatever repair crisis had arisen.

Colby closed the window and asked me which way he needed to proceed. I directed him to the block of apartments that contained Mimi's. The parking lot was relatively empty, so we could park close to her building.

Still, we dashed down the sidewalk through the continuing drizzle until we reached the front of her building. We jogged up the stairs to her door. Colby slipped the key into the lock, and we ducked inside. I scanned the apartment. It looked as if nothing had changed since my last visit.

"Doesn't look like anyone has been here," I remarked, relieved. I walked over to Mimi's work area and picked up the receipt from the gallery I had seen earlier. "I'm going to search for all of the receipts she has from Edric. Do you want to look around, see if anything else makes your cop spidey-senses tingle?"

He came up behind me, put his arms around me, and whispered in my ear, "I can think of a few things that make me tingle." I couldn't help myself, I giggled and felt the heat rise through my body. My best friend was missing, and two men were dead, yet Colby could get me to forget all about that with a few simple words. I was going to hell.

I pulled one of the accordion files from Mimi's well-organized desktop file sorter. Baby blue and labeled with her neat handwriting, it read: MEADLER ACQUISITIONS. It was thick, indicative of a busy year of work. I pulled out the papers and thumbed through them.

Organized by date, I had to sift through the entire stack before I found the Lancaster Gallery receipts. There was a handwritten sticky note that seemed promising. From Edric, the writing was full of swirls and artistic flourishes. It stated he had possession of one of Tom's prospective purchases, along with the expected return date. He listed the recommended cleaning and repairs, along with costs. He also noted his preliminary appraisal of the work.

Curious, I skimmed Mimi's notes to see her appraisal. Her numbers were considerably lower than Edric's. I found that interesting, but it didn't illuminate why Edric had kidnapped my friend.

Once I had pulled all the invoices related to the Lancaster Gallery, I sorted them alphabetically by artist. I thought that would make it easier to check them against the artwork I had photographed at the gallery. I opened my photo files, enlarged each photo in order to see the signatures clearly, and tried to match the various pieces to the receipts.

A few minutes later, Colby returned from deep within Mimi's expansive closet. "Are we sure no one tossed that closet?" Colby asked.

I laughed. "That's just Mimi. Hates all things laundry, including folding, hanging, and putting away. Ironing is of the devil."

He joined me at the desk and peered over my shoulder. "Did you have any luck?"

"So far it's a bust. Nothing in Tom's file matches any of the forgeries at the gallery." I replied as I placed the pile neatly on the desk, leaving it for Mimi to re-file when she returned. I was sure she would understand that we were on a mission and time was of the essence.

I placed the receipt she had left out, on the top of the pile. It still felt like a vital link, but beyond that hunch, I didn't know what it meant.

"I didn't see anything here that helps us, either," Colby said, walking over to the desk.

"Except for the receipt she left on her desk, nothing stands out." I was trying to swallow my disappointment and remain positive. Colby, seeing through my brave facade, pulled me into his chest. He held me close. I relaxed into him and breathed in his scent, regaining at least a modicum of hope while wrapped in his arms. "What's next?" I whispered into his shirt.

Before he could answer, my phone buzzed. Scrambling to disentangle myself so I could retrieve it from my back pocket, I almost screamed when I saw the photo on the screen. I answered and put it on speaker.

"Mimi! Where are you?!" I shouted loud enough for the entire complex to hear. What can I say? I was overjoyed.

"Teej," came a whispered response. And then the line went dead.

"No!" I screamed as I stared at the now blank screen.

Colby gently took the phone from my hand and swiped the screen a couple of times. He turned the phone around so I could see - the red dot was back. And it was in the exact location it had been before.

"Let's go!" I urged as I sprinted to the door.

Colby held up a finger as he pressed a number on his phone. A moment later he said, "Bobby, we got a call from that number I asked you to ping. Can you see if you can get me a precise location?" He listened for a moment. "Great, shoot me the info when you have it." He disconnected and joined me at the door. "How far is Venice from here?" he asked as we let ourselves out, and Colby locked the door behind us.

"About thirty minutes if traffic is light," I told him.

He stopped at the manager's office, and I ran the key to the drop box. Then we were off at a brisk pace to Venice. Colby had activated the navigation. With luck, it would detour us around any severe congestion or accidents.

We still encountered heavy traffic, but it moved at road speeds, so we made good time. I watched as the distance between the red dot and the green arrow narrowed. For the first time since I found Tom's body, I felt hopeful.

We were going to find Mimi, and then maybe everything would make sense again. Even if the police continued to treat her as a suspect, we could fix that, Colby and I. I glanced at him, grateful he had come into my life and insisted on staying.

I fidgeted in my seat, anxious for the two disparate symbols to meet up and reveal my best friend. Finally, we arrived at the beach parking lot again. The rain was steady, but the fog had lifted, giving us a much broader view of the area.

Just like last time, Mimi's red pin was just out of reach of my green arrow. I jumped out of the truck and ran to the barrier wall. I climbed onto it and scanned in all directions. There were businesses and condos to the east, lifeguard stations to the north and south, and the fishing pier leading from the parking lot to the ocean.

I looked at my phone. The red dot was stationary. It was not positioned on the street, but just as before, it was beyond the parking lot, toward the water. I knew this wasn't a precise tool, so I was doing my best to guess the most likely place she could be located.

The beach, the parking lot, the pier, and the ocean were all essentially deserted. In the stalls nearest the beach, there were two cars parked that had not been there before. I saw no sign of the occupants. Colby was making his way to the closest one, and I knew he would check them both. My focus kept returning to the lifeguard stations on either side of me.

They were both closed, and if I were going to stash someone, that seemed a logical place. Especially if Edric had planned to come back shortly, not anticipating his death would have prohibited that. They were equidistant from the fishing pier, close to the water and out of sound range from the parking lot. Even if Mimi screamed, the ocean waves crashing to the shore would drown her out on a stormy day with few people walking past any of them.

I was about to jump down to the sand and check one of the stations when Colby jogged over to me.

"I checked both cars, they are locked and empty," he explained. "No response when I knocked on the trunk and the hatchback."

"Good." I grabbed his hand as he jumped up to join me on the wall. It was narrow, and I briefly worried he wouldn't maintain his balance. I shouldn't have. For a big man, he had the reflexes of a cat. "We should check out the lifeguard stations next, don't you think?" I asked.

"Until someone calls us with a more precise location, I agree," he said as he looked to the north.

Just then, both our phones rang. I almost dropped mine as I scrambled to answer it. It was Mimi again. My hands shook as I put it up to my ear so that I could hear her over the waves, wind, and rain.

"Mimi! Where are you?!" I screamed into the phone. In my peripheral vision, I saw Colby step down and move away. Probably so he could hear without me shouting next to him.

"TJ, I'm not sure," Mimi shouted, probably because I was shouting. "I'm on a small boat. It's really rolling with these enormous waves. I'm in the cabin, and somehow the door is jammed or locked and I can't get out. There are a couple of small windows, but all I can see is water and rain. I have no idea where I am," she sounded close to panic.

"Colby is here," I reassured her. "We tracked your phone as best we could and we have people working on finding your exact location. We are coming to find you, if it takes the entire FBI and Marshal Service. I swear." I promised her.

"It was Edric, TJ," she sounded justifiably angry. "He drugged me or something, and the next thing I knew, I woke up on the floor of this boat, taped to the leg of a table. It took me forever to get free. And when I did, I found my phone, but it had powered down." She paused, and it sounded like she was trying to maintain composure. "When I turned it on to call you, the battery died. I tore the galley apart until I finally found a charger. Why did he do this?" She was spiraling a bit. I could hear the tears as she demanded an explanation as to why he would do this to her.

I needed her to keep talking, believing that if I kept her talking, she would stay calm enough for us to figure out the next steps. She needed to stay composed. Panic might lead to unwanted consequences.

Before I could look for Colby, he was beside me. He was at my elbow, listening to my side of the conversation. I had been so intent on speaking with Mimi, I didn't even feel him flank me. "Mimi, hang on, Colby and I are going to get somewhere that we can both talk to you, where it's not so noisy."

"Don't hang up!" she pleaded.

"No, honey, I'm right here. Keep talking." Colby and I jogged back to his truck while I listened as Mimi told me how she had gone to meet Edric at the gallery because she had a question about a piece he had cleaned and authenticated for Tom.

"And things got weird quickly," she explained.

I cut her off gently after Colby and I were in the truck. "Mimi, we can go into all of that once we get you off that boat. I'm going to put you on speaker phone so Colby and I can both talk with you."

I had never used such care in engaging the speaker as I did in that moment, afraid my shaky hand would accidentally disconnect her. Once we were on speaker, I let Colby talk to her first.

"Mimi, it's Colby. We are in the process of finding you. My team pinged your phone just off Marina Del Rey, so that is where we are going to start the search. Okay? It will have to be by boat, because a helicopter can't go up in these winds. But I'm going to guess, the boat you're on is one of a very few out on the water right now. We are coming for you."

He nodded to me to keep her talking while he did some quick texting. I asked her if she had anything to eat or drink. If someone had drugged her, it was essential to at least keep her hydrated.

"There is a well-stocked refrigerator onboard," she said with a tired laugh. "Once I was free, I drank a couple of cans of very expensive sparkling water. I'm a little nauseous with all the listing, so I stayed away from any of the food. Although I may have to break open the crackers soon," she tried to sound upbeat, but I could hear the fear and exhaustion in her voice.

"Mimi," Colby interrupted. "Can you open the windows?"

There was a long pause. I assumed she was checking.

Finally, she said, "Most of them are sealed plastic. But there's one window that is hinged, so I can open it."

"Good," Colby encouraged her. "Can you open it without risking waves crashing in?"

"I think so, the cabin seems well above the water line." Another long pause. "Okay, I have it open."

"Great. With the wind and waves, it might be difficult to hear, but if you do hear a speedboat, I want you to alert us. It will help them pinpoint your location."

"Alright, I will." Her voice was getting quieter the longer we spoke.

I needed to keep her focused and talking. As much for me, as for her. I didn't want to lose touch with her again. I was not going to relax until I could hug her.

"Mimi, honey, are you injured in any way? Does your head hurt?" If Edric hadn't drugged her, he might have hit her hard enough to render her unconscious.

"I'm a bit bruised and bloody from the stupid tape. But other than the seasickness, I think I'm fine. Although I might be blind from all the fluorescent orange duct tape he used to tie me up."

"Did you say fluorescent?" Colby asked excitedly.

"Yes, there is a huge roll of it on the table. That's what he used on me."

I could see Colby smiling as he spoke. "Mimi, can you make something large enough with it to hang outside the window?"

"You mean like a flag?" She sounded excited, too. "I see what you mean, so they'll see me. I can do that."

I beamed at Colby. Not only was this brilliant, but it gave Mimi something to focus on, a project to complete. That would help. I muted the phone.

"Any idea how long it will take to find her?"

SIXTEEN

In a couple of days, you're going to have the most wonderful breakdown - DIAL M FOR MURDER

I looked out the rain-streaked windshield, irrationally trying to see Mimi now that I knew she was out there, somewhere.

"Once the FBI discovered he had a slip at Marina Del Rey, they were able to identify his boat," Colby explained. "There aren't that many crafts out in this weather, but I have no idea how far beyond the harbor he has her anchored. I don't think it could have been far. Ailani said all he had was a small dinghy to get back to the slip."

I was trying to stave off the dark thoughts, but after everything I had seen in the past couple of days, it was difficult. "Colby, if Edric hadn't been murdered -"

He cut me off. "I don't think he was going to kill her, TJ. Whatever he was into, he needed a plan to keep her quiet. It probably involved an offer of a lot of money."

He was trying to reassure me, but I wasn't sure I believed him. I did find it difficult to envision the cranky little man I met a few days ago committing murder.

"Okay, I have made a large square of tape and secured it outside the window," Mimi said, interrupting my dark thoughts. I quickly unmuted her. "The wind has calmed down a bit, and the boat isn't swaying as much."

I looked out at the street, and it appeared the rain was finally subsiding, along with the wind, though everything was still gray.

"Good job," Colby told her. "Keep an ear out for the speedboat."

I decided I should continue to keep her talking, still unsure if she had suffered any injuries during her ordeal. I was on alert for slurred speech, disorientation, and signs of a head injury or lingering effects of a drug overdose.

It was also important to reassure her we were still here, and we weren't going anywhere until she was safely on land. Everyone needed a distraction to help pass the time until her rescue team arrived. "Can you tell us why you were meeting with Edric?" I asked.

"It was strange, TJ," she began. "There was a notification in my email when I got home yesterday. I have an app that keeps track of artwork that is scheduled to go up for auction or private sale. It helps me scan for anything I think Tom might be interested in acquiring," she paused for a long moment.

"Mimi? Are you there?" I asked anxiously.

"Yes, still here. I thought I heard something," she said when she spoke again. "Anyway, there was a painting coming up for sale next week. TJ, it was weird. It was a painting Tom had purchased about six months prior. Edric had certified it as the real deal. The paper trail was legitimate. Nothing out of the ordinary. We sent it to the Edric's gallery a few weeks after Tom took possession of it. He was to clean it and do a few minor repairs." She paused again, and I assumed it was so she could listen for her rescuers. She continued, "There was nothing unusual about the authentication or the sale. I did everything by the book." She sounded defensive, and I understood. With our jobs, our reputations were everything. "It all checked out. The seller was reputable, the auction house was reputable, and Edric signed off on it, so I had no doubts it was authentic. But here it was, up for private sale when I thought it was in storage. It looked to be an overseas seller, which set off my radar."

"Was it possible Tom had already decided to resell it?" Colby asked.

"He rarely turned them around that quickly, and usually he has me assist with the resale. But I thought he might have decided suddenly and just forgot to tell me. He has been traveling a lot recently. So, I checked his inventory list. He keeps two warehouses, one in Long Beach and one in the FTZ."

"What's the FTZ?" I asked.

"It's a foreign trade zone where his foreign purchases are exempted or tariffs are deferred until he resells them. And his other warehouse is not far from there. We keep an online inventory of everything so we can locate works easily when he wants to resell them. It wasn't like him to deviate from our system. He's a meticulous kind of guy."

"I guess I didn't realize he was so heavily into retailing his purchases," I replied. I knew some people traded artwork as others traded stocks. That wasn't the world in which I worked, and it puzzled me. I wasn't aware that was Tom's business model, though Mimi seemed comfortable in it.

"He has a knack for it," Mimi said. "He buys a lot of items and then resells them for quite a profit." I saw Colby's eyebrows raise, and I couldn't wait to hear his explanation for what I now assumed was a nefarious enterprise. "When I got home, I checked the online inventory, and the painting was still listed at the FTZ warehouse. I texted Tom to double-check, but I never heard back."

I swallowed hard. Having to tell her that Tom and Edric had both been murdered was not something I wanted to do. I would put it off as long as I could. At least until a doctor checked her out, and we got some food into her.

"Hey! I hear the speedboat," Mimi suddenly exclaimed. "Over here!" she yelled.

"Mimi, can you move the flag or wave it?" Colby asked.

"The window opening is too narrow to get my hand out. The flag is so damp, it really won't move now," she explained. She sounded scared.

"It's okay" Colby reassured her. "I'm going to tell them that they are in the right location." Mimi and I listened as he made the call and told them they were at the correct boat. He disconnected and returned to speaking to us. "Mimi, they are going to board the boat and figure out how to get the door open. You might want to stand back as far as you can in case it flies open."

Mimi said nothing. I suspected she was listening intently to her rescuers. I muted the phone. "Are they going to take her to Marina Del Rey?"

"Yes, they have EMTs waiting to check her out. Ailani is going to meet us there so she can question Mimi before the LAPD gets wind of all of this."

"We should be there," I said urgently.

"Agreed," Colby said as he started the truck and pulled out of the lot.

I continued to listen to Mimi as she conversed with the agents on board. I was relieved when they finally managed to open the door. From what I could hear, Edric had jammed it with the handle of a fishing net, so it was easy for them to open from the outside. Once she knew she was safe, she ended the call so they could load her into the rescue vessel.

We arrived at the marina while the boat was en route, and Colby parked alongside the rescue units near the Coast Guard station. We exited the truck, walked past the rescue units, and over to the building. Several paramedics and two people in rain gear with FBI logos were standing under the building's awning. Colby showed his badge, and I watched him explain the situation to them.

The rain had finally subsided. I looked toward the water, straining to see anything. Anxious, I needed to keep moving. I left the group and walked to the boardwalk. The security gate was open, so I made my way to the police dock. I figured if anyone objected, Colby would set them straight.

I paced the dock, listening for the diesel engine that meant Mimi was close. All the pent-up stress and anxiety flooded my body. My heart raced, and I found it difficult to breathe while I waited.

"You okay there, Kit-Kat?" Colby put a reassuring hand on my shoulder as he came up behind me. I stopped pacing and leaned my back against his sturdy chest. He wrapped his arms around me and held me tight.

"Yes. No. I don't know," I replied and then turned to him, leaning my head on his chest. Relaxing a bit as I listened to his heartbeat while he held me tight. I soaked in his strength and serenity. My breathing eased, and my heart rate slowed.

I swear the man was steely in the most stressful of situations. The same could not be said of me.

After an eternity, there was a flurry of activity. The paramedics rolled a stretcher to the end of the dock. The Coast Guard boat arrived at the marina, killing its engine to a snail's pace as it moved toward the dock.

Disengaging from Colby's embrace, I ran down the boardwalk in anticipation of the boat docking. I must have looked deranged. I did not care.

They put Mimi on the waiting stretcher and began to wheel her to the parking lot, where EMTs could examine her. I rushed over and held her hand while we made our way to the ambulance, resisting the urge to pepper her with questions. Instead, I let the medics do their work. After a thorough going-over, they released Mimi with a caution that she should see her doctor in the next day or so as a precaution.

Then, despite my protestations, the police and sheriff's deputies took over. They tried to push me aside as they swarmed Mimi and peppered her with questions. That was until Ailani arrived. She swooped in like a superhero, her black SUV part of a caravan of three that parked in the middle of the lot. Doors flew open before the vehicles had completely stopped.

Ailani stepped out of the vehicle. She walked slowly and with purpose to the officer in charge. Everything about her body language said, "fuck with me at your own risk." Surveying the scene as she walked, she sized up the situation instantly.

Mimi was sitting on the edge of the stretcher. I put my arm protectively around her, and she leaned into me for support. Looking directly at Ailani, I made sure she knew she would have to go through me before she upset my friend.

Ailani pushed her way through the uniformed officers until she was standing directly in front of us. “Special Agent Ailani Kekoa,” she began, showing her badge. “I need to speak to Ms. Weber about an ongoing investigation.”

“I appreciate that,” the slightly flustered officer countered. “But we have detectives on their way who want to discuss the murder of Tom Meadler with her.”

“Tom’s dead?!” Mimi exclaimed hoarsely, looking up at me. I squeezed her hand.

“Can we get some water for her?” I asked sharply. And then I made a decision. I stepped in front of Mimi, blocking her from view. “And I need to talk with my friend, alone,” I emphasized, “before any of you continue to harass her.” It was a demand, not a question. I was in mama tiger mode, and I would not allow anyone to upset her after the ordeal she had endured.

Someone handed me a bottle of water. “Thank you,” I said to the unknown water-giver. I unscrewed the top, turned and handed it to Mimi. Then I took a deep breath and returned my attention to the crowd. “I mean it. I want a few minutes with my friend. Otherwise, I’m going to advise her not to speak to any of you without a lawyer present.”

I felt Colby step behind me, and I swore if he so much as tried to rescue me and play the hero here, I would kick him in the groin. This was my fight, and I was not about to be pushed around by a bunch of unfeeling badge-wavers.

I waited, still squeezing Mimi’s hand while she downed the water. We both remained still and silent until every one of them backed off and gave us space to talk in private.

"What happened to Tom?" Mimi whispered to me.

I didn't want to tell her, not right now, but that idiot officer left me with no good options. Steadying myself, I explained as gently as I could. "When I got to the house for dinner on Monday," I began, in equally hushed tones. "I found him dead."

"Oh, my god!" And then realization hit Mimi. "Wait, they don't think I had anything to do with it, do they?" Mimi looked a bit stunned. I didn't relish the rest of what I had to tell her.

"Well, they did because you were missing, but I'm pretty sure being tied up on a boat is a decent alibi. I'm not sure exactly when he was killed, but you and I were together until you left to meet Edric. And he was dead by the time Edric kidnapped you."

"And when they find Edric, his activities will prove I wasn't anywhere near Tom," her voice broke as she continued, "I can't believe he's dead."

I sat down next to her on the gurney. "Honey," I said gently. "There's more. When we were trying to find you, we went to Edric's gallery."

"Oh, no, do you think Edric killed Tom?"

I looked at her for a moment. That thought hadn't even crossed my mind. I guess I was too stunned by his death and Mimi's disappearance. "Do you think he had a reason to kill him?"

"I'm not sure," Mimi said. "I mean, I don't think Tom knew what Edric was doing —"

"What do you mean what Edric was doing?" I asked. "What did you find out?" It had to be something pretty serious if Edric was willing to risk prison to keep Mimi quiet.

"I'm still not sure, and I would have to see the painting in Tom's warehouse, but I don't think it is the same painting we gave Edric to restore. I think he was authenticating artwork and then replacing it with expert forgeries. It's possible that Tom figured it out before I did." Mimi leaned against me, exhausted.

"Well, that might explain what happened to Edric. We found him badly beaten and shot to death at the gallery," I finally said.

"This is some kind of nightmare, right?" Mimi said, near tears. "I'm going to wake up, and none of this happened, right?"

I hugged her tight, and Colby slipped in and handed her another bottle of water. "You should probably drink this one, too," he said gently before slipping back into the background.

"What next?" she asked before she took a sip from the bottle.

I looked back at Colby. "How much does she need to tell the authorities right now?"

"If she gives everyone the basics of her kidnapping, the rest can wait," he said firmly.

I nodded. "Tell them she's ready to talk to them now." I squeezed her hand and asked, "Are you okay with that?"

"Yes, I want to get it over with so we can go home, and I can shower and change." She screwed the lid back onto the bottle. "And food...I just realized I'm very hungry."

"Colby, do you have a protein bar in your magic bag?"

"On it," he replied as he jogged over to his truck. Along the way, he signaled to Ailani that Mimi was ready for her.

As Ailani walked over, I turned my back to her and whispered to Mimi that Agent Kekoa was the woman I told her about earlier, the one I suspected was Colby's old flame. "She seems super competent, too, damn her," I added just before Ailani walked up to us. Mimi giggled, which, of course, was why I told her all of that to help ease the tension.

"Hi again," she began. Colby arrived with the protein bar and handed it to Mimi. "Do you need another minute, Ms. Webster?"

"No," she answered as she unwrapped the bar. "And it's Mimi. What do you need to know?" she asked before taking a bite.

"Can we start with you walking me through what happened to you?"

"Sure," Mimi began after unabashedly devouring her snack. The LAPD officer who blurted out about Tom's death joined us. Mimi eyed him suspiciously before she continued. "It started yesterday when I was alerted to the sale of a painting I had recently helped Tom Meadler acquire." She continued to tell her story of the last twenty-four hours and finished with, "And now I hear that Edric is dead, so I guess we can't ask him why he kidnapped me."

"No, we can't," Ailani agreed. "But I can promise you that we are going to find out why this happened."

"Do you think it had anything to do with why my boss is dead, too?" Mimi asked solemnly.

"We haven't been able to connect the two deaths yet, but we are looking into it." She gave the LAPD officer a look that would have frozen me in my tracks. If he had planned on asking Mimi anything, he thought better of it. "I think we should let you get some rest. There will probably be more questions, but they can wait until tomorrow. We'll keep you in the loop on our investigation. Thank you for your time."

She turned to go, then turned back to us. "Colby, do you mind walking with me?"

"Sure." He turned to us and handed me his keys. "Why don't you guys get settled in the truck? I'll be right there, and we'll get Mimi home." Then he caught up to Ailani, and they had an intense conversation all the way to her SUV.

"Let me help you," I said to Mimi as she slid off the stretcher. "Are you cold? Do you want my jacket?" We started our slow trek to the truck.

"I'm a bit chilly. Can we start the heat in the truck?" she asked.

"Even better, heated seats," I declared. She laughed, and I was so relieved to have my best friend back. "Listen, we need to talk," I said. "If you're going to continue to get kidnapped, I'm going to insist you get a tracking tag implanted on your ass, okay? Frantically searching for you twice in one lifetime is a little ridiculous, don't you think?" I said, referring to her other art-related kidnapping during our Boston adventures. I laughed and hugged her close before loading her into the truck.

She laughed with me. "I gotta say, I may need to look for a new profession. Dealing in art seems to be much more dangerous than anyone told me in college."

"Let's not be hasty. Danger is half the fun. Sometimes," I teased as I climbed into the back after I started the truck and turned on the seat warmers.

Colby wasn't far behind. "What did Agent Kekoa want? Or is it top secret?" I asked after he had settled into the driver's seat.

"She was giving me an update on our fugitive's status. Intel suggests he might still be in the area. They've found a second apartment in the name of one of his other aliases. It's in Santa Monica."

"Isn't that convenient, considering he had dealings with Edric," I replied.

"It looks like there was a substantial relationship between Edric and our fugitive. We are still looking into the full extent, but it does look like Edric was in deep." He paused for too long, and I waited for the gut punch. "And while we can find no connection between Meadler and their criminal activity, it does look like Tom was involved in money laundering. At least many of his clients were of the criminal variety."

Mimi was quiet for a long moment and then said flatly, "I'd like to go home, please."

Colby reached over and squeezed her hand before driving out of the parking lot and heading toward Mimi's apartment. "Are you hungry? Should we grab some dinner to take with us?"

I wanted to vote yes, but I left the decision up to Mimi, who agreed food was a necessity. We stopped at In and Out, ordered more food than we could possibly eat, including three shakes and extra fries, before we continued to Mimi's.

"Does this mean the police think I was involved in illegal activity?" Mimi asked while she munched on fries. "I mean, I might have been, unwittingly."

SEVENTEEN

A person doesn't change just because you find out more - THIRD MAN

With the rain having eased, traffic picked up. Colby expertly weaved through the surface streets while simultaneously reassuring Mimi. I loved a man who could multitask.

"Ailani is convinced you were unaware of Tom's activities," he explained. "Honestly, unless something significant turns up, they really can't tie him to any illegalities, either. But his clients were definitely some very unsavory people who were doing illegal things. Which makes the list of who might have killed him long."

This is one of the problems with collectors. Art is very subjective. Basically, it's worth what someone will pay. And no one really questions it when someone with an abundance of disposable funds spends lavishly on art acquisitions. I imagined that would make it appealing for money laundering. This made me wonder about something I had never even considered before: how exactly did money-laundering work?

Suddenly, I was very interested in that nefarious world. Then I almost laughed aloud as I imagined this was a world with which my father was very familiar. And here I was, wanting to delve into it. Genetics were something else.

We arrived at Mimi's gate, so my thoughts returned to food and taking care of Mimi. Colby lowered the window, typed in the code, we drove in and parked near her complex. Once in the apartment, we distributed our meals and sat down to continue analyzing all that had happened.

"I'm not even sure how to process the last twenty-four hours," Mimi said as she unwrapped her burger and pulled a tray of fries over. Colby slid her shake to her and then opened his double cheeseburger. He also grabbed one of the fry containers.

"Let's focus on getting you fed and a good night's rest," I told her. "I'm going to sleep better now that you're home safe. Tomorrow, we can start to sort things out."

"The painting!" Mimi exclaimed suddenly. "Do you know what happened to it?"

I shook my head as I arranged my burger and fries. "The last time I was at Tom's, the police were just beginning to search the house. I have no idea if anything is missing," I scooped some fries through the ketchup I had squeezed into the tray and popped them into my mouth. "They are going to be glad you're back and can provide them with your expertise on the inventory. I was useless."

"I suppose I'll have to talk to the police about everything tomorrow," Mimi said as she absently twirled a fry around before popping it into her mouth. It sounded like the last thing she ever wanted to do.

Colby heard her reluctance and jumped in to help. "I'll make a few calls and see if we can't make this as easy as possible for you. Do you want them to come here, or do you want to find a neutral space?" Colby asked. "I'll see if I can break away and be with you when you meet with them."

That's my guy, taking care of those he loves.

"No, you don't need to do that. I'll be okay. You've got a job to do. I can handle it," Mimi assured him. I wasn't so sure she could, but I knew I'd be there. "It would be helpful, though, if we could meet somewhere neutral." Mimi continued. "I don't think I would be comfortable going to the station without a lawyer. Especially now that is apparent Tom was involved with a criminal element."

Mimi was speaking from experience. Even though she had nothing to do with our former employer's illegal operations in Boston, she and I both faced some tough questions before they cleared us.

"Colby, do you think you could convince them we should talk at Tom's house?" I asked. "That way, if they needed Mimi to look over the house and evaluate if anything was missing, it could be done then."

"I'm sure they would be willing to do that, especially if I suggest that otherwise you'll be waiting for legal representation." He finished his burger and crumpled all his trash into the bag. "Ailani will want to talk to you at some point, too. We can do that informally, maybe over dinner tomorrow."

"You'll be sticking around?" That was news to me and not unwelcome.

"I suspect that we are going to be doing a lot more investigation on our fugitive's moves around LA," Colby explained. "His exploits here might explain why we've been unsuccessful in locating him in San Diego, despite the condo he owns there and the informant's information."

"Do you think he's become aware of the police activity?" I asked, knowing Colby ran a tight ship. But there seemed to be quite a few agencies involved that he had no control over.

"Hard to say. There are a lot of moving parts and more than one confidential informant. Informants are not known for their discretion. There have been a few in my career who have played both sides for the right price. It's always a chance we take," Colby said, sounding as tired as I felt.

I added my refuse to his and then focused on my shake. Chocolate shakes were meant for dessert, an opinion not shared by everyone. "Do you want me to stay with you tonight?" I asked Mimi when I paused with the shake. It was delicious, but I didn't want to risk brain freeze.

"I'll be okay," she replied quietly. I didn't believe her and gave her a look that clearly conveyed that.

She gave me a weak smile. "Really, I will be fine," she reassured me. "I'm going to take a hot shower, take a fist full of aspirin, and crawl into bed. We should meet for breakfast tomorrow, though. There is a lot more I need explained to me before I face any police, but I don't think I can process anything else tonight."

I took that as the hint we should leave and let her get some rest. I stood up and gathered my things.

"Your car is part of a crime scene," I reminded her. "So call me when you're ready for breakfast, I'll come get you."

"Actually, I have one of Tom's cars here. He is...was...funny about appearances. He considered it a company car so that I would look the part when I was representing him." She wrapped up her half-finished burger and took it into the kitchenette. Leaning her elbows on the island, she looked exhausted. "If Tom really was involved in illicit activities, they're going to freeze his assets, aren't they?"

"It depends," Colby replied. "If they find any illegal transactions, they will most likely freeze, at least, his personal accounts. His company assets disposition will depend on how the company is structured. The complication here is his death. It will be up to the government and how many resources they want to expend on this now. If they can secure a list of his clients, that might be all they pursue, and put their energy toward investigating the living."

"I just worry about the people he employs. They shouldn't have to suffer because he owes them payments." Mimi sighed. She looked ready to drop.

"And that," I said dramatically as I walked over to her, "is all we are going to discuss tonight. You need sleep." I hugged her. "If you find you can't sleep and your mind won't shut off, you call me. I'll drive right over. Promise me." It was not a request.

"I promise," she whispered as she hugged me back.

I left reluctantly, but I knew Mimi needed time and space to process what had happened. Once Colby and I were driving back to my hotel, I realized how drained I was. My mind still raced, though.

"Colby, how does money laundering work with art?" I pulled my knees up on the generous leather seat, tucking my feet, and leaned in his direction. "I mean, it sort of makes sense, but could Tom have been involved without realizing that's what they were doing?"

"Whether he knew or not isn't really relevant," Colby began. "If his sales were above board, what his clients did to get the money they paid for the artwork is not his concern.

But I'll be honest with you. He probably knew who he was dealing with and how they came about getting their funds."

"Poor, Mimi," I sighed. "She can't catch a break with her employers." I sat back and found it very difficult to keep my eyes open. Luckily, we were blocks from a warm bed. A thought popped into my head. I sat up and looked over at Colby, realizing something. "You're staying with me tonight, right?"

"Absolutely. There is nothing more for me to do...well, at least regarding work." He reached over, squeezed my hand, and gave me that wolf grin.

Funny, I wasn't all that tired anymore.

Once upstairs and behind a locked door, Colby pulled me into him and kissed me. One of those deep, passionate kisses that made my knees go weak, even after all these years.

"I need to take a quick shower. It's been a day," he said when he released me. He walked into the bathroom, closed the door, and a moment later, I heard the water running.

I walked over to the mini-fridge and grabbed a water. I opened it, took a long sip, and wondered if this desire would last if we married. Or would everything change, and we could lose the spark we have now?

Those were thoughts for another day. I polished off the bottle and then joined Colby. This day, I would enjoy the tall, muscled, naked man in the shower.

An hour later, after we made our way back to the bed and Colby made me come my brains out, he snoozed peacefully beside me. He rarely snored, but made these rough breathing sounds when deep asleep. It was extremely comforting. Not unlike when Wyatt and Stevie were sleeping soundly together. My pack, all sleeping soundly next to me, that was all I needed in this world.

I should've been asleep, too. My body was devoid of any and all tension, and I was rightfully exhausted. But my brain refused to give up for the night. The visions of both Tom and Edric haunted me, lying dead on their respective floors. I needed answers. Unfortunately, my mind was only willing to provide more questions.

My biggest question was: were the deaths related? It seemed inconceivable that they would both end up dead on the same day and not be related. The very day Mimi had discovered Edric's fraud. But for the life of me, I could not connect them. Unless Tom was in on the scam and the same person killed them both.

But that made little sense. If Tom was raking in the cash with legitimate art sales, even if they involved unscrupulous individuals, I doubted he would risk it all by trading in forgeries. Even more unlikely was Edric killing Tom and then some random person killing Edric immediately afterward.

What reason would Edric have to murder Tom? I wasn't sure when someone killed Tom. However, I was certain it was before Mimi confronted Edric about giving Tom a forgery and reselling the original. The timing didn't work otherwise.

Mimi met with Edric just before she was to arrive at Tom's for our dinner. No way did Edric have time to take Mimi out to the boat and then drive to Tom's and kill him before I arrived. And if he panicked enough to dose Mimi and kidnap her, surely he wouldn't have left her at the gallery while he killed Tom. Besides, my instincts said Tom was long dead when I found him.

At that moment, I realized I hadn't learned when or how Tom was murdered. I had been so preoccupied with finding Mimi and the shock of finding Edric dead that I hadn't asked Colby about the details of Tom's death. I tried to walk through the scene, tried to remember if I saw any wounds when I stumbled on him. Were there any weapons nearby? Despite Tom's body being burned into my brain, all I could recall was his glassy-eyed stare and blood everywhere.

I made a mental note to ask Colby tomorrow if he had the details or if he could get them for me. Unless daylight brought some other trauma to us, which with our luck wasn't out of the realm of possibilities. I wanted as much information as the police had before we spoke to them. Exhausted, I finally drifted off, wondering how Colby's investigation tied into this mess and if Ailani, hopefully, had a boyfriend.

What felt like minutes later, I was startled awake by ringing. I sat bolt upright, worried it was Mimi, and scrambled for my phone. Colby rolled over, and the ringing ceased.

"Sorry, that was my alarm. Afraid I have to be at work early. Lots to do today." He leaned over and kissed me before getting up and walking bare-naked out of the room. Even sleep-deprived, I could appreciate that view.

I debated pulling the covers over my head and going back to sleep, but I had a big day ahead, too. Starting with breakfast with Mimi. I stumbled over to the coffeemaker and brewed a strong pot. I traded places in the bathroom with Colby. When I came out, he was dressed and getting ready to leave.

"I made coffee," I said, if only to delay him as long as possible. Who knew when we would see each other again.

"Thanks," he said and poured a cup. He kissed me on the top of my head, which spread warmth through me. "I have some news." He sounded serious.

Jesus, what else could happen? Hadn't we seen our quota of trauma in the past forty-eight hours? I braced myself.

"Your dad is coming to LA. The FBI wants him to look over Edric's gallery and see if he can give us more information on what they were doing there. Ailani is thinking of taking him to Tom's warehouses, too, as soon as we can get the warrants cleared. See if he can spot anything that would link Edric's forgeries to Tom's business."

I sat down on the couch. So today was going to begin that way, huh? Why not? It was as if each day was trying to compete with the day before in the trauma Olympics. Now my not-so-dead parent was coming to town. How was I supposed to process that information?

"Well, you know where I'm staying if he decides he wants to meet," I said with more than a hint of bitterness.

"I know this sucks. I'll make sure he has your contact information. Meanwhile, I'm going to get Mimi set up with the LAPD for an interview. I think your suggestion for you both to meet the detective at Tom's house is the best solution. I'll do my best convince the locals of that." He sat down next to me and handed me a cup. Then he put his arm around me, pulled me in close, and tucked my head under his chin. "I'll check in throughout the day as I can."

He got up, grabbed his things, and was out the door before I could even fully grasp the idea of my father arriving in town.

I decided there was enough on my plate today, and dear old Dad would have to take a backseat. Way in the back of the backseat. I called Mimi.

She sounded as if she had slept well and was rested, though, understandably, still traumatized by events. We decided on a place to meet for breakfast, and I dressed quickly, doing my best to look presentable. After a day of rain, little sleep, and lots of worry, it was not as easy as I wished it to be. Finally, I decided it was good enough, and I left to meet my friend.

Mimi had chosen a booth in a quiet corner of a local deli. She had already ordered a carafe of coffee. I joined her, and we both ordered cheesy eggs on a bagel and then got right down to business.

"Tell me all the information you have about Tom's death," Mimi began.

"Oh, crap. I meant to ask Colby to get me anything he had from the coroner." Scowling, I dug my phone out of my bag. "I was sidetracked when he told me my dad was arriving in LA today." I tapped out a quick text.

"That's disappointing. I would have hoped you'd been distracted by more pleasant things," Mimi said with a smile. It was good to see her smile.

"That was last night. This morning, we were right back to business." My phone chimed, and I read the text. "He'll check on that and get back to us, along with the meeting info for the LAPD."

"I'm not looking forward to that," she sighed and sipped her steaming brew.

While we waited for our eggs, I told her everything I knew about Tom. How I arrived late because of traffic, and with no sign of her. I waited as long as I could and then finally rang the doorbell.

"The gate was unlocked, and the front door ajar. I thought maybe he wanted us to walk right in or something. Which I know makes no sense because you have keys, but I wasn't necessarily thinking clearly. I was more worried about having an awkward conversation with him while we waited for you."

I told her how I found him and then backed out of the house and waited for the cops to arrive. "It wasn't until after they arrived that it even occurred to me that there was no chef preparing dinner. Then I completely panicked and fell apart, thinking there might be more bodies in the house, including you. I was so relieved when they cleared it and said Tom was the only casualty," I squeezed her hand. "Little did I know it was going to get worse."

Our breakfast arrived. Eggs smothered with cheese sandwiched in buttery sliced bagels.

"I forgot how huge these are," Mimi said as she cut into hers. "We could have shared one."

"Speak for yourself. This looks perfect, and I'm famished." Mimi snickered, and I told her to get her mind out of the gutter. "It's delicious," I mumbled between bites.

"So you didn't see the rest of the house?" Mimi asked as she wiped cheese from her chin.

"No, I didn't go back in after the police arrived. They sent me on my way pretty quickly once they had my information, and it was fairly obvious I wasn't the perpetrator."

"Why was it obvious?" Mimi asked, probably wondering why they let me off the hook yet considered her a suspect until she turned up kidnapped.

"No blood," I said flatly. "I don't think whoever did it got away without at least some blood spatter." I looked around. We were speaking quietly, but I wanted to make sure no one could overhear our gruesome conversation. "There might have even been footprints, I'm not sure, but there was no blood on me anywhere." Mimi nodded. "But that's why I have no idea if the place was ransacked or his valuables stolen." My phone rang. It was Colby.

"I have information for you."

EIGHTEEN

We've been in worse jams than this, haven't we, Hildy? -
HIS GIRL FRIDAY

I got up, slid into Mimi's side of the booth, and hit the speaker button on my phone.

"I was able to get the detective on Tom's case to meet you at Tom's house for an interview," Colby began. "His name is Moscovitz. I gave him your number, and he'll text you a time. Seems like a standup guy. But if Mimi has any trouble, you call me, okay? I'm not going to let her get bullied after everything she's endured," Colby said firmly. I squeezed Mimi's arm, so grateful to have Colby in my life, looking after those I loved. "There is an update on the autopsy - Tom's - " he paused a moment. We were all still in denial that we could be discussing more than one autopsy. "His time of death was sometime before noon. He had been bludgeoned with a heavy object. Strong enough that it didn't break or leave any particulates when it struck him. They have yet to find that item."

"That's awful." Mimi sounded heartbroken. "We left before ten-thirty that morning because he took that phone call and then told us he had an urgent meeting," Mimi explained to Colby. "And he was going to call Chef Ritchie after that meeting to arrange dinner for us."

"I suspect that meeting led to his death," I interjected. "He obviously never called the Chef, otherwise he would have discovered the body before I did," I added. "That has to mean he never had the opportunity to make that call after his mysterious meeting."

"This is the information Detective Moscovitz will find helpful," Colby said. "I believe he's also going to have a uniform officer take you through the house for an inventory." There was a pause. "I'll be right there," he said to someone. Then he said to us, "I have to get going. You two be careful today. Don't go Mystery, Inc-ing it." He said something unintelligible, clearly responding to a question in the room. Back to us, he added, "I might be able to swing dinner tonight unless something breaks our way this afternoon. I'll text you." And with that, he disconnected.

I looked at Mimi. "Looks like we have our work cut out for us today. Are you ready for this?" She was quiet, but nodded. "You okay?" I asked, trying to gauge her stress level.

"I think I am. Still trying to process all of this - Edric, Tom - I can't absorb it. I wish I knew why Edric...did what he did. If he had lived, do you think he would have come back and killed me?"

"I don't know, and I'm very glad we don't have to worry about that now," I said. "Shoot, I meant to ask Colby if they had any updates on Edric." I squeezed Mimi's arm again, before she returned to my side of the booth. "I guess we can ask him tonight."

We returned to eating our delicious breakfast, but I could see Mimi was still struggling. "What else do you want to ask me?" I asked gently. "I'll tell you everything I know."

"Why do you think Edric was killed?"

I paused before I answered her. Since Colby and I found him, I had given this a lot of thought. I had no idea what kind of criminal element he was involved with, but from the condition of his body, it was personal. And that person was full of rage. "It wasn't a robbery. Mimi. He was badly beaten - that may even have been the cause of death - then he was shot twice. We found a hidden room filled with everything you would need to create forged paintings. I'm no detective, but this feels like a job gone wrong or partners turning on each other."

"Money laundering and art forgery," she said flatly. "And here I thought I was just helping some rich guy amass an art collection." She poked at the remainder of her bagel before pushing her plate aside.

"If it helps at all, Colby said that Tom may not have known who he was dealing with in regards to his art sales. And that so far, it looks like, at least on his end of the transactions, everything was above board."

"I guess it helps," she said, and then sighed. "I really have lousy luck with bosses, don't I?"

She appeared so despondent, and I hated to see her beat herself up. "To be fair, there have been good people in between the criminal activity," I pointed out. Mimi nodded but appeared skeptical. "Look, you like a challenge. Doing the same thing day after day bores you." I wondered which of us I was describing, Mimi or me? "Trevor and Tom both offered you the chance to do something different, challenging, exciting. Of course, you jumped at those opportunities."

I thought about the job with Trevor in Boston. Up until he went all Bruno Lohse on us and kidnapped Mimi, when we discovered his scheme, the job had potential. "If it's any comfort, I would welcome any opportunity to shake up my nine-to-five." I surprised myself with how true that statement was for me.

After I finished the last bite of my breakfast, I pushed my plate aside and reminded Mimi of the facts. "I barely gave your offer for this trip a critical thought before I said yes. I was mentally packing with scant details. It was going to be something challenging and, most importantly, different than anything I had done recently. I didn't even hesitate."

"Mimi, I'm restless and bored most days. I can't explain it, but I need more." Our server stopped at the table and topped off our mugs. I picked up my cup, took a sip, and then continued to reassure my friend that this was not her fault. "Look at all the fun you've had these past few years in LA. Anybody would envy your experiences." Over the rim of my mug, I gave Mimi a mischievous grin. "I mean, what's a little murder and mayhem. No job is perfect," I teased.

Mimi smiled a genuine smile for the first time since we located her. I breathed a sigh of relief. She was going to be okay. It was going to take time, but she would bounce back. Her phone buzzed, and she flipped it over.

"We have a meeting time," she said as she piled her utensils on her plate and took a last sip of her coffee. "Detective Moscovitz would like us to meet him in forty-five minutes." She waved down our server and asked for the check. "By the way, you're going to have to pay because I realized my wallet is in my bag, and that is in my car. Do you think Colby can convince the FBI to allow me to retrieve it?"

"I'm sure he can do that. I'll text him." Our server returned with our bill. I swiped my card, signed the tablet placed in front of me, and said a quick thank you. Then Mimi and I made our way to the parking lot.

We decided to drop Mimi's car at her apartment, and I would drive. Seemed prudent, as she was without any identification and driving a dead man's car. I was also driving a dead man's car, but at least I had a driver's license and a passing relationship with the cops investigating his murder.

We arrived at Tom's house early. It was jarring to see the crime tape across the entire front expanse of the fence - a stark reminder of what transpired beyond the gate. I parked on the street. It might not be legal, but I doubted the cops we were here to meet would be issuing us a ticket. I stole a glance at Mimi. She was staring at the house.

"You okay?" I nudged her. She nodded but didn't look away from the yellow-trimmed gate. I let us sit in silence until she was ready. It took all my restraint because nerves and stress make me chatty.

Finally, an unmarked, dull, beige sedan pulled up behind us. It practically screamed, *cop car*. The man who emerged was as nondescript as his vehicle. Dressed in tan slacks and a short-sleeved navy polo shirt, his balding pate was shiny in the after-the-storm humidity. He telegraphed cop even without the badge clipped to his belt. Mimi and I opened our doors, and he waited for us to exit.

"Good morning, ladies." He reached out his hand. "I'm Detective Moscovitz. We introduced ourselves, and he shook Mimi's hand first and then mine.

"Let's go inside," he said and lifted the yellow tape. He saw Mimi hesitate. "Are you okay with that? We can avoid the room where Mr. Meadler passed."

"It's okay, I'll be okay," Mimi replied. She seemed a little shaky to me, but she was determined to do this, so I kept quiet.

The detective held the yellow tape up with one hand and opened the gate with the other. We ducked under and then through the gate. We walked up to the door in silence. Moscovitz put in the code, and we entered the breezeway.

I felt Mimi tense as we walked toward the entry. I kept a close eye on her. She had been through the wringer the last two days. At some point, I expected she would reach her breaking point. I feared seeing the aftermath of Tom's murder might be it.

The house was cool, bordering on cold, when we walked into the hallway that divided the two wings of the mansion. I shivered involuntarily. The detective noticed.

"The techs turned the air conditioning temperature down until the next of kin can get a cleaning crew in here. It's difficult enough for survivors, and it's a simple act."

Next of kin, I wondered who that might be.

"Mimi, do you know who his family is?" I asked.

"Honestly, to the best of my knowledge, he didn't have any," she paused and thought for a moment. "He never mentioned any." She turned to Moscovitz. "Were you able to find his family?"

He was quiet for a moment, probably deciding whether he should reveal details of an ongoing investigation. "Ms. Webster, we are not even sure that Tom Meadler was his real name."

I saw her freeze for a second and then shake her head. I was again reminded of her prescient vibes. How she felt something was off with her boss.

"I have most of his passwords, where he kept the keys to his file cabinets, and the combinations to his safe and lockbox. I guess he has more secrets locked away, but that should at least give you a place to start." She sounded resigned to the reality that the man she worked for was an enigma.

"That would be very helpful," Moscovitz replied. "The more of his life we can unlock, the more likely we are to find his killer." He had stopped walking. "I would like to start in the theater if that's all right with you," he said.

When Mimi nodded, we descended the stairs and navigated the interminable hallway to the screening room. Moscovitz said nothing as he opened the big double doors and stepped back. Mimi and I stepped inside and gasped simultaneously.

Everything in the room had been upended. The tall shelves that had held numerous pieces of memorabilia were emptied. Contents were strewn about the floor. The long tables were pitched onto their sides, throwing items in all directions. The boxes that had sat beneath them were thrown across the room, scattering items along the way. And then there was the room itself. The velvet recliners had been slashed, curtains torn from the wall, and the big screen at the head of the long room had long gashes in it.

"It looked like a mob of angry chimpanzees spent a day in here," I said without thinking. "I mean, it doesn't look like robbery. It looks like revenge," I clarified. Moscovitz nodded in agreement.

Mimi had said nothing beyond her initial gasp. But when she finally recovered from the shock of the scene, she picked her way over the chaos on the floor. She grabbed the closet door handle and attempted to turn it. It didn't budge. In all the destruction, it had remained locked. She looked relieved, and then her face clouded.

"Crap, the key is in my bag," she said and turned to me. "Which, of course, is still with my car." She thought for a moment and then brightened. "I think there might be one in Tom's office upstairs," she said to the detective.

"Damn, I completely forgot," Moscovitz said, chagrined. "A nice FBI agent dropped off your bag to me this morning, knowing I was going to meet with you. I'll be right back." With that, he jogged down the hall, leaving us to survey the rubble.

Mimi leaned against the closet door. She looked as dazed as I had ever seen her. "The painting has to be okay. I feel responsible for it," she said.

"Well, unless this," I waved my hand over the mess, "was some ploy to distract us from the theft. I'm betting it is safe and sound behind that door."

"Who could have done this?"

"It absolutely looks personal, doesn't it?" I speculated.

Mimi looked overwhelmed by the disaster. "I wonder if the rest of the house looks like this?" she replied. "The artwork in the home is worth millions. It's irreplaceable if it has been as vandalized as this room."

"I was focused on other things the last time I was in the house. But I don't remember seeing any damaged paintings on my way in, and I was too stunned to notice anything on my way out," I said ruefully. "Do you think any of this is salvageable?" I looked more carefully at the items at my feet as I asked.

"It looks like everything was dumped, not smashed or slashed, unlike the rest of the room. Most of it may be okay with some restoration." Mimi surveyed the space. "But who would it be restored for? I mean, with Tom dead, what happens to all of this if they can't find a next of kin?"

"It would go into probate if we don't find anything illegal in Mr. Meadler's dealings," Detective Moscovitz replied as he reentered the room with Mimi's purse in his hand. He handed it to her."We'll continue to look for next of kin, or maybe the FBI can turn up something on his real identity. It's a process."

Mimi was digging through her bag for the key ring with all of Tom's keys on it, and when she found it, rushed over to the closet. It took her a couple of tries for her nervous hands to get the key into the lock. When could finally unlock it, she threw the door open and stepped inside.

"Thank God," I heard her say from deep inside.

I breathed a sigh of relief. Our painted lady was safe. Mimi stepped out, struggling with the large container. I joined her to offer assistance, and together we brought the wooden box into the room. "Is it okay if we open it?" she asked Moscovitz.

"Absolutely. I know you're anxious to check on it."

We pulled the canvas out of its box and scrutinized it. Once we were sure it was unharmed, we returned it to the container and secured it.

"Is it extremely valuable?" Moscovitz asked, looking dubious.

"It could be," I replied. "If we can authenticate it as the real painting. That's why I was here, working with Mimi and Tom."

"More importantly," Mimi explained. "It is not Tom's. We had the loan of it while we worked on authenticating it." Mimi put the boxed canvas back in the closet and locked the door. "Will I be able to return it to the owner?"

"As soon as we release the house, it shouldn't be an issue."

"Good," Mimi said, sounding relieved. "Does the rest of the house look like this?"

"No, it doesn't. Except for this room and the crime scene, the house seems untouched. Which is something I hope you'll be able to verify. If you are up to a walk-through," he stated.

"I'm ready," Mimi said, and it sounded like she meant it.

We did a quick scan of the lower level, and the detective was correct. Everything looked in order. As we ascended the back stairway, Moscovitz began to question Mimi. He started by inquiring about what she did for Tom. She explained how she assisted him in purchasing artwork for his personal collection. And occasionally buying and selling for his fine art sales business.

"Were you aware he had a warehouse in Long Beach?"

"Two, actually. One in the FTZ and another inland. He did was a lot of buying and selling. Tom was good at making a profit on the items he flipped. He had a good eye for current trends. He would buy and restore damaged works, purchase lots from estate sales, and buy from people who were liquidating for financial reasons. Then, sell them or hold them until their value appreciated. I mostly concentrated on his private collection. That was his true passion." We had reached the top of the stairs. Mimi paused, waiting for direction from Moscovitz.

"Let's start down this way," he said, directing us away from the kitchen area.

Probably deciding to put that off as long as possible, knowing it would be difficult for Mimi. I wasn't looking forward to revisiting the scene either.

"So, the warehouses weren't for his private collections?" he asked as we walked to the back of the house.

"Tom stored a few there, but most of the art in his personal collection is here at the house or at his space in Venice. He had to open a gallery there at some point in time." I noticed her voice caught, and she paused before she continued.

"I think he thought of himself as the next Getty," she explained. "He would send me information on anything he was interested in, and I would check it out, have it authenticated, and then negotiate the sale. I had them cleaned and restored, as needed, and then I assisted in curating them throughout the house. Over the past year, he would swap a few pieces out from the space in Venice, and I would facilitate the exchanges. The long term plan was to finish the remodel in the Venice building within a year and hopefully open the doors to the public within two."

"I'm curious about the space in Venice. We somehow missed that when we pulled his financials."

"I took care of all of it. I worked with the real estate agent, filed all the paperwork for the new LLC, and organized the remodel. He started storing art there about...four months ago." Mimi turned and walked back to the stairs. "I have everything filed in his office." We followed her to the third floor and into the dark room.

NINETEEN

I don't care who loves who, I won't play the sap for you - MALTESE FALCON

Mimi walked over to the wall of built-in cabinets and shelves. She reached up and pushed one of the shelving units, and it slid to the side, revealing a unique filing cubby system. She pulled out one of the vertical wooden drawers and grabbed a stack of files and handed them to the detective. "That's everything on the Venice location."

Moscovitz took them from her as his phone buzzed. He set the files on the highly polished desk and pulled the phone from his pocket.

"Moscovitz," he said as he stepped out of the room. "Got it," his voice echoed in the cavernous hallway. "Give me about forty-five minutes, and I'll be there." It sounded as if he had ended that call and made another. He walked back into the office, still on the phone. "I'll need two uniforms at this location," he paused to listen, while indicating to us with a finger that he would be a moment longer. "Okay, thanks." With that, he disconnected and returned the phone to his pocket.

"There has been an incident nearby, and I'm going to have to assist. Do you mind if I take these files with me?" he asked.

"Let me make you copies. I'd like to keep the originals in the event I'm required to assist with the sale of the space."

Mimi took the file from him and slid the bookshelf back into place. Then she slid another bookcase to one side and revealed a large, expensive copier. She put the paperwork through the feeder, and the machine spat out copies in record time. She handed those to the detective.

"I'll put the originals back in the filing cabinet in case you need them later." She pushed the magic shelves around until she had returned the files to the cabinet. "What next?"

"If you are up for it, I would like to take you to the kitchen. You might see something we wouldn't, something that might be missing or out of place."

Mimi took a deep breath before she said, "Sure."

We followed Moscovitz to the first floor and through the large vestibule that bisected the two wings of the house. None of us spoke, all dreading the task ahead. Only the echoes of our footsteps broke the silence.

The kitchen was to our right, and I watched Mimi hesitate before crossing the threshold. As we entered, I found myself slightly dizzy when I saw the dried blood on the floor. I could still see Tom there, even though he had long been removed from the scene. I closed my eyes, and when I opened them again, the spinning had subsided, and the floor was devoid of dead bodies.

Mimi was quiet. I stole a glance at her. She was staring at the blood. I decided it was time to distract her. I walked over to the counter where once had been a fantastic breakfast spread, now sat molding on the counter. Flies had embedded themselves in the spreads, the bagels had grown green patches, and a slick had formed on the top of the coffee in the carafe.

"Whatever happened," I said to Mimi, "Tom didn't even have time to put away our breakfast." That snapped her out of her freeze, and she joined me by the island.

"You're right," Mimi agreed. "He would have put everything away. His housekeeper wouldn't come until Tuesday because he was out of town all weekend. And clearly, he hadn't even called the chef yet to make dinner plans," she added.

"What time did you both leave?" Moscovitz asked.

"We were gone before eleven," Mimi replied. "We had come over for a breakfast meeting at ten-thirty, and we had barely prepared our bagels when he received a phone call." She turned around and looked toward the seating area, as if she was remembering that last morning with Tom. "He stepped out on the patio for the call. When he came back, he told us we had to postpone until dinner."

"And that conversation was heated," I explained. "We could overhear some of it," Mimi nodded in agreement.

"Any idea what the conversation was about?"

Mimi shook her head, and I added, "We could hear the argument but not what was said, if that makes sense."

"It does, and that helps us confirm the time of death. It does correspond to what the coroner estimated," Moscovitz explained. "And now we'll see if we can find out who that last call was from. His phone is locked, and we are in the process of getting a warrant for his call records."

"I have the phone code," Mimi said, and Moscovitz looked like she'd just handed him a winning lottery ticket. "It's 04-04-20." Moscovitz scribbled that into a small notebook. "He said it was his grandfather's birthday, so it stuck with me. Which was good because, on occasion, he'd toss his phone to me to answer a call or text or look something up."

Moscovitz's cell buzzed. He pulled it out and read something. "I'm going to have to get going. There are two uniformed officers on their way. What I'm hoping, if it's okay with you, Mimi, is could you go through the rest of the house? Get us information on anything else looks out of place or is missing. We can tackle an inventory of the movie room on another day because it sure looks like that may take a while to assess. But it would really help us to understand the killer's motive if we had more details on the contents of the home."

"I can handle that," Mimi replied. "Honestly, anything I can do to help."

"Thank you," he said, then shook our hands and left.

Mimi sat down on one of the upholstered bar chairs at the island. She stared out at the ocean, saying nothing.

"You doing okay?" I asked. I'd seen my share of blood-soaked crime scenes. She had not. From my experience, I knew it was a jolt to the system.

"I guess. I'm still in denial that Tom is gone. Blood evidence to the contrary." She stood up, walked to the sliding doors, and slid one open. "My mind is spinning with all the things that need to be done now that...now that he's dead."

"Well, all of that is for another day." I reminded her. "Getting the detective the information he needs and the painting back to its owner is our priority."

"Agreed. Let's start upstairs and work our way down," Mimi said as she strode purposefully across the room. I followed. Keeping busy was the best way to cope with trauma, and we had plenty in front of us to distract us for the rest of the day.

We did a quick sweep of the upstairs rooms. The guest rooms were spotless and untouched. In the primary bedroom, Tom's bed was unmade. A jacket was neatly folded across an upholstered chair in the corner. His travel bag was on a suitcase stand, waiting to be unpacked. The rest of the room was immaculate.

We took another quick look in his office. This time, Mimi focused on anything that might be missing. She slid the last of the bookshelves over to reveal a safe and proceeded to punch in the code and open it.

"Looks like everything is still in here, too," she said before relocking it and sliding the bookcase back into place. *This town sure loved its secret walls*, I thought.

Downstairs, we tackled the first wing, and just as we were about to check the other, a chime rang.

"That's the door alarm. The officers must be here," Mimi said. We detoured to the main hallway to greet them, since it would probably be impossible for them to find us on their own in the interior maze.

As we reached the entryway, a tall, tanned young man was standing just inside. Dressed in gray shorts and a salmon tee, a mop of dark hair framed his sad face. He had such a quintessential LA vibe it took a moment for the gun to register. He was holding it in an outstretched, shaky hand.

Fearing any movement might startle him into using his weapon, I froze. I stole a glance at Mimi, wanting to warn her to be cautious. She appeared too relaxed for the situation.

"What are you doing here?" he snapped.

To my horror, Mimi stepped a little closer to him. I instinctively grabbed her arm to keep her close. "Ritchie, it's Mimi," she said calmly. "I work...worked for Tom, remember?"

She obviously thought he felt startled and confused. I sensed a different motive in his defiant stance. I was relieved she knew him, though. That might give us a chance to reason with him.

"Why are you here?" he asked again, ignoring her pleasantries, shaking the gun at us as he spoke.

He was making me very nervous. I doubted he had ever held a gun, much less used one. That's a dangerous combination. Too easy to make a simple mistake and fire a round wildly.

I was scrambling to find a safe way to defuse the situation. This was difficult because I had no context for why he was here or who he was.

"Ritchie," Mimi began. "Are you okay? What's going on?" It was clear she knew him, but I didn't think she understood he was not behaving rationally. I squeezed her arm, trying to signal to her that something was wrong. You would think the gun would have been her first clue, but she'd had a rough few days. I couldn't expect her to react to more danger logically. Regardless, I felt she was too cavalier with a man holding a deadly weapon on us.

Ritchie stepped toward us, gun still raised. I made a snap decision. I pulled Mimi with me as I retreated slowly down the hall, never turning my back on Ritchie or the weapon. Hey, it is supposed to work with wild animals, right? Don't turn your back on the panicked gunman seemed like good advice. Especially since I had no other plan.

We crept through the hallway, Ritchie matching our gait but keeping his distance. I had no idea how we were going to get away. He stood between us and the front entrance. The ground floor had multiple egresses, but as far as I knew, they all led to a heavily fenced yard. There we would definitely be trapped.

"No one is supposed to be here," Ritchie said as he followed us. His voice rose in pitch and volume, but he kept his distance. He was unraveling, and I felt helpless on how to stop it. Suddenly his steps quickened, his gaze focused past us and down the hall.

We were near the kitchen now. Now I had to worry that the sight of the bloodstain might be enough to push him over whatever emotional cliff he was teetering on. I scrambled to think of a way to lead him in a different direction, but he was laser-focused on that room.

I pulled Mimi to my side as Ritchie angrily waved us into the kitchen. As he forced us further into the sitting area, I could not see a way past this madman. As he stood over the bloodstain, tears streaming down his face, still holding the gun on us, I knew I had to defuse this before whatever control he had eroded completely.

"Ritchie, I'm TJ, I'm a friend of Mimi's. Can you tell us what's wrong? Why are you here?" I asked in the calmest voice I could muster under the circumstances. "Maybe we can help."

"Why are you here?" he repeated, as if I hadn't spoken.

Mimi gave it a try. "The police asked us to look after the house because Tom died," she paused, smartly gauging his reaction to that news. I noted he didn't flinch when he heard

Tom was dead. "Did you know he died? It's very sad for all of us."

"Of course, I know he died!" Ritchie wailed as he waved the gun wildly. "I know!" He sat down on the edge of the white divan and dropped his head into his hands. The gun was still pointed in our direction, so I remained motionless. He took a few ragged breaths and then looked up. Something outside by the pool mesmerized him. Then he spoke so quietly, I almost missed it when he said, "I loved him, ya know? Really loved him."

"I'm so sorry for your loss, Ritchie, I really am," Mimi said with sincerity. I had to hand it to her. After all she had been through, she was calm and composed in the face of this new danger. "Let's get out of this room. It's a terrible reminder. Are you hungry? We could drive down to Marcos, grab something to eat, and talk about how much Tom meant to us."

That was clearly the wrong thing to say. Ritchie was up in a flash. Gun pointed at Mimi, anger contorting his face. Mimi stepped back, and I saw the first hint of panic cross her face. I wanted to step between the two of them, but I was afraid any movement would force him to act.

"Meant to us?! Us!" he seethed. "Were you sleeping with him, too? I always suspected. He never stopped talking about you." His voice was getting louder and angrier as he spoke. He paced around the room while he ranted. I was ready to grab Mimi and bolt when he began waving the gun ever more erratically.

He continued his tirade, almost screaming now. "Raving about how you were so good at your job, really knew the art world. Knew how to handle tough negotiations, always raving about how you made everyone feel like they had won." He stopped to catch his breath. I did not take my eyes off his weapon.

"Ritchie, I can assure you, I only worked for Tom. We had no relationship outside that," she tried to reassure him.

"Bitch!" I wasn't even sure he heard her as he continued his attack. "I worked for him, too. That's how it all started."

He returned his gaze to the pool and patio. Gun still pointed in our direction. He stood like that for a long moment. When he turned back to us, there were tears streaming down his face. "I didn't mean to do it. I didn't. I loved him." He used his gun hand to wipe his face.

Every time he swung it erratically, I held my breath. One thing about living with a cop, gun safety was drilled into your head, along with horror stories of improperly stored weapons or careless handling of firearms. Even experienced cops have had misfires. I was trying to make a plan, but it was difficult, not knowing what direction or mood he was going to swing to next.

"You didn't mean to do what?" Mimi asked gently. I didn't think that was a good idea, but she knew him, and I didn't. However, I was reasonably certain of what he had done.

"I was just so angry," Ritchie said, doubling over as if he were going to be sick. But then he stood again and trembled as he pointed the gun at us. "I told him. I told him again and again that I wanted him to stop sleeping with..." he waved the gun wildly around the room, and I stepped closer to Mimi. He didn't seem to notice. "....everyone!"

Then, once again, he pointed the pistol directly at Mimi. "Is that too much to ask? I mean, he said he loved me. He said he loved me." He looked down at the bloodstain. "But when I complained about all the people he slept with, he brushed it off. He said it was just recreation. He said I shouldn't be so jealous."

"I'm sorry. That's awful," Mimi said with compassion. I wasn't sure she should be engaging him. I worried he still believed she was sleeping with Tom.

"You know," Ritchie lowered the gun for a moment. "You could tell me. I mean, if you were sleeping with him. You could tell me. Although you are a little younger than he liked his women," he said with a laugh. "I never understood that. Maybe he had mommy issues." He sobered again and looked around the room. "I hated him for not loving me enough to stop fucking around. I should have been enough."

He was beginning to unspool again. He returned to pacing around the room. "Well, I was done with his screwing around. It was bad enough all the random hookups, but then he started hitting on my friends. We fought about it. And he laughed. He laughed when I told him he had to choose."

Ritchie stopped pacing, standing between the coffee table and the open sliding door. "He laughed," he sounded almost sad. He wasn't shouting now. Instead, he spoke almost matter-of-factly. "So I grabbed the sculpture that sat here," he pointed the gun at the coffee table. "It was called The Lovers," he glared at Mimi. "But you probably knew that." His voice rose again. "You knew everything about the art he loved. Loved more than me. And then you found that painting, that stupid movie poster that he dreamed of, and all he cared about."

As he fixated on Mimi, I was ready to pounce, to do what I had to do, to end this standoff. I needed to get us out of here safely. I scanned the room, looking for any way out.

"All that stupid, fucking movie crap," he screamed. "That's what got him hot, that's what made him..." Ritchie let out a piercing sob. "What have I done?" He was sobbing hard now, and I made my plan. I would get Mimi behind the island counter so I could push her down if he lunged for her. I had no doubt that was his next move.

"What did you do?" Mimi prodded.

Goddamn it, Mimi, I thought. *Don't provoke him.* I was trying to figure out how to maneuver her when Ritchie exploded.

"I killed him. That's what I did!" He was shaking, and the gun was moving wildly through the air. "I took that sculpture, and I bashed in his fucking head. Over and over until he was on the ground," he gasped through sobs. "Until he stopped moving."

He was crying out of control now and making deep, primal sounds. He raised his hands and pressed them against his skull as if to shut out the memories of what he had done.

And then he bolted. But instead of coming for Mimi and me, he ran out the patio doors and to the pool. Mimi followed him, and I would have shouted for her to stop, but I didn't want to startle Ritchie. Instead, I chased after her. I couldn't wait to explain that decision to Colby. If we lived through this.

"Ritchie, it's okay. You were angry. Tom had hurt you," she said with genuine empathy when she stopped on the opposite side of the pool from him. "Everybody will understand."

Ritchie raised the gun, and I panicked because I didn't see anywhere for Mimi and me to run to if he began shooting. Instead of pointing the gun at us, he raised it to his temple.

“Ritchie, no!” I screamed. Then Mimi ran toward him before I could stop her. I blindly lunged for Mimi, grabbing her shirt, and we tumbled over a chaise.

When I looked up, I saw Ritchie falling backward over the glass deck railing to the cliff below.

TWENTY

You know, when I was a kid, I always thought I'd grow up to be a hero - BUTCH CASSIDY AND THE SUNDANCE KID

Ritchie's screams echoed off the rocks and houses until they abruptly ceased. Mimi and I rushed over to the glass railing. Below us, he lay motionless, gun still clenched in his hand.

The drop-off was not as precipitous as I had imagined. Below the deck, the hillside had a gradual rocky slope, but also a lot of low-growing scrub. I could see blood on his head and on a small boulder near him. But his chest rose and fell, so he was alive. I was sure the heavy foliage had broken his fall when he flung himself over the rail. I hoped the bushes slowed his descent enough to minimize the head injury.

Mimi was dialing 911 when two uniformed officers came running out of the house.

"Are you okay," one of them asked, weapon drawn.

"Yes, we are," I said quickly to avoid any undo gunfire. "But the man down there is not. He's going to need immediate medical attention."

The second officer radioed for a rescue unit while the first joined us at the railing.

"Is that a gun?" he asked as he looked down at Ritchie.

"It is. He was holding us at gunpoint until he decided to throw himself over the railing," I explained. The officer looked skeptical.

"As soon as we get him stabilized, I'm going to need the complete story," he said firmly.

"You might want to have Detective Moscovitz come back, too," I told him, and then pointed at Ritchie. "That's who murdered Tom Meadler."

The second officer joined us. "Fire Rescue is three minutes out. Let's get down there and assess him."

"You two, don't go anywhere," the first officer said firmly. He seemed more than a little suspicious of the events as I described them.

"Wouldn't think of it," I said with just a touch of impertinence in my tone. I was exhausted and cranky. I glanced at Mimi, wishing more than anything that she wasn't going through any of this. I sat down in one of the chaise lounges. Mimi came over and sat in the other.

"Should you tell Colby what's going on?" she asked.

"Probably," I answered, but didn't make any effort to follow through. I was still trying to understand what the hell was going on and how I had come to be involved. "So, who is Ritchie? You said he worked for Tom, but in what capacity?"

"He cleaned the pool and took care of the plants. If he did anything else for him, I was unaware." Mimi sounded as exhausted as I felt.

"And clearly, they were in a relationship," I said.

"Clearly," Mimi concurred.

"Were you aware?"

"I had no idea. But then I didn't involve myself in Tom's private life," she said flatly. "Maybe I should have, then I would have seen this coming." She closed her eyes and breathed deeply.

I wanted to say something reassuring, but I didn't know what that would be. In the last two days, her entire world had blown up. I had no way of making that better. I pulled out my cell and texted Colby that he should call when he had a moment. This was not something that should be shared in a text.

Twenty minutes later, the rescue crew had transported Ritchie to the ambulance. He was still unconscious when they finally left for the hospital, but his vitals were strong, and they assured us he would probably recover.

With Ritchie gone and the scene secured, it was our turn to answer as many questions as we could. We returned to the kitchen and then went back out to the patio. Exhausted, we sat in the chaise lounges and watched as the investigators combed through the rocky brush, impatiently waiting for our turn to be interrogated.

Detective Moscovitz finally arrived, and he brought snacks. "I thought you might be hungry. Turkey clubs, sliced strawberries, and crème fraiche." He handed us two bottles of sparkling lemon water and pulled what looked like bento boxes out of a large handled bag. "Why don't we sit down over here, if that's okay?" He led us over to the larger patio table. He dropped his box and water on the table and then opened the umbrella.

Mimi and I sat down and opened our boxes. Everything looked amazing. I refrained from attacking it like a ravenous wolf. "Thank you for this. Breakfast was a long time ago, and I suspect we are going to be here for a while, answering questions," I said.

"I figured since the department was buying, I'd splurge and go to the fancy place in the village." He opened his box and took a bite of his sandwich. "Where should we start?" he asked before taking a drink.

I looked at Mimi and decided I would answer as many questions as I could. She looked like she was as close to shell-shocked as I've ever seen her. She had yet to take a bite of her food.

"We were going through the house, as you asked," I began. "We had finished the upstairs and were on the main level when we heard the door alarm chime. We thought it was the officers you sent over. Instead, we were confronted by a man with a gun." I continued to take him through the events and explained how Ritchie seemed to unravel before jumping over the railing. "I think he had come here to take his own life when we startled him. And in the end, he lost the nerve to shoot himself and jumped instead."

Moscovitz had been taking notes as I spoke. He set his pen down when I finished and took another bite of his club before he continued with Mimi. "Ms. Webster, what do you know about," he checked his notepad, "Ritchie Sandler? Had he worked here long?"

Mimi had finally found her appetite and finished chewing before she answered. "I don't know how long for sure. I've been here a little over a year, and he worked for Tom before that. I would run into him occasionally. He was friendly and outgoing." She looked over the railing where he fell. "I would have never expected this." She sounded understandably sad.

"And you heard him admit to killing Mr. Meadler?" he asked, probably to confirm my account.

"Unfortunately, yes. He said he took a marble sculpture from the coffee table and struck Tom multiple times. The sculpture is definitely missing from the table, and we haven't run across it yet."

"It's probably not here. The techs gave the place a good going over looking for a murder weapon before we released the residence to you. Can you describe it? It might help when they process Sandler's home."

I was betting they were going to find it in the hillside brush just off the deck, where the techs were now searching. Ritchie struck me as someone who was impulsive and would want to throw it away as soon as possible.

"It was about two feet tall, white marble, an abstract piece that looked like two bodies entwined," she explained. "I might be able to locate a photo of it," she added before staring out at the hillside again.

"If you find it, it will probably be blood-stained. Blood is a real bear to get out of stone objects," I added. When Moscovitz gave me a suspicious look, I elaborated. "It's my job to know these things. I work in museum acquisitions."

He nodded. "Yes, I think I remember that from your initial interview with the officers."

"You'd be surprised at some of the things we find on art pieces...or maybe not," I corrected myself, remembering his actual job.

He smiled. After that, we chatted about unimportant things while we finished our food. A bit of respite before we returned to the situation at hand.

"You said earlier that you didn't think Tom Meadler was his real name. What led you to believe that?" Mimi asked as she finished her strawberries.

"Until five years ago, he didn't exist. His identification is all government-issued, but so far, we can't find a birth certificate, next of kin, or any trace before that."

"That's interesting because, according to his biography, he sold his shares in a tech company five years ago and moved to Los Angeles," Mimi said.

"Well, that's a place to start." Moscovitz gathered up our boxes and trash and returned them to the bag. "I suppose you both would like a break before finishing the house inventory?"

"Actually, I'd like to finish today," Mimi said. "If that's alright. We are almost finished, and I'd prefer not to have to come back here again anytime soon." She paused. "At least until it's time to turn everything over to probate," she sighed. I think she realized her work had just begun.

"We would appreciate that because then we can release the house to his estate," Moscovitz said. "Oh, and I spoke to my captain. She said that you can return the painting to its rightful owner. Please get a signed receipt for it for our inventory files."

"Oh, that's a relief. I'll make sure to have them sign for it," Mimi agreed. "Their contact information should be in Tom's papers. I arranged the pick up, but I don't know anything else about the owner."

My phone chimed, and I saw Colby's picture pop up. "Excuse me, I have to take this," I explained and walked to the far end of the patio. I answered the call with a cheerful "hi!" as if nothing interesting had happened since we parted this morning.

"Oh, no, what happened?" Colby asked cautiously.

"What makes you think something has happened?" I teased. The silence on the other end said he was not in the mood for jokes. "Well, Mimi and I were held at gunpoint by Tom's killer, and then he tried to kill himself by jumping off the deck, but it looks like he'll live. And how is your day going, honey?" Dark humor was my best defense.

There was a long silence, and when he spoke, his voice was measured. "I don't know how you manage to find yourself in these situations." I had to wonder who else was with him, listening.

"It's a gift," I said lightly. "Look, it's not my fault a crazed lunatic showed up at the mansion while we were doing inventory for the cops."

"And you are both okay, right?" He sounded tense, and I took the hint.

"We are fine and even had a pleasant lunch with Detective Moscovitz. We can talk about the details later," I replied. "I take it you are in the middle of something super important."

"I am. Glad you're both okay and we will talk about this later. Guarantee it." And with that, the call disconnected.

I did not take his abruptness personally. He knew I could take care of myself, that there were cops on the scene, and that Mimi and I were safe. I knew he was in the midst of something significant with his case, and even returning my call was probably a distraction. The last thing I wanted was my lawman distracted while working. I preferred he returned to me without bullet holes.

I walked back to the table.

"Was that Colby?" Mimi asked.

"Oh, yes. Sounds like he and his team are deep in it right now, but he was glad we were safe," I replied.

The detective stood up and pushed in his chair. "I will let you get back to the inventory. Officers will be here until you leave." He looked around at all the activity. "Although, I doubt you will have any trouble going forward. Unless something turns up in our interview with Mr. Sandler, I believe this case is wrapped up."

"Thank you for everything," Mimi said. "You'll let me know if you find next of kin, won't you?"

"I will," he said, and then gently added, "Do you want updates on any other personal information we obtain on Mr. Meadler?"

"Yes, please," Mimi said with another sigh. "I suspect I'm going to be left cleaning up his mess, and I'd like to know what I'm getting into before I do."

"If either of you need anything, call me, okay?" With that, he walked over to the sergeant in charge and chatted a bit. Then he was off. Probably to work on the other case he had responded to earlier. I did not envy him his job.

Mimi and I returned to inventorying the residence. We trudged upstairs and continued with the bedrooms. I tried not to be awed by the sheer amount of artwork in each room. There were large framed canvases on every wall. Sculptures and small paintings on easels were on every dresser and shelf. One room held what I swore was a Daniel Rozen, but I knew that wasn't possible. However, it was a good homage to his work.

On the main floor, I could not help but gawk at the floor to ceiling paintings and large sculptures in each of the rooms.

Unlike the bedrooms, though, the art in these main rooms was sparse, letting the larger paintings and sculptures shine.

The lowest level had the fewest pieces. Mostly it was the pieces hanging along the long hallway. The other rooms were the most utilitarian: gym, laundry, storage, and, of course, the home theater. We made our way quickly through all but the theater.

With the exception of the missing sculpture in the kitchen area and the ransacked media room, nothing else had been touched. Back in Tom's office, Mimi found the contact information for the painting's owners. She entered everything into her phone. Then we returned to the theater.

"I don't even know how or when I will be ready to deal with this," Mimi said as she pushed the doors open.

"Do you even know all of the items he had in here?" I asked.

"Nope, and I don't know if he had an inventory written down," she replied as she walked over to the closet and unlocked it. "But, since we know who trashed the room and why, I honestly doubt anything is missing. Smashed to smithereens, sure, but I don't think anything was removed."

I stood the toppled easel up as Mimi pulled out the boxed canvas. I helped her lift the box onto the easel. She pulled out her phone and dialed the number she had found in Tom's office. I wondered how she would explain the painting's sudden return.

While she spoke with the owner, I wandered through the room, trying to gauge how much had been destroyed and how much could be recovered. I spotted the Art Deco phone I had admired earlier. It had been tossed onto the floor, its receiver sprawled the length of its cord away.

I picked it up, looked it over, returned the headset to the base, and then placed it back on a now empty shelf. It looked unharmed, and I wondered how many movies had featured someone dramatically sweeping it off a desk or angrily slamming down the headset after an unpleasant call. It was probably unfazed by a jealous murderer throwing it to the floor.

I felt a little like that phone.

Mimi disconnected and walked over to the shelves. "Did the phone survive?"

"It sure did. I suspect this was nothing it hadn't seen before," I replied with a laugh. I gave the phone a friendly pat. "Mimi, I have an idea, and I hope you'll agree."

"You want to take the painting over to Joslyn Ellis and let her look at it before we return it," she said.

"I do." Not at all surprised that we were both thinking the same thing. "I think if we put the paintings side-by-side, we'll know for sure if it's the real deal. And then we can let both Joslyn and the owner know."

"It would be great if I could broker a deal between them. I could use a sizable commission now that I'm unemployed." She picked up the painting and distributed the weight so that she could walk with it. "Can you close the doors behind us?"

Once we were in the hallway, I helped her carry the painting out of the house. We slid it into the back of the Porsche, which had a surprisingly roomy hatchback. Then we began the drive to Joslyn's house.

Along the way, Mimi called her and let her know we had the painting. She asked her if she would like to see it. Her answer was an enthusiastic yes.

"So what are you going to do now?" I finally asked as traffic slowed to a crawl. If this was the time to ask, I wasn't sure, but I needed to know how she was coping.

"I have no idea, except I'm getting the hell out of LA. Taking care of Tom's belongings is probably the right thing to do and the financially responsible choice." She sounded resigned to the responsibility. "But after that, I have no clue what will be next. If I knew anything besides art, I would pursue it. Because I may be done with the art world forever."

I hoped that wasn't true. Like me, she lived and breathed art and was good at her jobs. She just needed to find the right opportunity. I was sure of it.

Traffic finally returned to a decent pace, and we arrived in Joslyn's neighborhood. I wended my way through the narrow streets at the direction of the little British dude in the dash, as I fondly referred to the car's GPS. The beauty of the area still caught me by surprise.

It was an entirely different world. Peaceful, dreamy, and far-removed from the surrounding city. Relaxing as we passed flowering bushes and vines under the canopy of tree-lined streets, I could almost forget the horrors of the past few days.

"I wonder if they will ever find out why Edric kidnapped me and what he planned to do to me," Mimi mulled beside me. Obviously, the flora did not have the same impact on her psyche. I reached over and squeezed her arm in support.

We had arrived at the Ellis residence and were buzzed in quickly. Joslyn greeted us warmly and cooed at the large box we were wrangling through her door. She led us to the sunroom where we had viewed the other Limon.

It was still there, but next to it was an empty easel Joslyn had prepared for us. Mimi began to unbox the painting, and I jumped in to assist. Joslyn looked like a small child on Christmas morning. She was practically vibrating with anticipation.

I have to admit, I felt the same way.

Mimi and I lifted the painting onto the easel. The canvas was so large that we had to shift the easel a few feet away from the other painting. Once it was in place, we all stepped back.

After just a moment of observation, I knew.

TWENTY-ONE

It isn't enough to tell us what a man did. You've got to tell us who he was - CITIZEN KANE

There was no doubt in my mind. The beautiful lady in the painting was an original Limon, which practically guaranteed it was the missing movie canvas. My job here was done.

"Oh, she's beautiful," Joslyn whispered. "What do you think?" She turned to me. "Do you think she's authentic?"

"It sure looks like it," I said cautiously. "We were in the process of having the paint analyzed, but with what we know now, I wouldn't trust that source, even if the work had been completed. I have a lab I work with in Virginia. If the owner wants me to finish the evaluation, I would recommend sending a sample to them."

"I am happy to pay for that service," Joslyn said. She turned to Mimi. "Do you think you could broker that sale for me? I would like to purchase this."

"That would be something I would be happy to do," Mimi replied. "I would love nothing more than to see this painting go to a good home. She's very special, and I've grown attached to her the last few weeks."

"I trust you'll broker a fair offer," she said to Mimi. "And you will complete the authentication," she instructed me. "I will pay whatever the costs for that." I nodded.

She offered to have us stay for tea and cookies. As tempting as it was to spend more time with her and hear more of her fascinating life, I knew Mimi was eager to return the painting to the owner. With the day we had, it was one burden we were grateful to relieve.

We packed up the portrait and said our goodbyes. Mimi promised to be in touch soon, after she conferred with the owner on the details. Then we were on our way.

Mimi put the next address into the navigation, and we began the drive to Beverly Hills. I was a little excited to venture into one of the most famous neighborhoods in the country. The late afternoon was lovely. Sunny and warm, great for a drive down Sunset Boulevard. Blossoming trees and flowering bushes lined the road, so I lowered my window to take in the intoxicating scent.

"I wasn't expecting Sunset to be so wild," I remarked. I maneuvered around another curve, trying to focus on the road and not all the beauty.

"This end of it is mostly neighborhoods beyond that natural barrier of trees and bushes. The closer we get to the city, the more it looks like it does in the movies," she replied.

As we approached our destination of Beverly Hills, the tree barriers gave way to sidewalks, stucco privacy walls, and beautifully sculpted eucalyptus trees. Those gave way to towering palm trees. Our GPS directed us to turn down a quiet neighborhood street, and suddenly, we were plunged into the land of mansions. The opulent homes sat on spacious lots. Some were gated, while others had privacy hedges for protection.

"I forgot to ask in all the running around," I said, suddenly remembering an important detail. "Did you tell the owner about Tom's death?"

"Yes, I did," Mimi replied. "I couldn't think of any other way to explain why we were returning the painting. I didn't tell him Tom was murdered, though. So maybe don't mention that if he asks."

I nodded. I turned again, as instructed, and we found ourselves in a neighborhood with smaller homes. Well, smaller compared to the surrounding neighborhood. Finally, our GPS informed us we had reached our destination.

I pulled up to the iron gate and rang the bell. Then, I explained to the garbled inquiry that followed that we were indeed expected. The gate inched open at a glacial pace, and finally we were allowed to proceed down the horseshoe-shaped driveway. We stopped at the entrance to the house, where a tall, well-dressed older gentleman was waiting.

Mimi stepped out of the car and introduced herself. I followed and stood behind her, unsure of my actual role here.

"Ladies, it is good to meet you. I'm Terrance McNeil, the owner," he explained. "I was terribly sorry to hear about Mr. Meadler's passing. Terrible shock. Terrible."

I opened the hatch. Mimi and I retrieved the painting, struggling, as usual, with its unwieldiness. Mr. McNeil joined us, and I noticed his gait was unsure. I hoped he would not be chivalrous and offer to help us carry the unwieldy container.

"My dears, let me have Marco grab that," he said, and I breathed a sigh of relief. Suddenly, a young man appeared. We stepped aside as he pulled the box out of the car. He disappeared with it into the house. "Thank you for returning her," he said. "I guess I'll have to start from scratch now."

"I may have someone else who is interested," Mimi said. "If we can authenticate her, that is."

"That would be wonderful. I'm hoping you'll be able to determine that the painting is genuine."

"May I ask how you acquired the portrait? I'm TJ Wilde," I explained. He took my outstretched hand in both of his for a warm greeting. "I was working on authenticating it before Mr. Meadler passed," I explained. "The new prospective buyer has asked me to continue with the authentication if you'd allow it."

"Oh, yes, I definitely want to continue because I would still like to sell the piece," he said enthusiastically. "It is actually my wife's painting. We found it when we were clearing out her mother's home. Lovely lady. She passed last year, lived to be a hundred and two. It was in the attic, along with a few other vestiges of film history." He paused and pulled a handkerchief from his pocket, and sneezed into it.

"Allergy season. I love all blooms. They do not love me," he said with a laugh. "My wife and I are busy downsizing our belongings, and as lovely as the painting is, we don't really need it. In my prime, I was a film critic, so I suspected its significance when I saw it. Do you think my suspicions are valid?"

"They might be," I said. "We have a signature that appears to be authentic, and the frame and canvas are from the right period. I would like to explore a few more avenues to make sure, but I saw it next to another Limon painting and that was revealing. It does appear to be the real deal," I explained. His validation of the provenance had sealed it for me, but I didn't want to jump the gun just yet.

"If we can finish the authentication, I believe we can make a deal with an interested buyer," Mimi said, and pulled a card out of her bag. She handed it to McNeil. "This is my information. I'll keep you informed of our next steps."

McNeil smiled and turned the card over in his hand before slipping it into his jacket pocket. "I think we can come to an arrangement," he said.

With business taken care of, we said our goodbyes and left. Back on the street, I stopped and looked at Mimi.

"What do you want to do about dinner? I am hoping Colby will join us and give us an update on his day. I'm very curious to know what they have found out about the Edric case. Are you up for it?"

"That sounds like a plan. Let's go back to my apartment, and I'll get my car. Then we can go back to your hotel. I'd love to sit on the deck, drink heavily, and watch the sunset," she sounded wistful. "Then we can check with Colby about dinner."

She looked exhausted, which was not surprising. No matter how stressful the last few days had been for me, I had not been kidnapped and stashed on a boat. Alcohol and sunset sounded perfect to me.

After I dropped her off, I made a snack and alcohol run. I bought a nice bottle of wine for Mimi and a six-pack of Colby's favorite beer. For myself, I grabbed a six-pack of Diet Coke. I wanted to keep a clear head and hoped the caffeine would combat my ongoing fatigue. I added strawberries, a nice sliced cheese platter, and a box of crackers to my haul and then made my way back to the hotel.

In the car, I realized I had no real glassware. I called Mimi and asked her if she had left yet.

"No, I decided I wanted to change clothes. I'm leaving in just a few minutes."

"Great, I bought some wine and snacks but realized I don't have glasses or plates," I explained.

"No worries, I have a picnic basket I bought on a thrift store excursion that is equipped with all the essentials. I'll bring that," she said.

We disconnected, and I proceeded leisurely through the neighborhoods of Santa Monica. Luckily, I had Jeeves to navigate the journey because my mind was elsewhere. While Tom's murder seemed a tragic case of love gone bad, that didn't explain his mysterious identity. With the killer in custody, would the police even look further into his business dealings, his background, or how he acquired his wealth? I was highly suspicious that any of it was this side of legal.

It appeared unlikely that there would be an extensive investigation. The LAPD appeared to be too busy with other cases to investigate a white-collar crime when there was no one left to prosecute. Maybe they would stumble across a handy-dandy list of criminals who had transactions with Tom, but even that possibility probably wasn't enough motivation. It would be a lot of man-hours without the assurance of any convictions.

I was not going to be satisfied with unanswered questions. Answers were probably even more important to Mimi. I suspected that even the hint that she might be complicit in illegal activity distressed her. No amount of reassurance from Colby or me was going to assuage her concerns. I felt a responsibility to help her find answers. I just wasn't sure how.

Hopefully, Colby would have some suggestions. It would be ideal if Tom's actions garnered the attention of the Feds. They would have the resources to investigate him fully. The downside was, it could cause trouble for Mimi. Even though I was sure her actions were completely legitimate, having her entire life turned upside-down while the Feds did their thing would be traumatizing.

As I pulled into the parking lot, I realized there were no good scenarios for getting to the truth. I climbed the stairs to my room, discouraged and tense. All that washed away when I opened the door to see Colby sprawled on the couch, flipping through channels. He hopped up to help me with the groceries.

"Hi, honey, I'm home," I said as he took the bags from me. "Did your day wrap up early?" I asked, knowing his response would not be the answer I wanted.

"Unfortunately, just a dinner break. I'm afraid I'll be on an overnight surveillance team later."

I kissed him, and he pulled me in close. When he was out in the field, I tried not to worry. It was, after all, our everyday life. He had a good team, and he was excellent at his job, but there was no denying that his job was dangerous. It felt good to be wrapped in his arms, and I didn't want to let go, but my phone buzzed.

"That's Mimi. She might need help carrying things," I sighed before I answered the call. Colby jogged downstairs to help her. I brought the food out to the patio table, and before I had it set up, Colby had returned with Mimi.

Mimi set a beautiful vintage wicker picnic hamper on the table and snapped open the clasp. It opened like a suitcase and revealed everything we would need, including checkered cloth napkins.

After we had set everything out, it was time to get down to business. I wanted to know what Colby knew. I handed him a beer and waited until he opened it and took a drink before beginning my interrogation

"So, what can you tell us about Edric's murder?" I asked.

"And do you know anything more about Tom's identity or business?" Mimi added.

Colby laughed, took another long swallow. "Shouldn't we think about dinner first?" We both gave him the look. He would not distract us from our concerns. "I think we should have pizza," he said, ignoring our stern faces. He looked at his watch. "It should be here anytime now."

His phone buzzed. He looked at it and smiled. I knew that smile. Something was up. I probably would not be happy about whatever it was. "Pizza is here," he said before jumping up and heading down to the gate.

I looked at Mimi and raised an eyebrow.

"What's he up to?" she asked warily.

"I have no idea, but I'm sure I'm not going to be amused."

Then we saw it. Colby climbing the stairs carrying three large pizza boxes and Ailani close behind him. I plastered on my polite, happy face. I suspected Ailani was a good enough cop to know it wasn't genuine.

"Dinner has arrived," Colby announced. I stood up and rearranged the appetizers to make room on the table for the boxes.

"I hope you don't mind me crashing the party," Ailani said before sitting down. "Colby thought you would both want information on the state of our investigations, and I was happy to give you an update."

I was suspicious. Convinced that her take would be a lot of runaround without many answers. But I was willing to give Colby the benefit of the doubt. He knew me well enough to know I would not tolerate bureaucratic runaround. Nor would I be quiet in my distaste for it.

"What can I get you to drink? Wine?"

Ailani eyed Colby's beer. "Do you have another one of those?"

I walked inside, pulled another from the mini-fridge, and returned to the group. I handed it to Ailani, grabbed a slice of pepperoni, and sat down, waiting to hear her out.

"The not-so-great news is about Meadler," Colby began after he grabbed a couple of slices of pepper and onion and slid them onto his plate. "We have run into a dead end on his identity. He didn't just carve out a new identity. He appears to have paid big bucks to have his old life erased."

"Is that possible?" Mimi asked.

"With enough money, it is," Ailani replied. "Eventually, we would figure it out. Unfortunately, unless we can connect him with an actual crime, there isn't a lot of motivation to continue to dig into it." She grabbed a slice of the mushroom pizza and sighed. "I wish it weren't the way, but it is."

"The good news," Colby said to Mimi, "there is nothing suspicious that we can find in any of his art transactions. Everything you did was with his legitimate business. He worked with some unsavory characters but kept his dealings on the up and up."

"I guess that's good news. But I don't like the idea that I helped bad actors clean their money." She pushed her pizza around her plate before getting up, walking over to the rail, and looking out at the ocean.

Colby looked at me, and I shrugged. There wasn't anything either of us could say to make her feel better. At least not yet. It was going to take time for her to make peace with this.

"So, what's the news on Edric?" I asked, assuming that was really why Ailani was here.

She looked over at Colby, and I felt my stomach knot.

"I don't know how much you know of why your father entered WitSec," she began.

"Very little." I tried not to sound resentful, knowing both she and Colby were privy to the entire tale. The truth was, once I learned my father was alive and that he continued to choose not to contact me, I feigned disinterest in his history. It was easier that way.

The less I knew, the less I missed his presence in my life. The fact was, he had been out of WitSec most of my adult life. At any point after that, he could have shown up at my door and reintroduced himself. I had given up the fantasy long ago of the two of us discussing our mutual love of art or of him wanting to paint something for me for the joy of it.

Ailani interrupted my pity party. "Long ago, your father fell in with a dangerous group while forging artwork."

"I thought he went into WitSec because of an insurance scam."

"He did. He testified against the man who hired him. But that man was part of a larger operation. It wasn't just art forgery. It was counterfeiting, drugs, extortion. If there was an illegal way to make money, they were into it. Things your father didn't sign up for. Once your dad testified, that man decided it would be best to turn on the crew for a better deal," she explained. "The head of the organization, a man named Bohgan, was convicted and sentenced to twenty-five years to life. His crimes were extensive. While he was being transported to federal prison, he killed a guard and escaped. We believe he had someone on the inside but could never prove it." Ailani looked over at Colby.

"Two weeks after he escaped, the man who testified against him was dead," Colby explained. "That's when it was decided it would be safer for your family if your father 'died.' He didn't want all of you to have to enter witness protection. He and your mom decided it would be better if everyone, including you, thought he was dead." Colby reached over and put his hand on mine. I nodded to let him know I was okay and that he should continue. "The task force I'm on, well, that your father and I are on, is tracking that man. Your father has felt that as long as Bohgan was a fugitive, you and your mom weren't safe. So he chose to stay dead."

"If you catch this guy, then my father can come out from the shadows?" I was unconvinced. I was sure he would always remain an enigma in my life.

"That's the plan," Ailani said. "And we are close. We just didn't expect the complication that was Edric Lancaster." She grabbed another slice of pizza.

"Do you want another beer?" I asked.

"Better not. We are working tonight," she replied.

"How is Edric part of all this?" Mimi asked. Giving me a *what in the Twilight Zone is happening?* look.

"Lancaster's involvement in art forgeries was extensive. His gallery was underwater. We are not sure yet how he hooked up with Bohgan, but he did," Ailani explained. "From Lancaster's records, it appears he stole from most of his high-paying clients. Replaced their paintings and a few sculptures, with forgeries, then resold the original artwork. Usually to overseas buyers with private collections, to keep the thefts from being discovered."

"It was very lucrative. Your father is working on tracking down the forgers. He believes, from the forgeries he's seen, that there were at least two," Colby added. "Professional forgers inhabit a small world, and your dad has stayed connected. I suspect he'll have them identified by the end of the week."

"So where is Bohgan now?" I asked, wondering how he continued to evade capture. Knowing he wanted to harm my dad raised the stakes and my anxiety.

TWENTY-TWO

I don't know if it will help saying this to you… some men in this world are born to do our unpleasant jobs for us… your father is one of them - TO KILL A MOCKINGBIRD

Colby opened one of the pizza boxes and added a pepperoni slice to my plate and a slice to his. "Bohgan is in the wind, and it is looking more and more likely he is responsible for Edric's murder."

"What?!" I had not expected that. I had assumed all along it was a disgruntled client who found out what Edric had been doing. "Why do you think that?"

"His fingerprints are all over the scene," Ailani said. "There were angry text messages exchanged between Edric and one of Bohgan's aliases. We are trying to track that phone, but our guess is he has dumped it already."

"He's not stupid or reckless. That's how he's stayed ahead of law enforcement all these years. He's usually not careless, but this murder seemed careless," Colby said before finishing his slice.

"And you think after all these years, he still cares about my father?" I was not wise in the ways of career criminals, but a thirty-year vendetta didn't sound terribly smart.

"Bohgan's entire crew was caught up in the arrests. His son and nephew were both sent to prison. His son died of cancer while incarcerated. I suspect that fuels his desire for revenge against your father," Ailani explained.

"But you're going to get him this time, right?" I demanded, suddenly understanding my father's absence. "Right?"

Colby reached over and squeezed my hand. "I don't think he's going to stay a fugitive this time. He's panicking and making mistakes," he reassured me. "He has a bungalow in Venice. We have it staked out. As well as his condo in San Diego. The net is tightening."

"We have LEOs looking for his vehicles in three counties and the border patrol has been notified in case he tries to leave the country. It's just a matter of time, TJ," Ailani said so confidently that I was almost convinced they would find him.

But he had managed to elude them before, and I wasn't as confident as she was that they would be successful this time. The thought of him doing to my dad what he had done to Edric made me dizzy with fear. I may not have seen my father in years, but he had made his presence known and had helped me when I was in some dangerous situations. And if I were honest with myself, I still held out hope that we would be reunited.

"Where is my father now?" I looked at Colby. "You have him protected, right?"

"He is working with Brody on tracking the forgers. You know he's not going to let anything happen to your father."

I knew that. Brody was Colby's right-hand man and an excellent marshal. I trusted him with Colby's life, and I knew I could trust him with my dad's, too. I relaxed a bit and let the warm ocean breeze wash over me. Despite my better judgment, I briefly fantasized about my father walking up the stairs and knocking on my hotel door to greet me once Bohgan was in custody.

"We should get going," Ailani interrupted my reverie. "I hope we get lucky tonight and find the SOB."

Colby stood up and kissed me on the top of my head. "You two aren't going to go out and find more trouble tonight, are you?" He said it teasingly, but I knew he was also concerned. Who could blame him? It had been an eventful trip.

"I don't know about TJ, but I am going straight home to bed. There are a few days of sleep I need to catch up on," she assured him as she stood up and stacked the boxes and trash on the table.

"Oh, I almost forgot," Colby said to her. "You can pick up your car tomorrow. They've cleared it. You've got the keys, right?"

"That's great. TJ and I can run over there tomorrow," she said. "And the keys were in my bag that Detective Moscovitz returned to me, so I'm all set."

I shooed Mimi away from the table and told her I'd finish cleaning up so she could get home. We said our goodbyes, and she followed Colby and Ailani to the parking lot. I bagged up the trash, took the leftovers and stashed them in the mini-fridge.

And then I was alone. Alone with my thoughts. There were a myriad of them. I turned on the television to stave off their intrusion and the sudden emptiness I felt. Colby was a big presence, and the void when he left always unsettled me. Surfing through all the channels mindlessly, I finally hit the off button. I could not quiet my mind.

I stepped out onto the deck to look at the lights on the pier. The Ferris wheel lights blinked and danced, as strobe effects chased around the spokes. Though tonight it seemed quieter. No rappers or laughing groups strolled the path below. There was only the rumbling of the boardwalk rides with the occasional laughter and screams from the passengers, and the crashing waves.

I was restless. I wanted to go for a run to clear my head. But that seemed unnecessarily risky at this time of night. And I had promised Colby I'd stay out of trouble. I looked wistfully at the lights reflecting off the water. Then I went inside to continue to wrestle with my thoughts.

While I washed my face, I wondered where my dad was and if he would be safe. As I brushed my teeth, I thought about the Limon painting. I wanted to finish the job we started with it. I had grown attached to our femme fatale, and I wanted her to have resolution.

Thoughts of death intruded while I changed into my sleep shirt. The images of Edric and Tom flooded my brain, along with all the *what-ifs* if we hadn't found Mimi in time. I reminded myself sternly that Mimi was safe and probably sound asleep right now.

Finally, as I crawled into bed, my mind turned to my little four-legged family in Virginia. I missed them and made a note to call Abby in the morning to check on the crew. That was the last thought I had before I finally fell into a deep sleep.

Sometime before dawn, Colby quietly crawled into bed next to me. I briefly thought of asking him how his night had been, but instead returned to my dreams when he wrapped an arm around me. I slept peacefully, comforted by his rhythmic breathing as I nestled into him.

He was still sleeping soundly when a very persistent mockingbird in a tree near our window woke me. I slipped out of bed, grabbed my running clothes, and closed the window to silence our feathered alarm. Figuring Colby needed all the sleep he could manage, I pulled the curtain across the casement that separated the bedroom from the remainder of the room. Then I went to take a shower.

I toweled off and dressed. As I peered in the mirror over the sink, I thought I looked much too tired for someone who had just slept a solid eight hours. When I stepped out of the bathroom, Colby was sitting on the couch, reading something on his tablet. So much for letting him sleep.

"Coffee's ready," he said. "And I swiped one of your yogurts."

"What time did you get in this morning?" I asked as I poured milk into my coffee.

"A bit before four." He sounded tired. "We called it a night when there was no sign of Bohgan at his bungalow." He stood up, walked over, and wrapped his arms around me. I had to juggle my coffee, so I didn't spill it all over him. It felt good to be wrapped in his warmth. But when he pulled away, I knew he had something to tell me.

"What's on your mind?" I asked.

"Your dad is in Brazil with two agents. They flew out late last night. We tracked one of the forgers to San Paulo. Local authorities have detained him, and your father has gone down to interview him. If he is indeed part of Edric's crew, we'll start extradition. That might get us some answers."

"I can't say I'm not relieved. He's likely safer there than here."

"He's not in as much danger here as you might think. There is no indication that anyone even knows he's working with us," Colby reassured me.

I wasn't convinced, but let it slide. "And what will you and your team be doing today?"

"We've got agents and deputies watching both his residences. The FBI picked up his girlfriend yesterday and one of his cohorts early this morning. All his financial avenues are under surveillance, so the walls are closing in on him. He's bound to show up somewhere."

"You think he'll try and leave the country?"

"I do, but we are ready for that," he said, putting his cup on the counter. "I am not letting this fugitive escape. He's been on the run far too long and hurt too many people." He had that look on his face that I understood to mean that any and all criminals should be afraid. Very. Afraid. "What's your plan today, dear?" he teased.

"I believe that Mimi and I will have a quiet day, NOT filled with any more dead bodies or threats on our lives. Kidnapping is also off the menu." I joked.

"Good plan. I'm going to shower and then I'll be out for the rest of the day. It would be best not to plan on me for dinner."

"I'm sure I'll manage," I said, trying not to sound disappointed. I was enjoying having him around my little kitschy beach hotel. It was possible that all I needed was a change of scenery and a little danger to remind me of how lucky I was to have him by my side. Marriage looked a little less scary from this vantage.

After he left to shower, I texted Mimi.

> Are you up? When do you want to get your car?

Her reply was swift. She had a few things to organize this morning and asked me to pick her up around eleven.

> Then we can have lunch and retrieve my car. I also hope you'll help me plan the next steps for Tom's estate.

I let her know it all sounded like a good plan. A free morning was welcome, as there were a few things I had to do as well. First up, I had no idea how long Mimi had booked my room, or how much longer I would need to be here. I would have to check with the front desk on my options.

And then there was the car. I still wasn't sure how I felt about driving a dead man's vehicle. I supposed that was a problem for another day. But eventually, if I had to extend my time here, it would have to be addressed.

Also, I needed to check in with work. I had to update my boss on my timetable. And see if there was any further information on the possible estate sale in Santa Barbara. That could make for a pleasant diversion for Mimi and me.

Since I was wearing my running gear, I decided to use that as an opportunity to go for a run on the beach. It was a cool morning, and low tide made for a pleasant run on hard-packed sand. Once I hit my stride, I could clear my mind. I focused on my breathing and the beauty of the morning. Once again, the dolphins joined in on the fun and swam just offshore.

As I walked back to my room, I felt renewed and ready to help Mimi in any way I could. After I changed, I headed to the hotel office, expecting to let the clerk know I would pay for the room going forward, since Tom was dead. Instead, I found out the room had been prepaid for two full weeks.

So, now I was staying in a room paid for by a dead man, while driving a dead man's car. But at least that gave me time to assist Mimi and maybe even finish what I came out here to do. Validate the legitimacy of the Fiona Limon painting. I had to admit I was fully invested in finding the answer and seeing her find a home with Joslyn.

Back in my room, I made a few notes on the next steps for authentication. With Edric gone, my professional sources were our best option. It would take longer, but we could trust the results. I called my contact and arranged to send the samples. My next call was to my boss, and then it was time to pick up Mimi.

As I drove to the apartment complex, I lowered all the windows and enjoyed the warm air whipping through my curls. Mimi buzzed me in. I parked and jogged up the stairs to her unit. She opened the door, and I was stunned to see her formally tidy living space in a complete shambles.

"Were you ransacked?" I asked as I stepped over the threshold.

"Very funny," she replied. "I couldn't sleep, so I was up before dawn and started looking through my paperwork on Tom's sales. Trying to figure out what the hell he was up to, but everything looked legit." She waved her arm around the studio. "So, then I started sorting the things I wanted to take with me when I leave."

"Wow, so you're definitely leaving?" It didn't surprise me. That was Mimi. She knew what she wanted, so she pointed her ship in that direction and sailed straight ahead.

"No reason to stay after I finish closing out Tom's affairs." She walked over to her desk and pulled her bag from underneath a mound of papers. "I already spoke with his attorney this morning, and we are going to meet the day after tomorrow to discuss next steps. She thinks it will be fairly straightforward once the DA makes a decision on whether or not to end the investigation."

Mimi shuffled through a few more papers, looking for something, then walked into the kitchen and scooped a set of keys off the counter. "There they are. Are you ready to go?" She was a woman on a mission.

"Let's go," I said and opened the door. "I'm hoping lunch is the first item on our agenda because I am famished."

"Of course," she said as she locked the door behind us.

We stopped at a small Mediterranean restaurant and had a lunch filled with homemade goodies and the freshest tabbouleh I had ever eaten. Mimi had obviously frequented the establishment, as the owner greeted her by name and waited on us personally. She was a charming woman, and I imagined she had colorful stories to tell, but the restaurant was busy, and she had others to serve.

"Amazing food," I remarked as I dug into my lamb and rice.

"I eat here more than I want to admit. It's close, it's inexpensive and delicious," she said as she scooped up tabbouleh with fresh pita.

"Do you think we'll be able to finish up the work on the Limon painting?" I asked. "I know it's the last thing on your mind right now - "

"No, it is absolutely on my mind," she said firmly. "It feels like a mystery we should be able to solve, and I need that right now. I was thinking I'd contact the owner later today, but first, I want to speak to Joslyn."

I knew what she was thinking, and it was an eloquent solution. Mimi would let Joslyn know the owners were still interested in selling and then gauge her interest in the purchase. She could then negotiate a deal that would cover our costs and get the sellers a fair price. She was excellent at her job.

"Do you think Joslyn will still be interested if the price is as high as I think it might be?" I asked.

"In my opinion, she should at least have the chance at first refusal."

I agreed. There were plenty of collectors out there, but there was no denying Joslyn had an emotional connection to it. And I felt obligated to honor that.

We finished our meal and then began the drive to Lancaster Studio. Traffic was heavy, which was fine by me. I was in no rush. I wasn't looking forward to returning to that crime scene, but at least we wouldn't have to enter the building. Colby had said there were still agents there going through Edric's files.

They would eventually have to contact all the clients to ascertain whether they bought a forgery or an original. It was going to be a mess to sort out, I was sure of that. And as I thought about that, a spark of an idea began brewing in the back of my mind. But that would have to wait until after I helped Mimi. And we made sure my dad was safe with Bohgan back behind bars.

"I want you to know that I can stay here for as long as you need. I have plenty of vacation time and it turns out my room has been fully paid for the next two weeks," I looked over at her and smiled.

"Better safe than sorry," Mimi laughed. "I didn't know how long our project would take and then I wanted to make sure you had some actual vacation time once we were finished." She looked out the passenger window for a moment before turning back to me. "Thanks for going with me to the studio. Not sure how I feel about it. I mean, the last time I was there, I was drugged, kidnapped, and left alone on a boat."

Reaching over, I squeezed her hand. "Of course. And I'm here if you get the screaming meemies, or need to throw up all over the parking lot. We'll get through it together."

We finally reached our destination. The parking lot was filled with black SUVs, crime scene vans, and agents milling around. Mimi's car was in the same spot as it had been during my previous visit.

I pulled the Porsche up next to it. Before I even put the car in park, an agent walked over. I exited and explained who we were and why we were there. Keeping a sharp eye on Mimi the entire time, in case the trauma should overtake her. She was steadfastly ignoring the studio and all the police activity.

Satisfied after looking at our IDs, the agent rejoined the others and left us to retrieve the car. Mimi unlocked it and hesitated before getting in. She looked over at the studio and froze. I put my hand on her back, reassuring her that I was there.

"Will you be okay driving home?" I asked.

That was enough to jolt her back to the present. "I will be. Thank you. Thanks for everything," she said, turning to hug me. "I don't know how I would get through this without you." I hugged her back. Steady again, she got into the driver's seat.

"I'll follow you back to your apartment," I said.

"No, that's not necessary," she insisted. "Go enjoy the rest of the afternoon. Let's meet for dinner tonight. I could use a good nap before then. Still catching up on lost sleep." She closed the door, and I stood by my car and watched her drive away.

I opened the driver's door and leaned against it. With the studio in direct view, I tried not to imagine what horrors had happened inside. To Mimi. To Edric. Anger washed over me, mixed with fear of what could have happened to Mimi. I couldn't help but wonder if the man who had kept me from my father was responsible for all this misery.

In the car, I turned on the navigation. I needed some whimsy. Deciding that a long drive might be just the solution to a cluttered mind, I programmed in my destination. Taking the long way back to the hotel, via Mulholland Drive, would surely be a pleasant diversion.

Instead, it almost killed me.

TWENTY-THREE

This guy who is following you, he is very persistent! - ROMANCING THE STONE

It was a lovely drive. I had all the windows down and the sunroof open. The wind whipped through my hair, creating a hazardous distraction. Finally, I jammed my sunglasses up on my head to keep my unruly strands from my eyes. The navigation took me through Laurel Canyon, heading up to Mulholland Drive. Mimi was right. With the recent rain, the scent of eucalyptus filled the car.

As the speed limit fell, road and wind noise diminished. Suddenly, I heard a loud scream and almost slammed on the brakes. Then it repeated, and I realized it was a birdcall. It had to be peacocks. Their calls were loud, harsh and as audacious as their feathering. I would have to remember to ask Mimi about it tonight.

I don't know when I realized I was being followed. Once I did, that voice in my head said the black Cadillac Escalade had been there for quite some time. I felt stupid that it hadn't registered before I was well into the narrow canyon. I had been too busy enjoying myself and had become inattentive.

In my defense, heavy traffic makes it difficult to spot a tail, especially something as ubiquitous as a black SUV. But now that we were in the canyon, with its narrow two-lane road, it became apparent. The driver was aggressively staying within visual range, sometimes crossing over the double yellow line or, in one case, swerving dangerously past a stationary left-turning vehicle.

They were not trying to hide the fact that I was their target. But I had no idea why. I asked my mobile butler to call Colby.

"What's up?" he asked when he picked up. I was relieved he didn't let the call go to voicemail. That's my guy, making me a priority even deep in an investigation.

"Don't freak out," I could literally hear him tense on the other end of the line. "I think someone is following me."

"Give me details," he said calmly, which dropped my heart rate from potential stroke to a more moderate, high level of anxiety.

"Black Cadillac Escalade, new model. California plates. Tinted windows, it's difficult to see the driver. Not making it a secret that they are following me." I replied as calmly as I could. The adrenaline was kicking in, and my grip on the steering wheel tightened.

"Where are you?"

I looked at my GPS. "Coming up on the turn onto Mulholland Drive from Laurel Canyon Road." I didn't know the area well enough to give him cross streets, and I didn't want to take my eyes off the road long enough to look longer at the dashboard map.

"Hold on, let me check something," Colby said, and I tried not to panic at the silence on the line.

Here is a fun fact about being in a long-term relationship with a cop. Conversations veer into topics ordinary couples might not find interesting or romantic. How to stay vigilant, how to spot a tail while walking or driving, and what ordinary objects make suitable weapons, counted as a love language.

A couple might enjoy practicing self-defense, or spend a Sunday at the FBI driving course practicing evasive maneuvers. To be fair, Colby knew more about the art world and had been to more art museums than he ever expected, too. Love is, after all, about sharing your passions.

I had a decision to make. The GPS, as I had programmed it, would take me back to Santa Monica via Mulholland Drive, a long, scenic route. There were cross streets ahead, but I did not know where any of the streets would take me. With an unfamiliar car on unfamiliar roads and with my adrenaline cranked up to eleven, it seemed prudent to stay the course. Perhaps Colby would have a better suggestion. Until then, I followed the GPS and turned onto Mulholland.

"Honey," Colby's voice sounded pinched. That was not good. "Can you see the SUV now?"

I looked in my rearview mirror. "Yes," I replied, trying to sound calm and confident.

"Any chance you can see the plate number? Without putting yourself in danger," he added hastily.

I looked hard. He was staying just far enough away that I couldn't read his plate. "I think it starts with a 9X - fuck!"

"What happened? Are you okay?" Colby asked urgently.

"I'm fine. It's a curvy road. Distractions are not my friend. The other letter I could see was a W," I stated flatly. "9XW."

I was going to have to keep my focus on the road. What was supposed to be a nice, scenic drive through the canyon was now going to be a white-knuckled, laser-focused trip. I had a sinking feeling that my stalker was waiting for one of the more dangerous curves to make a move, and I would have to be ready.

"TJ, I have Deputies and LAPD units en route. Just stay on Mulholland if you can, then they'll know where to find you. I'm tracking your phone right now," he reassured me. There was a long pause, and I could feel him making a decision. I wanted to shout, *just tell me!,* instead, I focused on the road and waited. "TJ, I don't want you to panic, but we think that SUV belongs to Bohgan. The partial plate matches one of his aliases."

My focus was on a long, sharp curve with an even sharper drop-off on one side, so it took more than a moment for me to comprehend what Colby had said.

"What the fuck? Are you sure?" I was incredulous. How would he even know who I was or where I was going? "Does he think I'm Tom Meadler?" I couldn't think of any other reason for him to be following me. "I mean, it would make sense, wouldn't it? If Tom was involved with what Edric was doing, and it's unraveling, could this guy be tying up loose ends?"

Colby's long silence was telling. And when he spoke, it took everything I had to stay on the road. "We think he found out you're Thomas Joseph's daughter."

Once I regained my composure and the curves eased, I demanded, "How?" Anger overtook fear. My father had spent most of my life protecting me from this, and I wanted to know who was careless enough to undo his efforts.

"We don't know yet," Colby said. "I promise you, I will find out, and there will be a price paid. But for now, I need you to stay focused on the situation at hand. We need to resolve this safely."

"You think he's going to try and kill me, don't you?"

"I don't know his intent, but whatever it is, it's not good. I need you to stay defensive. He may try to run you off the road and you have to be prepared for that," Colby said calmly. He was in cop mode, and I imagined it took everything for him to remain impassive. Cop mode was good. It kept me calm and focused on the task at hand. "Keep the line open. I'll let you know when the officers are close."

After that, we didn't speak. I needed my entire focus to be on the road and on the SUV.

I glanced in the mirror. Creepy was still keeping his distance. Traffic was moderate at this point in the drive. I closed all the windows, preparing for the worst. I hoped that whatever he was going to try, he would do it when there were few cars on the road. It was one thing to kill me. It was another to take out a family of four when he did it. I prayed help would arrive before he had that chance.

The curves became sharper, and if I hadn't been in this dire situation, I would have had time to admire the way the Porsche handled. Graceful, nimble on the curves, and hugging the road like an excellent performance vehicle should. I doubted Mr. Bohgan was having a similar experience. But with his intentions, weight and size were to his advantage.

Before I could finish that thought, the SUV sped up and closed the distance between us. I pushed down on the pedal and accelerated, pulling out of his range quickly.

The advantage of an electric motor, zero to sixty is a couple of seconds. His combustion engine, combined with the Cadillac's lumbering size, slowed him down, but not for long. Again, he gained on me and closed the gap.

I wasn't comfortable speeding much faster through the unfamiliar curves. There is no telling when I might encounter heavy traffic or a turning vehicle. Speed would not get me out of this. I needed a plan.

I stole a glance at the map on the screen. The canyon was opening up now, with a steep drop-off on my side of the road. The view of the city would have been stellar if I had the time to look.

Ahead there was a sharp curve and immediately after, a pullout for overlook viewing. I stepped down on the accelerator, inching up my speed. He matched my speed and increased his enough that he was dangerously close to my bumper. I feared he was waiting for that curve to make his move.

I didn't wait, slamming the pedal to the floor. The Porsche did what a Porsche is meant to do. It practically flew down the road. As I approached the curve, I prayed the road beyond it was clear. The SUV fell behind, and I watched as he pushed it and began to catch up. I was counting on the pullout being substantial enough for me to make a defensive maneuver that the SUV could not duplicate.

I took a deep breath, tested my seatbelt, and gripped the steering wheel. The moment I spotted the turnout, I aimed for it and slammed on the brakes. The car fishtailed, but held its ground. By the time I had fully stopped, I had done a one-eighty on the narrow dirt patch. I found myself facing the SUV, and Bohgan was coming straight at me. Fortunately, his vehicle was not agile enough to match my moves.

I was preparing to merge back onto the road to make my escape when an oncoming sedan rounded the curve at a high rate of speed. At the same time, Bohgan had crossed the double yellow line, into its path, in an attempt to follow me into the pullout. He had no choice but to swerve to avoid the advancing vehicle.

The SUV lurched onto the narrow shoulder to avoid the sedan. Unfortunately, at the speed Bohgan was going, the SUV fishtailed and tipped precariously. He over-corrected, and his now completely out-of-control vehicle swerved off the road and over the steep incline. It flipped several times until it came to rest at the bottom of the ravine.

I wasn't sure what to do. My instinct was to rush down the rocky hillside to assist him. Luckily, before I could act on that, the next vehicle around the curve was a dark SUV with red and blue lights flashing.

Mimi and I were sitting on the beach in the beach chairs she had brought over after she heard what had happened. She also brought two pints of ice cream. That's a good friend for you, knows the right junk food for any situation. As I spooned the creamy goodness into my mouth, I reflected on the previous hours. Grateful to be here, listening to the waves, sitting next to my best friend.

After the Marshals had secured the scene on Mulholland, I stepped out of the car and threw up. Nothing like a shot of adrenaline to wreak havoc on your body. Someone handed me a bottle of water, and I nodded my thanks. After that, the rest was a blur.

I honestly didn't remember anything until Colby pulled up in his truck and hugged me. After making sure I was unharmed, he had a deputy drive me back to the hotel, telling the uniform in charge I would be available to answer questions tomorrow.

He arranged for another officer to bring the Porsche back to the hotel. I called Mimi on the way, which was why she was waiting at the hotel with treats when we finally arrived.

We didn't say much as I changed my clothes, and we walked to the beach in silence. We set up the chairs, soaking in the late afternoon sun. Once I had a few bites of strawberry shortcake swirl, I related what happened.

"Do you know if he survived?" she asked gently.

I sucked in my breath. I had been actively avoiding thinking about what lay at the bottom of that ravine. "I don't know," was all I said. Then, we finished our ice cream in companionable silence.

After an hour of sun and sugar, we returned to my room. Colby was waiting for us.

"I was about to call you and see where you had gotten off to," he said before taking me into his arms. He squeezed me tight, and I realized he had been deeply concerned. He released me and handed me the keys to the Porsche. "It's back in the lot." He walked over to the refrigerator, grabbed a bottle of water, turned, and leaned against the counter. He paused long enough that I held my breath in anticipation. "Bohgan is dead," he finally said. "He was ejected from the vehicle and died on impact."

The room spun a bit with the news, but I regained my equilibrium quickly, relieved that the danger to my father was over. "And you're sure it's him?" I asked, thinking it could not have been a pretty scene down there.

"It is. Fingerprints confirmed it."

I sat down on the couch, not sure how I felt about any of this. "Does this solve Edric's murder, too?"

"We think so, but they'll continue the investigation to ascertain if anyone else was involved." Colby came over and sat next to me.

"Do you think Bohgan knew he was following me?" I asked. Not wanting to ask the real question. If he were, how did he find out who I was?

"Yes. We pulled traffic cam data once I knew where you were this afternoon. He had to have been watching the studio when he saw you there. He followed you as soon as you left."

"That brings up two questions then. Why was he watching the studio when he knew you were looking for him?" I took a deep breath. "And how did he know who I was, and why did he want me dead? I'm assuming his intention was to kill me."

"We are going to find out how he knew. I don't think it was something he stumbled upon randomly." He put his arm around me. The implications of a leak somewhere were sobering. "I'm afraid that as we retrace his movements today, we'll find he was following you before you stopped at the studio."

I knew from experience that any type of law enforcement corruption weighed heavily on my lawman. I had to hope it was just a low-level employee somewhere who wanted to capitalize on the information.

"Does my dad know what happened?" I asked.

"He does. I had the unpleasant task of relaying the information to him. He's on his way back to the States. They are extraditing the forger, so he's returning to continue to look for the rest of Edric's team."

Mimi had been awfully quiet, sitting in the chair by the window.

"Mimi, you okay?" I asked.

"You could have been killed this afternoon and it's my fault."

"I'm sorry, what?!" I asked sharply. "How do you figure that, friend?"

"I'm the one who invited you out here. If you hadn't come to help me, this wouldn't have happened," she explained.

"Hold up. First of all, however this unraveled, it is not on you. What I see is that the man who threatened my dad and his family is no longer an issue. And that happened because I was here. I'll take that, however it occurred." I said adamantly.

"And secondly," Colby interjected. "If TJ hadn't been here, you might have perished on that boat before anyone found you. I'll be honest, we don't know Edric's intentions. Or who else he was working with who might have harmed you. I'm grateful TJ was here to insist you were in danger and helped me find you."

I wasn't sure if any of this cheered her, but she didn't look as distressed as she had a moment ago. "Mimi, I would go on any adventure with you, no matter the danger. So banish those dark thoughts, and let's get some dinner," I implored. Ice cream or not, I was hungry.

We decided on a Korean restaurant. Once settled and the appetizers had arrived, it was time to figure out what was next for all of us.

"How long do you think you'll have to be here?" I asked Colby.

"My part is mostly complete. I was tasked with fugitive apprehension. The FBI will continue the investigation into Bohgan's recent crimes. I do know there are several warehouses of artwork that need to be sorted through, and they will need to figure out what is forged and what is original."

"Oh, really?" This was news. And it fanned a spark of an idea I had been tossing around in my mind for the last few days. "Will my dad help with that?"

"He might. It's a bureaucratic nightmare. Who is going to pay? Who will actually do the authentications? Do they need to get bids? You know the drill." Colby explained. I did. Anything with the government came with a mound of paperwork. "Anyway," he continued. "I should be home in a couple of days. How about you?" he asked me. "Have you determined if that painting is the real deal?"

I looked over at Mimi. "Well, my hotel room is paid for another week. We are still working on the details of the painting, so I'm here for whatever Mimi needs." We both looked at her expectantly. "I suspect you'll need a team to close out Tom's affairs."

"I meet lawyers tomorrow. After that, I'll know what the estate needs me to do and how much they'll compensate me for it," she said with a shrug. "I've already decided my fee will be exorbitant, as will any contractors I need to hire," she said and then grinned at me.

I had to admit, staying in LA longer, even though I would miss Colby and the critters, had appeal. Investigating and classifying Tom's artwork would be work, but it would also be invigorating. Spending more time on the beach would not be a hardship either.

What a freaking trip, I mused. I wanted more excitement. That was undoubtedly what I got. Missing art treasures, art forgers, car chases, and murder made for quite the vacation.

It was going to be difficult returning to my mundane desk job after all of that.

After dinner, we watched Mimi drive away from the hotel. She promised she would text me when she was safely at home. Still a bit traumatized by the past few days, I needed to know my tribe was safe and secure. Colby put his arm around me, pulled me into him, and kissed me.

“What did you have in mind for the rest of our evening?” I asked. I had a hefty amount of pent-up tension I was sure he could help me alleviate.

“Honestly?” He gave me that wolf grin. “I’d really like to ride the Ferris wheel.”

TWENTY-FOUR

You're not much of a detective, are you? - AFTER THE THIN MAN

The next ten days were a blur. Once Colby left for home, I focused on helping Mimi inventory Tom's house. She hired a crew to carefully pack the catalogued artworks and move them to one of his warehouses. Those items would stay there until Tom's estate was settled. At which time they would most likely be sold at auction unless an heir could be located.

We left the furniture and personal items in place while his lawyers continued to search for next of kin, who could then deal with the remaining contents of the home. I suspected the house and all its contents would end up on the auction block as well. Tom would remain an enigma.

With the bulk of the house inventoried and the artwork removed, it was time to tackle the Hollywood memorabilia. Both of us dreaded that task. We would walk by the closed double doors every day and share a knowing look. We could only put off the inevitable for so long.

The room had remained untouched since the vandalism. Neither of us could face it in the beginning. It was a stark reminder not just of Tom's passion, but also of his murderer's violence. However, as the days ticked by and we had become accustomed to the emotions around dismantling a man's life, and there had been time to process the murder, clearing the theater became conceivable.

Piece by piece, we examined, catalogued, and photographed everything. The plan was to have one of the local Hollywood memorabilia experts prepare a valuation of the entire collection. Like Tom's artwork, it would then be sold at auction once the estate was settled.

We cleared off one of the large shelving units to be used exclusively for items that had been damaged and needed repair. The hope was that the same expert could offer guidance there as well. To my untrained eye, it looked as if most of it could be salvaged.

Finally, we tackled the warehouses with a small crew of competent and efficient professionals, provided by Tom's law firm. The movers had already transported the few items at his gallery space in Venice to one of the warehouses.

I was stunned by the volume of the cache. In all my time working with acquisitions, I had never seen this much artwork in one private collection. Despite my love of art, I couldn't imagine the desire to amass all of this.

Our final task was to examine the works Edric had access to, and except for the piece Mimi had already flagged, they were authentic. That ended the involvement of law enforcement. They had their hands full with the forgeries.

They did not have the time, manpower, or inclination to determine how Tom acquired his pieces. That would be for someone like me down the line to explore before anything was purchased at auction.

And since the FBI was unable to determine Tom's true identity, the chance of finding a next of kin was slim. With no apparent criminal activity, they considered the matter of his mysterious identity closed.

Now it was up to the lawyers. They had a year to continue their search before the state claimed it all. Then everything could finally be auctioned. That would be an auction I would love to attend.

In addition to helping Mimi, I continued my quest to validate the Limon painting. Once I had the report on the paint analysis and after a more extensive interview with the owners, I was confident it was the real deal. Finally, I sought the opinion of the expert we had brought in to examine Tom's memorabilia.

He practically drooled as he looked it over and agreed with my assessment that it was truly an original Limon. Armed with all that, Jocelyn was happy to meet the buyers' asking price. Mimi and I delivered the painting ourselves.

It was great to see her one last time before I had to return to my real life in Virginia. And to see our beautiful lady, that both Mimi and I had grown so attached to, in a home where she would be appreciated for all the right reasons.

We were well compensated for all our efforts, including a nice commission on the sale of the portrait. Which was going to help because I would be leaving my current position once I returned home. I was ready to start something new and exciting. And I had an idea simmering, though I wasn't ready to share details with anyone, yet.

Mimi and I spent my last night in LA discussing what would come next for her. She would have to stay in LA a while longer, finishing up Tom's estate details. But after that, we decided she should come to Arlington and we would go into business together. She agreed without even knowing what I had in mind. It was no wonder that we were friends.

Explaining that I needed to ruminate on the business idea a little longer before I sprung the full concept upon her did not deter her. I had fingers-crossed Colby wouldn't think it too audacious. Though I was sure I could count on his support, regardless.

The next day, Mimi and I drove Tom's Porsche one last time, to the airport. I hated leaving her alone in LA to continue to deal with the fallout without me. I hugged her and reminded her I was a phone call away if things got too heavy.

As I grabbed my luggage, Mimi stopped me with one final question, "Have you made a decision about marriage?"

I pulled up the handle on my rolling bag, hung my carry-on over it, and smiled at her. "I have," was all I said before dashing off to my terminal. Grateful that I was going home to those I missed terribly.

Once I was home, I gave Stevie and Wyatt the requisite attention before I tossed my suitcase on the bed, vowing to unpack later. For now, I was exhausted. I couldn't remember ever being this tired before.

Maybe I was coming down with a virus after such a tense few weeks. It would be a predictable result after all the trauma and the long days of hard work. Whatever it was, I was definitely run-down.

I didn't relish the idea of going back to my job. My boss would not be happy when I told her I would be leaving. After almost a month away, I would be giving her only two weeks notice. Barely enough time to start interviewing for my replacement. But it was time.

Flying home, the new business idea came fully into focus. Art recovery and restitution was big business, especially when you had a direct line to law enforcement. It probably wouldn't involve mobsters or tech-bros, but that was always a possibility. More than likely, our clientele would involve burglaries, family disputes, and misplaced family heirlooms.

The idea of offering our services to track down lost art excited me. Mimi and I seemed to have an affinity for it. We definitely had a record of accomplishments between Boston and Los Angeles. I loved the prospect of an art detective agency.

We could call it something like *Webster and Wilde: Finders of Lost Things,* or *Webster and Wilde: Art Hunters.* Or maybe something as boring as *Webster and Wilde: Art Investigators.* In addition to being art detectives, we could also offer our consulting services to small museums and private buyers.

The endeavor would be a risk, but one I was willing to take. I could not see myself going back to my current job, no matter how respected I was or how much I enjoyed the people there. Too much had happened in the past few weeks.

I settled in the overstuffed chair and flipped on the television to catch up on the news. And there was Colby, his boss, and some FBI dude I didn't recognize, taking questions on another case. Then they ran B-roll of Colby leading a guy away in handcuffs.

Damn, he looked handsome on camera. I supposed I should marry him just so some gold digger didn't snag him with her dubious charms. Honestly, I had no idea what I would do without him in my life. I only wished he was happy to live in sin with me, like a normal man.

That anxiety was for another day. My current focus was on the thousands of pieces of artwork in Los Angeles that would need to be authenticated and cataloged before the inevitable trials in the Edric case. He might be dead, but the forgers and their network still needed to be held accountable.

Stevie jumped on the arm of the chair and rubbed against me before settling in my lap. Demanding that I continue to atone for my recent desertion. I absently petted her from chin to tail while formulating my career plans.

All that stolen artwork needed to be authenticated. Original owners needed to be located. Forgeries needed to be screened out. And it all needed to be organized and then cataloged.

I was confident that the government would have to contract out those services. And I was going to be at the head of the line for that job. They would have to take me seriously, what with my background and connections. Not to mention the fact that Mimi and I were integral in discovering the crimes.

All that was left was for me to convince Mimi that we could open our own business. No more criminal bosses, no more sitting behind a desk all day…maybe a few questionable clients. Can't have everything. I was sure it would be anything but dull.

Edric's situation made me think of my father. I wondered what he was up to in the aftermath, now that Bohgan was dead and the forgers were in custody. I supposed he was blending back into his environment like a chameleon, monitoring my life from a secret location. Never to walk me down the aisle while Colby waited at the altar. No taking his grandkids to the park or the zoo.

I definitely needed sleep because here I was, angry at my father for not playing with his imaginary grandkids or walking me down the aisle at a wedding I was avoiding.

I eased Stevie onto the couch. She complained, but then curled up and fell sound asleep, as cats do. I needed to unpack and then make some notes. Copious notes. While the ideas were fresh in my brain.

Wyatt barked in the backyard. I was about to shush him when the doorbell rang. Since I wasn't expecting anyone and we had just vanquished a major criminal syndicate, I let Wyatt in through the French doors and had him accompany me to the front door. The ancient wavy glass revealed the distorted figure of a man, distinguished and casually dressed. Something about him was familiar. I put my hand on the knob and turned, noting that Wyatt sat next to me, tail swishing gently across the hardwood floor. No hackles, no anxiety.

I pulled the heavy wooden door open and stared at the gentleman standing on the other side of the wooden screen door. Funny how you just know.

"Hi, dad," I said as if I had said it every day.

He grinned broadly. More rugged than in the photo I had, a challenging life etched on his grizzled and lined face. He was also more muscular than his younger self. I supposed a life on the run meant you had to stay in shape. But it was his Basset Hound-like eyes that captured me, looking just a touch vulnerable and expectant.

"Hi, Tammy Jean." I cringed as he said it, but bit back the reflexive correction. I unlocked the screen door, and Wyatt enthusiastically pushed it open to invite my father inside. "What a good boy," Thomas Joseph said as he petted him. "Gotta love a dog you don't have to bend down to give a good ear rub."

His voice was deep and warm, like a smoky Scotch, and Wyatt responded by melting into his side, leaning heavily on him while he scratched his ears.

"Come on in," I said, as if my father standing at my door was a normal Friday. Wyatt's tail wagged so hard I thought it would snap off. Traitor. I stepped back and directed my father to the sunroom. "We can sit in here. Can I get you something to drink? Tea? Sparkling water?"

He smiled again, and his eyes danced a bit. He may have been expecting me to be angry or, at the very least, cool and detached. I'm not sure why I was neither. It all felt surreal, like Santa and the Easter Bunny showed up for tea, and the Tooth Fairy provided the snacks. Of course, I would invite them in, and we would all chat amiably. We sat at the small table by the tall windows.

"I suppose asking you how you've been would be inappropriate," he said quietly. I nodded. Small talk seemed inappropriate.

"Why are you here?" I asked, hoping it didn't sound bitter or accusatory. My question was genuine.

"I thought it was time. With Bohgan gone, a great weight has been lifted, TJ, and I didn't want to waste any more time. I know I wasn't the best father, but I did what I could to keep you and your mom safe."

Funny, I did know that. After I found out he was alive, after I recovered from the shock, I was angry. But I knew it was better to have an absent father than a dead father, and even better to have an absent father who was doing so to protect me. I nodded my understanding, encouraging him to continue.

"And I wanted you to know that. I would do anything for you and I am angry I wasn't able to protect you from Bohgan. I'm sorry he came after you. He's lucky he's dead," my father said vehemently.

"It's okay. I know you did everything you could." Stevie jumped into my lap and curled up, soon to be fast asleep again. "Did they find out how he knew who I was?"

My father scoffed. "Would you believe one of Bohgan's associates had a girlfriend who worked in housekeeping at the hotel where we were staying in San Diego? She overheard a conversation between agents, and then she and her boyfriend leveraged it for a big payout from Bohgan. Via text. Criminals are rarely smart."

"Isn't that the truth," I agreed. It was an odd but apt dictum to bond over. With that, I felt it was time to let the walls down. "I appreciate all the help you've given me over the years and I'm glad I get the chance to tell you in person."

That appeared to lift whatever burden he had been carrying when he walked into the house. His shoulders relaxed, and his eyes brightened. Wyatt walked over and put his head in my father's lap. My father gently stroked it. Wyatt closed his eyes, relaxed and accepting. I felt that was a positive sign.

"That's good to hear. So good to hear," he said finally.

We talked for over an hour. We covered the gamut, talking about Mom and my job. I shared my desire to do something different. And then, the best news of all, Dad said he was buying a townhouse downtown and wanted to be part of my life.

"That is if you want me around," he said.

Oh, boy, did I.

I felt like a gigantic piece of my life puzzle had been found under the couch, all dirty and battered, and once it was dusted off, it fit perfectly. Bringing a little more of the puzzle into focus. Thoughts of having him over for Sunday dinner and strolling through the park with him and Wyatt flooded my mind, and I relished the hell out of them.

"By the way, Colby said you two are engaged. When's the big day?"

"I haven't decided, but I hope you'll be there when it happens." That elicited a huge grin from him.

Later, once he had given me his phone number and promised to let me know when he closed on the townhome, he hugged me. And it was the best hug I had ever had. We said our goodbyes, and I floated around the house. Finishing chores and wondering what the hell had just happened. I couldn't wait for Colby to get home so I could share the day with him.

Unfortunately, by the time he rolled through the door, I was sound asleep, with a cat curled up next to my pillow and a dog draped across my feet. I heard nothing until the sun peeked through the blinds, and a really, really annoying mockingbird sang through his entire repertoire on the branch outside the window.

Stevie sat on the sill, chirping at him, which I swear made the little feathered guy sing louder. I rolled out of bed, trying not to disturb Colby. He was tucked under a hundred pounds of dog as Wyatt had transferred his warmth and affection to Colby's feet.

I slogged my way to the kitchen, still feeling like I hadn't slept in a week. I needed to pull myself together because Mimi and I had a video conference scheduled for the afternoon. The ducks needed to be in a row if I was going to convince her my idea was solid. She was enthusiastic about our joint venture once I shared the details. Now I wanted to make sure she was firmly committed before I returned to work on Monday.

Next, I needed to determine what it would take to extricate myself quickly from my current career without leaving my boss in a lurch. Maintaining my reputation in museum circles was a priority. I would need all those contacts if Mimi and I were going to be successful in the private sector.

With my first cup of coffee at my side, I sat at the counter and opened my laptop. I began adding items to my already overwhelming list of to-dos. Colby padded into the kitchen with Wyatt close behind.

He wrapped his arms around my waist and kissed my neck as he looked over my shoulder. "Mmmm, coffee," he said before he kissed me again. He released me, walked to the back door, and let Wyatt out for his morning bush-watering escapades. He poured coffee into his mug and then topped off mine.

"Grab the milk, please?" I asked before he sat down next to me. "And an orange." He rolled an orange over to me, poured a bit of milk into each of our mugs, and then sat in the chair next to me.

"How was yesterday? Did you manage to unpack and get some rest?" Colby asked.

I closed the laptop and pushed it aside before I peeled the orange. "You are never going to guess who stopped by for a visit," I said, popping an orange section into my mouth.

After relaying the news about my father's visit, I then shared my wild plan with Colby while we made breakfast. He was enthusiastic. That was a relief. He said he had some crazy ideas, too, but wanted to mull them over a bit more before sharing.

He looked excited, so I was excited for him, no matter what changes that might mean. As long as he wasn't thinking of becoming a CIA assassin, we could handle whatever came next.

Later that morning, Colby started a load of laundry before settling on the couch to catch up on all the sports news he had missed. I would have loved to curl up next to him with a book and some tea, but there was a box of mail that had accumulated while we were away that needed to be sorted.

At my desk, I began the task, but my heart wasn't in it. Outside our office window, the big flowering dogwood was in full bud. It wouldn't be long before the blooms burst forth.

Spring was almost here, filled with new beginnings. I felt like the dogwood, ready to blossom. It felt as if our lives were about to shift dramatically, and I was ready for it.

I fiddled with the dial on the antique phone that sat on my desk. Mimi had given it to me as a thank-you gift. It was the one I had admired from Tom's movie memorabilia. I was afraid to ask her what she had paid for it. But it looked stunning on my desk. And it was a wonderful reminder of our LA adventures.

It was almost time for our call, so I jotted down a few more notes and flipped open my day planner to get a sense of timing for my resignation and her arrival. And that's when I saw it. I flipped back a few pages anxiously, and then a few more. Well, that was not good.

I called in sick on Monday morning. Mimi and I had sketched out a solid business plan. Things were moving in the right direction. I decided I needed to take an extra day to prepare before I faced my boss.

However, I had another, more pressing reason for staying home. As I watched the timer tick away, I buttressed myself for when the buzzer rang.

A geological eon later, the timer dinged. I looked down at the test stick in my hand.

"Well, I'll be damned."

EPILOGUE

Seven months later, Colby and I welcomed a beautiful baby girl. We named her after our grandmothers. Before her arrival, we had a small wedding ceremony. Well, as small as our mothers would allow us to have. It was filled with friends, family, and co-workers who wished us well and showered us with gifts.

Best of all, my dad walked me down the aisle. And even though it felt a bit corny, we shared a father-daughter dance. The moment he spun me around the dance floor was a moment I will cherish forever.

Mimi and I got the FBI contract for the Edric forgery case. It took a bit of finagling and calling in a whole slew of favors. But identifying and cataloging all that stolen art gave us a massive boost for the new business, which was flourishing. We even managed to get all the art returned to its rightful owners before the baby arrived.

I introduced Mimi to a really nice guy at the museum, but she fell for our FBI liaison. They've been dating for several months now. I have no idea if it will stick, but if it does, at least she'll have a professional around if she gets kidnapped again. He's a nice guy, for being with the FBI.

Colby upended our lives quite a bit. He decided to make a run for Congress. I might have preferred he started his political career a little quieter, say, in the state general assembly. But with all the positive publicity he received after the capture and subsequent guilty pleas of Bohgan's associates, the powers-that-be approached him for the congressional run. I was a little apprehensive that we traded the danger of police work for the danger of public life. But he's happier than I've ever seen him, so how could I do anything but support him?

Work took a backseat while I took time to get acquainted with our daughter. I'm afraid to say she arrived full of spunk and attitude. Our new adventure has begun, and I think I'm ready for it. She has Colby wrapped around her little finger, and he's a great dad.

When I go back to work, she'll go with me. It's never too early to learn about good art. And our company has a very generous bring your child and dog to work policy.

I can't wait to see what the future holds.

ABOUT THE AUTHOR

Annie DeMoranville has lived all over, including Boston and Los Angeles. She now resides in the shadow of the Rocky Mountains with a menagerie of critters. She loves to travel with a goal to see the most beautiful beaches in the world.

Up next: the second book in the **Duxbridge Mysteries** series. Catch up with Maggie, Jake, and all the quirky residents of Duxbridge, MA. Also in the works: **Blackout,** the first book in the new **Jennifer McCaffrey Mysteries** series.

For more information on her upcoming novels, visit
www.AnnieDeMoranville.com

Connect with her:
Facebook/AnnieDeMoranville.com
@anniedemoranville.bsky.social on Bluesky
#annieshortstories on Instagram

www.ingramcontent.com/pod-product-compliance
Lightning Source LLC
LaVergne TN
LVHW091114080826
845145LV00008B/1910
* 9 7 8 1 7 3 2 5 0 7 0 7 4 *